I would like to wish a special thanks to the following people for helping this dream come true.

Kevin and Jean Trapp for editing this book.
Robert Rogers for all his help.
Jeremy Potter for feeding me tons of ideas.
Ron Diller for being my guinea pig and holding on to what I gave him.
My mom for telling me never to give up.
My biggest thanks is to my wife and kids for being patient with me and encouraging.
My final thanks goes out to everyone who reads this book. I really hope you like it.

The Vampire Chronicles of Jack Holladay

(Crimson Nights)

By Steve Krebs

ISBN 978-0-578-04920-5

Chapter One

The name's Jack Holladay and I'm a pizza delivery driver. I know what you're thinking. What's so special about a pizza driver? Not much, at least not until the night I almost died. Luckily, someone was driving by when the attack occurred or I would be dead right now, or worse. His name is Shaun Miller.

I still remember the details about the night I met Shaun. It was in the middle of summer, about a month ago. It happened on the South side of Pueblo, Colorado in a new development. Lots of houses were being built in this area. It was a quiet neighborhood, quiet and dark. The street lights were not assembled yet. For the locals it was an awesome view of the stars, but for a delivery person it was just another nightmare. Street signs were very difficult to read and unless a house had its porch light on, the addresses were nearly impossible to see.

It wasn't only hard to see in the new development, it was also potentially dangerous. Not long ago a delivery driver was pulled over by a car load of punks with a shotgun. Luckily the driver was only robbed instead of beaten up or killed. I heard the driver quit his job afterward. Once a gun has been stuck in your face and you look down the barrel of an instrument of death, you begin to think to yourself. Your life doesn't pass before your eyes like many people say, all you think about is "Oh God, please don't let him pull the trigger."

I met Shaun in the same neighborhood. He saved my life from a nightmare far more frightening than any punk with a gun. The events changed my life forever. It opened my eyes to another part of the night, one that few get to experience.

I work for Aces Pizza. The shop is located in the Mid-Town shopping center. It's owned by a guy named Tom Dillon. Tom is a decent enough employer. He is willing to work with his employees. If you needed a day off it was usually easy to get, usually.

Tom has a pale complexion and blue eyes, much like me. His blond hair was always neatly trimmed and his clothes were clean and ironed. My hair on the other hand was dark blond and shoulder length. It wasn't messy, but neat was also a word I wouldn't use for it. My clothes usually looked like I dragged them out of the hamper, stains and all.

I've been working at Aces for about ten years and I wasn't at all happy about getting a delivery to the neighborhood where the other driver was robbed. This driver worked for another company, the newspapers were not clear on which one. Since the store has been open none of our drivers had been robbed. Frank, one of the assistant managers, wasn't so lucky. One night a few years ago, while all of the drivers were on deliveries, a man walked into the store and pulled out a gun. Fortunately, most of the money had been locked in the safe and the crook only made off with a small amount of cash.

The night my life changed it was a typical shift at Aces and I was the closing driver. I didn't particularly like my job, but it was the best one I could get with no college and little experience in anything else. I had other jobs, but none I cared to waste away in for the rest of my life. One day a good friend told me, "You may never find a job that you like, so until you do just do the job that you hate the least." I thought that it was good advice so I followed it and for the majority of the years I worked at Aces it got me by. Well, at least until I saw where my delivery was going to. At that time I had second thoughts.

Tom handed me the delivery and with a little edge in his voice he said, "Be careful. If you can't find the address or if they don't have a porch light on, call them on your cell phone. If there's no answer don't take any chances, just bring the pizza back."

"I'm touched," I said as a small smile snaked across my face. "You do care about me. What's there to worry about anyway? It's a rich neighborhood with hard working people and no street lights. What would thieves be doing lurking around a rich, dark neighborhood?"

Tom just shook his head and went back to tending the ovens. Then he said, "Just be careful. I don't want to be stuck closing for you tonight.

"Don't worry about me Kaun," I said as I put the pizza in a delivery bag. "You don't pay me good enough to take chances."

I called him Kaun. It was a personal nickname I had for Tom. Unless an employee was a long timer at Aces they wouldn't have a clue who I was talking about. He earned his nickname one day when he arrived at the shop with a personal sized serving of spicy cucumbers. He picked it up at a Chinese restaurant named Kaun's. The rest of the night he ate the cucumbers as he walked around saying, "Tom's Kauns." From that night on I started calling him Kaun and the name took.

I headed for the door, but noticed I forgot the soda that went with the order. Tom just bought a new computer system for the store and nobody was used to it yet. I went over to the cooler to grab a two liter and accidentally bumped into Pascal. The older driver looked at me and said, "Watch it, Jack.

Get out of my way."

Pascal Ferris is sixty two years old and severely balding. What little bit of hair he does have is gray. He also wears glasses that magnify his blue eyes. Pascal is one of those people that you love to hate. When he started to work for Aces about seven years ago he used to wear very strong cologne that could be smelled a block away. I used to harass him about the strong smell and after a few months he finally quit wearing it.

He lives in an old beat up trailer off Acero Street. I don't know for sure, but I swear Pascal doesn't have a refrigerator. Anytime a manager would make a crew pizza he is always the first to grab a slice. Sometimes, when a customer doesn't finish all their pizza, Pascal will dig the box out of the trash and eat what's left.

Pascal falls for every get rich quick scheme he comes across. Personally I can recall four of them and they have cost him thousands. Another thing he tries is mail order brides and like the money schemes he ends up losing thousands on those as well. I guess some people just don't learn.

Once I bagged up the two liter I walked out to the parking lot and saw Danny Perry getting out of his car, he was coming back from a delivery. Besides Tom, Danny is one of the few employees at Aces I would actually consider a friend. He is a rather cool headed and intelligent individual that has an interest in martial arts and playing the piano, he excels at both of them. He has long black hair, which he keeps pulled back in a tail and brown eyes. He isn't very tall, maybe around five feet six inches, but I saw some of his karate and I wouldn't want to mess with him. The height probably came from the oriental side of his family. His mother met a United States naval officer while he was over seas. The two hit it off and then soon after Danny's father went back to the States. Nine months later Danny was born, but his mother couldn't afford to take care of a baby so she dropped him off at a military base. From there he was put in an orphanage until he was adopted by an American couple.

"Daaaack!" Danny yelled as he saw me coming out of Aces. It was a nickname that he gave me and like most nicknames at Aces the name also took.

"D-man!" I yelled back. Which was the nickname that I and practically everyone else at Aces had for him? "Guess where I'm going?"

"I don't know, where?" Danny asked as he met me halfway in the parking lot.

"The new development up off Kingsroyal," I said and I could instantly see Danny's face darken. "It figures that I would get a delivery up there."

"That sucks," Danny said. "I don't think we should even go up there at night until they put the street lights in. You can't see the street signs half the time."

"I know, but you can't stand in the way of progress and the hungry public," I said as I walked over to my car.

It was a Hyundai Accent. I bought it new and it was a great pizza delivery car. It got thirty miles to the gallon and was great on snow and ice.

I drove across town to the new development. It was built on the Southwest edge of town; on all sides of it was open prairie. Wild animals have been known to wander down from the mountains some thirty miles away and into town. I could see the house lights far before I even arrived. I started searching the signs for the street I was looking for. It was so dark that I couldn't make any of them out and the little light from the moon wasn't helping any. I was tempted to get out of the car to get a closer look, but instead I decided to position it so I was directly facing the street sign. Once I turned on the brights of my headlights I made out the name.

"Kingsroyal," I said to myself as I stared at the street sign. "Then the street I want is just a few blocks away."

Happy that I looked at the map before I left the store, and a little relieved I was almost at my destination, I turned off my brights and started down the street. Within moments I turned down the street I was looking for and had little problems in finding the house. It was one of the few that had its porch light on, not to mention the large house number on the wall next to the front door. Even though I found the house I wasn't in a hurry to get out of the car. There were a lot of dark shadows where someone could be hiding. They would be able to see me, but I couldn't see them.

Once I was satisfied that no one was going to pop out from the shadows, I got out of my car and walked up to the house. The yard was nicely and richly landscaped, while the house had that new look and smell to it. I knocked at the front door and within a few moments an elderly man answered. He was probably a doctor; he had that family doctor look about him.

"How are you doing sir," I said as soon as he opened his door. "We have one large pizza; thirteen dollars and eighty one cents will be your total."

"Its kind of spooky out here without those street lights," the elderly man said as he pulled out his wallet and started to finger through it. "It must be kind of scary delivering to a place like this at night."

"It's not really that bad if we can find where we're going," I said as the elderly man handed me some money. "We can get robbed anywhere, day or night. You should see some of the apartment complexes we deliver to. Now they can be scary."

"Keep the change and be careful out there," the elderly man said with a smile.

He stepped back inside and closed the door. I counted the money on the way back to my car. He gave me twenty dollars, which equaled to a six dollar tip. Sweet!

I got back in my car and drove back the way I came. I was beginning to feel pretty good about this evening and then that's when it happened. First, something moved very quickly in front of my car, so fast it was almost like a blur. My first thought was that a deer darted across the road, but I dismissed that thought. Whatever it was it moved far too quickly. Then I thought a gust of wind blew some dirt across the road, but there wasn't much more than a small breeze five minutes ago.

As I drove down the road I contemplated what could have been so fast. Moments later there was a loud popping sound and my steering wheel jerked, almost right out of my hands. I held on tightly as I pulled over to the side of the road. I put the car in park and turned it off. I shook my head and swore silently to myself. Why now in the dead of night, on the same stretch of road the other delivery driver was robbed on, did I have to get a flat tire?

I really didn't want to get out of the car, it was pitch dark and I didn't have a flashlight, which was stupid for a delivery driver. I decided the first thing I should do is call Tom and let him know what happened. I dialed the number to the store and after a few rings Danny picked up and said, "Thanks for calling Aces Pizza, this is Danny. How can I help you?"

"D-man," I called him by his nickname. "Its Jack, is Tom available for a moment."

"Yea, hold on for a second," Danny replied before he put me on hold. I waited for about a minute and then I heard Tom's voice.

"What's up Jack?"

"I just blew out a tire," I replied after a depressing sigh.

"Oh great," Tom said in his regular calm voice, but I could tell from the years of working with him that he was mildly stressed over the matter. "Did you get the pizza delivered or do you need someone to come by and grab it?"

"No," I replied. "The flat happened on the way back, but guess where I am."

"Don't tell me you're at the location where the other driver got robbed," Tom said and I could hear a little concern in his voice.

"Yup," I said as a slight chill went down my spine. I really wasn't looking forward to changing the tire out in the dark. "Leave it to me to get a flat tire on the road no delivery driver wants to be on. And to top it off I don't have a flashlight."

"What kind of pizza driver doesn't carry a flashlight?" Tom asked in an astonished voice that made me laugh. "Do you need someone to come out there and help you?"

"No," I replied even though every fiber of me wanted to say yes. "Your already short one driver and you don't need to lose another. If for some reason I can't see good enough to change the tire or if I have any problems, I'll give you a call."

"Ok," Tom reluctantly said. "Just keep me posted."

I agreed and we hung up. As soon as I put the phone back in my pocket I wished that I was still talking to Tom or Danny or anyone, someone to help me calm my nerves. Outside my car was total darkness and I prayed that was all there was.

I put the hazard lights on and slowly opened my door. I looked around and didn't see anything within my ten feet of visibility. I listened and didn't hear anything besides a light breeze blowing through the prairie. As satisfied as I could get I got out of the car and closed the door.

I walked around the car checking the tires as I went. Once I got to the front passenger side tire I noticed that it was definitely flat. I felt around the tire until I came across a tear on the outer side wall. I wondered what could have possibly ripped open the tire like it did. It almost looked like someone sliced it with a jagged knife.

I haven't had a flat in years, so I wondered if I had a spare. If I did it was probably one of those stupid little doughnut tires. Good thing I bought a heavy duty floor jack several years back or I would be out here all night trying to lift the car with a standard complementary jack.

I walked to the back of the car and opened the trunk. It was really hard to see since the only light source I had was the moon, when it wasn't behind the clouds anyway. I reached in to grab the jack and heard a snap of a branch from somewhere out in the prairie. I immediately scanned my surroundings, looking everywhere because I didn't have any idea which direction the noise came from. Another chill went down my spine as I stared out into the darkness of night. I still saw nothing, but my gut feeling told me someone or something was out there.

I reached back in the trunk and pulled out the jack, it was heavy. I carried it back to the flat and happily put it down. I walked back to the trunk and felt around until my hand came across the lug nut wrench. I unconsciously gripped it like someone would a weapon, then I lifted the trunk mat to find the spare. Yup, it was a doughnut.

I carried the spare to the front, still clutching the lug nut wrench as a weapon. I set the tire down next to the jack and looked around my surroundings one more time before I knelt down in front of my task. I no sooner started to take off the lug nuts when I heard another snap, but this time it was right behind me. I jumped to my feet while holding the wrench out in front of me, but there was nothing there.

My body momentarily quivered with fear and I was starting to feel like prey being stalked by a predator. It wasn't uncommon for mountain lions to come down from the mountains looking for food. If I was being stalked by one of the big cats and it became brave enough to attack, I wouldn't stand a chance.

I tried to think of something I could use to keep a big cat at bay, at least long enough for me to change the tire. The only thing I could think of was fire. Problem is I don't have any matches and I quit smoking years ago. Probably for the best anyway, I most likely would have ended up burning down the prairie and myself with it. The only other thing I could think of was turning on the car's headlights and hope that it doesn't kill the battery.

I turned around to go back to the driver's side of the car, but as I did I saw it. It was crouched on the hood of my car directly behind me. First thing I saw was its glowing red eyes, glaring at me in the dim light. But these were not the eyes of an animal, nor that of a human, but something in between. It had the face of a human, even though it was distorted. When its mouth opened and I saw the fangs, I realized that my childhood nightmares have come back to haunt me. The creature crouched in front of me was most definitely a predator, but far more dangerous and deadlier than any mountain lion. It was a creature of the night that preyed on humans for their blood. It was a vampire.

I jumped back when I saw the vampire and it watched my every move. There was an evil intelligence in its eyes and at that moment I knew it meant to kill me. I clenched the wrench in my hand so tightly my knuckles began to turn white; the vampire hardly seemed to even notice the futile weapon. Fear began to overwhelm me and the creature seemed to sense it and in a way feeding upon it. My heart began to work faster and the vampire stared at my chest as if it could hear the beat.

Fear welled up inside me so intensely tears began to flow from my eyes and I lost complete control of my body. I heard a low growling sound come from the vampire's throat, then the creature hissed as it bared its fangs. I wanted to run but my body wouldn't move. Then, in a blink of an eye, it was on me. I didn't see it leap off the car, even though I was looking directly at it. I felt the force of its body as it slammed into mine, knocking me to the ground. For an instant I could feel its hot breath, then the penetration as it bit into my neck. Agonizing pain shot through my body as the vampire tore away at my throat, slowly draining away my life force. I couldn't move. I couldn't scream. All I could do was lay there as my consciousness slowly drifted into darkness.

I began to see the light people say they see when they nearly die. Only thing is this light wasn't above me, it was coming towards me from the road. As I watched the light get closer I felt my body being dragged away, out into the prairie. I saw the form of a man in the light and he pointed something long and thin at me. There was a loud booming sound like thunder, and then fire shot out from the end of it. I heard a scream and the pressure on my neck released.

The man walked towards me and within moments I was looking up at him. He wore a cowboy hat and long black hair flowed out from underneath it. His face was unshaven and he smelled of dirt and sweat. I heard him say as he knelt down beside me, "Hold on, the ambulance is coming."

I saw him pull a small vial from a pocket and he poured the contents on my neck. I remembered smelling garlic and then screaming as it began to burn, then everything went black and the darkness finally took me.

Chapter Two

I hear voices, unfamiliar voices. They drag me out of my slumber and back to consciousness. My neck hurts. My head hurts. Everything hurts. I try to open my eyes and I'm forced to keep them shut. The light, sunlight, it's too bright. What happened to me? Where am I? All I remembered were eyes, glowing red eyes telling me not to move. The eyes brought pain and with the pain came darkness.

I tried to open my eyes again and this time with success. The sunlight was still irritating them and my vision is kind of blurry, but at least I could see. I looked around my surroundings and even with the fuzziness I could tell I was in a hospital. There was an IV in my arm and my neck was wrapped up with medical gauze, so I must have had some type of accident. I tried to remember what happened last night. I went to work and took a delivery to the new development; no way could I forget that. I delivered the pizza and on the way back my tire blew out. I tried to remember what happened after that, but everything was blank except for the red glowing eyes. I don't know why, but they stuck in my head like a horrible nightmare.

The door to my room opened and a man that I didn't recognize stepped in. He wasn't wearing doctor scrubs so I figured that he didn't work here. He wore a cowboy hat and had long black hair. As he approached my bed I smelled dirt and sweat, then I remembered everything. The fear from last night welled up inside of me again and the man seemed to notice. He put his hands out as a sign of trust, trying to show me that he meant no harm.

"Calm down," the man said as he quit approaching. "You're still feeling the fear effects from last night. I'm the guy that rescued you. My name is Shaun Miller."

"Fear effect?" I asked and I didn't have any idea what he was talking about. "I don't know what you mean. What fear effect?"

"How much do you remember from last night?" Shaun asked as he walked over to one of the three chairs in the room and sat down. "Do you remember anything about the attack?"

"All I remember is that while I was trying to change my tire I was attacked by some lunatic," I replied as the memories from last night raced through my mind.

"Is that all you remember?" Shaun asked again as he pushed for more information. "Try to picture your attacker's face."

I did as Shaun asked, but at first all that I could picture were the glowing red eyes. Then I remembered the fangs and the full description of my attacker came back to me. The memories were so horrific that the fear effect took over again. I shook my head rapidly trying to get the images out. Several moments went by before I was in control again. Once I gained my composure I looked at Shaun and asked, "What was that thing?"

"Everything I'm about to tell you can not be repeated," Shaun said in a very serious voice. "There are things, creatures, in this world you never knew existed. Monsters from fairy tales, creatures from TV, and probably some of the things from your nightmares are out there. Yes, all the fictional ghosts and goblins we go to the movies to see are real, and darn few people know they really exist. I was in that neighborhood last night because I was tracking one of the supernatural creatures, and luckily for you I was. The thing that attacked you last night was a vampire."

"Vampire?!" I said a lot louder than was intended. I didn't know if I should laugh or search around the room for a wooden stake and some holy water. "You're insane. Everyone knows that monsters don't exist and if they did why doesn't anyone ever see them?"

"Oh, but they do," Shaun assured me while still using a serious voice. "Many of the people in the asylums or even the State Hospital here in Pueblo say they've seen monsters. At night you can hear them screaming in their sleep and some of them have retreated so deep in their own minds all you can see is the fear in their eyes. I, myself have seen more than my share of the supernatural."

"If you seen all kinds of monsters then why haven't you told someone?" I asked in my most convincing voice. I was of the mind set that Shaun was a fruitcake and it would take more than ghost stories to convince me otherwise.

"I have," Shaun replied and I heard anger rise up into his voice. "But they didn't believe me anymore than you do right now. I spent my time in a padded cell and now that I'm out I have been hunting the creatures down. I hunt them down and I destroy them. I will never stop until I have taken out the last one or until they kill me first."

I personally believed Shaun needed to be back in a padded cell, but this time throw away the key. I didn't know just how stable he was and in my weakened state I really didn't want to fight off a mad man. I hoped beyond hope that he was reasonable so I thought up a reason for him to leave. I yawned and looked as tired as possible and then said, "I hate to run you off so quickly Shaun, but I am still terribly weak from the attack. Can we talk about this some other time?"

Shaun just looked at me and without saying a word he stood from the chair. I didn't think he bought my ruse; he just walked to the door and put his hand on the knob. Before he opened it he looked back at me and said, "I just wanted to warn you before it's too late. If you choose to believe it or not you have been bitten by a vampire. If you are lucky it was the master I destroyed and you have nothing more to fear, but if it was a minion you will find out soon enough. Very soon, one of these nights, possibly even tonight you will be visited by a vampire. If it is the master he will try to turn you, most likely to make up for the servant he lost. But if it is one of his minions, then it will just try to kill you. It will drain every last drop of blood from your body until you are nothing more than an empty sack of skin and bone. Personally, for your sake I hope it was the master I killed. If not, and if I were you, I would hope for a visit by the minion. By the way, the police report says that you were attacked by a mountain lion, what you tell everyone is up to you."

Shaun walked out before I could say a single word. I thought I would feel better once he left, but I found myself wishing he was still here. He might be insane, but the man did save my life and for some reason I felt safer with him around.

I turned on the TV and tried to get comfortable, but no sooner than I did a nurse walked into my room. She was heavy set, with a little longer than shoulder length brown hair. She had a kind face, but I also saw a little bit of playfulness in her green eyes. She walked over to my bed with a tray full of needles and pills. I hate shots, more than anything in the world. I remember once, when I was a kid, I had to get a tetanus shot, and it took four orderlies, my mother and brother to hold me down. I still managed to break the needle and deck a nurse in the process. I felt terribly bad about it later, but when faced with a phobia people will lash out anyway possible to escape it.

"Hello, my name is Nurse Sutherland. How are you feeling this morning?" The nurse asked as she picked up one of the needles. I immediately began to get nervous and she saw this. "Don't worry, with the IV all I have to do is just inject the medicine into the tube."

"What are you guys pumping into me?" I asked as I did my best to ignore the tube hanging out of my arm. "How much longer until I can get this IV out."

"Someone woke up on the wrong side of the bed this morning," Nurse Sutherland said with a slight amount of sarcasm. "Well this right here is a pain killer. This syringe is full of vitamins and this clear stuff right here is you're breakfast, yummy. Let me know how it tastes?"

I wasn't amused and she couldn't care less. Sounded like the beginning of a great friendship. I watched her inject the serums and I took the pills she handed me. I didn't make anymore smart remarks towards her since I saw her as my equal in that department. In my drugged out stage she would annihilate me. I found it best to just be quiet and let her do her job.

"Is there anything you need this morning?" Nurse Sutherland asked and I saw that playful look in her eyes again. She expected me to make a smart remark and when I didn't she seemed surprised and then a little disappointed. Instead I just shook my head, but when I did pain shot from the wound in my neck. "The pain killers that I gave you should help with that. When I come back in later I'll check you're bandages. Well, if you change you're mind about needing anything just use the little buzzer on the side of the bed."

Nurse Sutherland left the room carrying her tray of needles. I could already feel the pain killers kicking in and for a while all my problems melted away. I tried to watch TV and couldn't keep my concentration on it. The drugs made my mind wander and soon I drifted off to sleep.

I woke a few hours later after having a dream I had to use the bathroom. I found out after I woke up the dream was true. Those are one of the most annoying and possibly embarrassing dreams. No matter how many times you use the bathroom in you're dream you still need to go. The whole dream usually consists of you trying to find a bathroom.

Once I woke, I tried to get out of bed, but everything went black and my head started to get fuzzy. I didn't want one of those catheters hanging out of me so I buzzed the nurse and did my best to compose myself. I was sitting on the side of my bed when Nurse Sutherland came in. She looked at me and I didn't have to say a thing. She knew what I wanted and I swore she took great pleasure in teasing me about it; at least I hoped she was teasing.

"You have to go pee, don't you," Nurse Sutherland said as she walked over to me. She offered me her arm and helped me off the bed. "You know if you can't make it to the bathroom we will have to attach a catheter to you."

I looked at Nurse Sutherland, but I didn't say anything. She had a slight playful smile on her lips and a twinkle in her eyes. I could tell she was trying to be funny and she wanted me to say something, anything to give her room to work. Like I mentioned before, any other day I would have happily sat here and banter with her for hours, just today I wasn't up to it.

Nurse Sutherland helped me to the bathroom and made sure I was steady and the IV wouldn't get in the way before leaving the little room and letting me do my thing. I was relieved to see I didn't have any problems going to the bathroom; the last thing I wanted was another hose hanging out of me. Once I was finished I heard Nurse Sutherland outside the door talking to someone, then I heard the familiar voice of Tom. I flushed and washed my hands. As soon as I was finished Nurse Sutherland gently open the door and moved to my side. I looked around the room and saw I had three visitors, Tom, Danny and Steve.

Steve is the youngest manager at Aces; he is twenty one years old. He started working there five years ago as a pizza maker. He proved his worth so well that Tom offered him a manager position and, with it, a pay raise. Steve has short brown hair and is built like a body builder. He did a lot of weight lifting in high school while he played football. Normally I would have a hard time being managed by someone younger than me, but over the years Steve has proved himself and earned my respect. I even gave him a nickname, I call him Scooter. I really don't know why. I guess it was because he has kind of a child's face and when I look at him I imagined a kid riding a scooter. Don't ask me why, I'm not a psychologist.

"What's up guys?" I asked as Nurse Sutherland helped me back to my bed.

"You tell us," Tom replied as he watched the nurse help me. "I had a couple police officers stop by the shop last night and say you were in some kind of accident and had to be transported to the hospital. I asked them what kind of accident and the only thing they would tell me was the investigation was still going on and no other information could be revealed at that time."

"I was attacked," I started to say, and then I stopped. Tom, Danny and Steve stared at me with big eyes, even Nurse Sutherland stopped what she was doing to listen. I wondered if I should continue with what I was going to say, and then I remembered what Shaun told me. He said he told the police a mountain lion attacked me. I wasn't sure what to tell everyone right now. I didn't want to end up in a padded room, so until I knew more I figured it was best I just stuck to Shaun's side of the story. "While changing the flat last night I was attacked by a mountain lion. It sneaked right up in the darkness and attacked me. I never heard or saw it coming. Luckily someone was driving by and scared it off or I would have been its dinner for sure."

"Wow," Tom said in an astonished voice as he looked at the bandages on my neck. "Leave it to Jack to get attacked by the only mountain lion within thirty miles. Well it looks like you're going to be off the schedule for a few days."

"Then that means that the D-man is going to have to cover you're shifts," Danny said in an overacting discouraged voice. I knew he was joking, but I still felt bad about someone having to give up their spare time to work for me. "Thanks a lot Jack."

"I still say Jack is faking," Steve said playfully with a big grin. "We all know how much he hates to work the closing shifts. He probably staged the whole thing and even paid off the cops with a pizza to say he was attacked. That way he could get a few days off."

More questions came about last night and I made up lies to answer them. Nurse Sutherland checked the wire that was connected from my left index finger to one of the beeping machines, and then with a final look at me she left the room. The conversation lasted for about another thirty minutes then Tom said, "Well I have a lot of stuff to do so I better get out of here and let Jack rest."

Yeah, same here," Steve said as he stood up from one of the chairs. "I'm due in at Aces in less than an hour. I don't want to be late, even though I'm sure that Frank can handle it a few minutes without me."

"My girlfriend wants me to go shopping in a bit so I'm off also," Danny said and all of the sudden I didn't feel so bad. I did that once before with a past girlfriend and swore next time I would rather just walk out in front of a bus. "See ya Daaaack."

"Laters D-man," I said as I watched them walk out the door and Danny shut it behind him.

I was once again alone in the room and even though the silence was nice I still wished that I had some company. My nerves were still rattled from last night and visitors seemed to give me a moment of peace.

A few hours after the three stooges left, Nurse Sutherland opened the door to my room carrying her tray. I didn't complain this time; actually I was kind of happy to see her. The pain in my neck was starting to throb again, so I decided that I would put up with her banter for some pain killers. I guess in a way I was trading one pain in the neck for another.

"How are you feeling?" Nurse Sutherland asked as she injected serums into the IV tube. "Are you still in a lot of pain?"

"My neck is starting to hurt again," I replied and it kind of ached to talk. "Besides that I'm alright."

"We don't see many attacks like yours around here," Nurse Sutherland said as she handed me a couple pills and a cup of water. "The police and medical report both say the attack was done by a mountain lion, but you're eyes and voice says different."

"What do you mean?" I asked and I wondered if Nurse Sutherland actually knew more about the attack than what she led on. "I don't understand what you are trying to say. What do you mean by my voice and my eyes say different?"

"Its nothing I'm sure," Nurse Sutherland replied as she noticed I was getting upset. "It's just that when someone gets in a really bad trauma situation like you did, they don't like to talk about it. When they do try to talk you can see the fear in their eyes and hear it in their voice. When you talk about you're attack there isn't any. That usually means you were not traumatized by the attack or you're not telling the truth."

"Are you trying to say that I did this to myself?" I asked as I was trying to think of a lie to get me out of this one.

"Of course not," Nurse Sutherland replied and I could tell that she was worried I was offended. "I was just wondering if you were that it was a mountain lion that attacked you."

I thought about telling her the truth that it wasn't a mountain lion at all. I thought about telling her it was some kind of super fast madman with fangs and glowing red eyes. I wanted to tell her the truth instead of the ruse I was using. I wanted to tell her the creature that attacked me was a vampire, but I didn't want to spend the rest of my life in a padded room. I didn't even like delivering to the State Hospital; I surely didn't want to live there.

I just looked at Nurse Sutherland without saying a word. I didn't want to have this conversation with her. Something told me that she would know if I was lying or not and I really didn't want to take the chance of ending up in a padded room, so I kept my mouth shut.

"Well my shift is ending and I won't be back until tomorrow morning," Nurse Sutherland said as she checked my bandages and then picked up her tray. "You're neck looks like it's begun to heal. It's a good thing the cat missed anything vital or we wouldn't be having a conversation right now. Anyway, if you need anything Nurse Francis is here and just a button push away."

I thanked Nurse Sutherland with a smile as she left the room. I went back to watching my program, but the drugs were starting to kick in and I felt sleepy. My eyes were beginning to droop so I figured it was futile to resist the side effects of the medicine. I turned off the TV and the lights. I closed my eyes and within a few minutes I drifted off into a deep sleep.

As I slept I started to have nightmares of vampires. I saw their red glowing eyes staring at me from the shadows. I tried to run from them, but everywhere I turned I could still see their eyes. As I ran I could feel the fear effect swarm up inside me. Up ahead I could see my car parked on the side of the road. If only I could make it to the car, then I could drive away and leave this nightmare behind me. I ran as fast as I could and I heard them laughing from all sides. I heard their laughter echoing inside my head to the point I thought I must scream or go insane.

I finally reached my car; oh thank God I made it. I searched my pockets for the keys and thankfully they were there. I got in the car and tried to start the engine, but it wouldn't turn over. I tried again, but the car was dead. Looking out the windows I saw the vampires. They circled my car like caged animals. I didn't know what to do. I wanted to yell for help, but my voice wouldn't work.

I heard scratching at my window and when I looked I saw one of them, staring into my eyes as it clawed at the window with its long sharp claws. I noticed every time the vampire did this it left gouges in the glass. I knew the window wouldn't keep them out, but I had no way of stopping them.

Suddenly I woke up in the hospital bed, but I still heard the scratching sound. I looked over to the window where the noise was coming from and to my relief I saw a tree branch scraping against it. I let out a sigh of relief; apparently I was letting Shaun's stories mess with my head.

I sat up in bed and my heart was still pounding. I've had many nightmares before, but none of them had ever been so frightening, so real. I stared around the room, but my vision still hadn't adjusted to the dark. The room looked the same as before, at least what I could make out. The little light from the moon which came in through the windows didn't help out much. I was just about to lay back down when I saw the slightest bit of movement out of the corner of my eye. I glanced in that direction and what I saw made my heart skip a beat. Red glowing eyes were staring at me from across the room. My breathing became rapid and the fear factor whelmed up inside of me again.

I couldn't think straight. I didn't know what to do, so I did the first thing that came to mind. As fast as possible I reached for the button to summon the nurse, but no matter how fast I moved it wasn't fast enough. The vampire was across the room in a heartbeat, one hand clenched my arm and the other had my neck. Pain shot through my body and I couldn't breathe. The creature's amazing supernatural strength was crushing my arm and windpipe. I knew that the vampire had to be playing with me, because if it wasn't I would have been dead by now.

The vampire brandished it's fangs as it ripped the bandages off my neck, and then it leaned forward to tear out my throat. I heard the creature breathe in deeply as it smelled the blood, then I felt its lips brush against my neck. I knew this time my life was over and no matter how much I struggled there was nothing I could do about it. As ironic as it sounds I now knew I should have listened to Shaun. Then for some unexplained reason the fear effect stopped and I found myself not afraid of the vampire any longer. The danger of the moment was still very evident, but I was no longer scared and the vampire sensed it. The creature stopped just centimeters from my neck, then it raised up to look me in the eyes and for the first time I saw it was stunned. I tried to use the opportunity to break free from the vampire's grip, but the creature's amazing supernatural strength had me pinned.

The vampire had been feeding off my fear. It looked at me in confusion and I saw its lips part as it began to speak, but the only thing the creature was able to say was "How...?" Then a crossbow bolt erupted from the vampire's chest. The creature looked down at the protruding piece of wood, then as if by some magical effect it turned to dust and imploded until nothing remained except for a little black marble that fell onto the bed.

I looked in the direction the bolt came from and I saw Shaun standing in the doorway with a crossbow in his hands. He looked at me and saw the surprised look on my face. He walked over to the bed and picked up the little black marble and put it in his pocket. A small smile came across his face and then he asked, "Now do you believe me?"

The only thing I managed to do was nod. Shaun walked over to the same chair as earlier and sat down. He looked at me, but didn't say a word. I guess he knew I was still stunned from the attack and probably wouldn't have heard much he said anyway. Then after a few minutes he asked, "What did you do to the vampire right before I shot it?"

"What do you mean?" I asked because I didn't understand what he was talking about.

"It looked shocked," Shaun said as he laid his crossbow on the chair next to him. "The only times I have ever seen a vampire look shocked was when I killed one. It was about to rip out your throat and it stopped. You had it so confused it didn't even notice me enter the room, and those blood sucking freaks have extraordinary hearing and senses."

"I don't know," I said and I really didn't have a clue. "I just quit being afraid of it. The vampire froze up a minute and stared at me. I think it was going to ask me how, but before the vampire could finish what it was saying you shot it."

Shaun was quiet for a while, contemplating what I told him, and then he said, "You have been suffering from the fear effect from the other vampire and it finally wore off."

"This vampire was using its fear effect on me?" I asked and I wasn't really sure what I was talking about. "When it stopped working, wouldn't the fear effect from this vampire taken over?"

"Yes," Shaun replied and I heard the astonished tone in his voice. "That's what is supposed to happen anyway. At least that's what happened when I've witnessed it in the past. We have bigger things to worry about right now anyway."

"What bigger things?" I asked as I wondered what Shaun meant. "What the heck is happening now?"

"A second vampire has been killed and the master will definitely not be happy," Shaun replied and when he did I knew this was far from being over. "The master will most likely be the one who comes after you this time. Two of its minions have been killed and I'm sure it will want to replace them. If for some reason the master doesn't come it will send more minions, but this time more than one will come. I will do what I can to protect you, but I don't know what I can do against a master. I have never fought one, but I have seen what they can do. If by some miracle we survive until you are released from the hospital we will have a better chance of fighting them on the street.

"How will I contact you once I'm released?" I asked and I didn't like the idea of having to depend on Shaun for my survival.

"Don't worry about that," Shaun replied as he disassembled his crossbow and stood up. He walked over to my nightstand and placed a little piece of paper on it. "I took the liberty of fixing your car and brought it here. It has been valet parked and can be picked up when you are released. This paper is the ticket to retrieve it. Just show it to the valet when you are ready to leave."

"What was that black marble you picked up off the bed earlier?" I asked and my neck hurt again. I put my hand on the wound and felt liquid. When I pulled my hand away blood ran slowly down it.

"It's what vampires turn into once they die," Shaun replied as he showed me the little black marble. "The negative energies that help vampires exist turn into this marble when they implode. I started collecting them. Oh, and you had better get you're neck bandaged back up. Some of you're stitches have been ripped open."

With those final words Shaun walked to the door and left, once again before I could say anything. I pushed the buzzer on the side of my bed and a few minutes later there was a knock at my door and Nurse Francis stepped in. She was younger than Nurse Sutherland and a little on the petite side. She wasn't particularly pretty, but she wasn't really ugly as well. Her long brown hair was the same color as her eyes and unlike Nurse Sutherland she had a more serious look about her. As soon as Nurse Francis entered the room she asked, "Was there something you needed?"

"I think that I struggled in my sleep and tore my bandage off," I said.

Nurse Francis turned on the light and when she did I heard her make a small gasp. The wound on my neck had bled onto my hospital smock, making things look far worse than they really were.

"Oh my," Nurse Francis said as she walked over to my bed and started examining my wound. "Looks like you tore a couple stitches loose, but it doesn't look bad enough to bother a doctor. I should be able to stick it back together with some surgical glue. Give me a moment and I'll have you back together in a jiffy."

Nurse Francis left the room and came back a few minutes later with a tray and two syringes. She took one syringe that was full of a clear gel and I noticed right away that it didn't have a needle. She started applying the gel onto my wound and I felt a little bit of pressure. Pain surged through my neck and down my spine. I stiffened up and gritted my teeth. Nurse Francis looked at me and said, "I'm so sorry. I didn't realize the pain medication had worn off."

Nurse Francis took the other syringe, this one had a needle. She injected the serum into my IV and after a few minutes she began to work on my neck again. It still hurt at first, and then the pain killer began to kick in. Once Nurse Francis was finished patching me up she helped me to the bathroom and handed me another hospital smock to wear. I changed and did my business; then she helped me back to bed. Once I was back in bed and snug as a bug Nurse Francis asked me, "Is there anything else you need before I return to my station?"

I shook my head and thanked Nurse Francis, then she opened the door and shut it quietly behind her. My life had taken a total twist. I now knew supernatural creatures existed and I was going to be hunted down by them until I was killed. Geez, I may never sleep at night again.

Chapter Three

My mom and sister came to visit me at the hospital, talking about a pain in the neck. My mom was hysterical. After hearing about the mountain lion attack she was convinced my job was too dangerous and I needed to find a different one. It took me a half hour just to get her to realize I wasn't going to quit. What happened to me was a freak accident; well that's what I told her anyway.

My sister's name is Janet. She is seven years older than me, but we get along great. She has long, straight brown hair that she parts down the middle. I'm not sure, but I think she has had the same hair style for as long as I could remember. She is fun to be around and always seems to be full of energy.

I also have an older brother, whose name is Andrew. He is three years older and almost completely bald. He started balding at a young age and over the years his hair seemed to disappear from his head and reappear on his back. Janet used to say Andrew's hair is making a b-line to his behind. As children, I never really got along with Andrew, but now that we are older I think he is trying to make up for lost time.

My mom's name is Karen and she has curly purple hair. Well not exactly purple. She dyes it black, but in the light it looks purple. She's blind from a car accident that happened when I was a teenager. It was a really nasty accident. We were on our way home from Oklahoma, where my sister and her husband Brian Quest lived at the time. Brian has short brown hair and kind of bulgy blue eyes that makes him look like he's surprised all the time. He is clean shaven and has several tattoos on his arms. They weren't covered with ink; he just had about three or four small ones on each arm. Brian was kind of built in his younger years, but he is getting kind of flabby in the mid-section.

Brian was in the military and about to go out into the field for a week. Janet didn't want to stay home by herself so we drove to Oklahoma and picked her up. Andrew drove on the way home. It was raining and I was sleeping in the back seat. Janet and my mom were sitting in the front with Andrew. No one was completely sure what happened, but the car swerved off the side of the road and into a ravine. I was awakened by being thrashed around in the back seat and when all was still I saw that everyone was unconscious. My mom and Janet were badly injured, while Andrew and I only received minor bruises from the accident.

Some people stopped to help us, but little could be done until the ambulance arrived. My mom and sister were transported to a hospital and then flown by helicopter to Kansas. Everyone survived the accident, but my mom was blinded and had to have her face surgically reconstructed. Janet lost an eye and broke a collar bone. She was in the hospital for around three months, but my mother was there a lot longer.

As the years went by Janet and Brian left the military life and moved back to Colorado. Andrew got married and moved to Wisconsin, where he and his wife live happily. My mom learned to cope with her handicap and now lives alone ever since my dad died a few years ago. He smoked most of his life and finally died from cancer. She only lives a couple miles away from Janet and even less from me.

I was released from the hospital a few days after my mom's visit and without anymore attempts on my life. I was almost convinced the vampires decided I wasn't worth the effort, but Shaun didn't agree. He figured they were waiting for my release so they could get me on the streets. Not a very comforting thought.

I got kind of close to Nurse Sutherland over the last few days. She was actually a very nice person. I still kept to my mountain lion story though; I personally didn't think she could handle the truth. Anyway, the least she knew about what was out there the better. Most people go their whole lives without even seeing a supernatural creature. It's just the few unlucky ones, or the people who are hunting for it that get to experience the true dark side of the night.

Once released, Nurse Sutherland walked me outside to the valet and they brought my car down. The doughnut was on my car so the first thing I had to do was buy a tire. I said my goodbyes and drove to a discount tire shop near the mall. Thirty dollars and thirty minutes later and I was on my way home.

I pulled up in front of my house and couldn't wait to get inside. It was daytime so I doubt there were any uninvited vampire visitors inside, not to mention if any of the old legends were true vampires couldn't enter without permission anyway.

When I reached the front door I saw a business card tacked to it. It was to a nightclub downtown on Main Street called the Crimson Chateau. There was some writing on the card which said, "I found the lair. Meet me at nine-o-clock tonight, Shaun."

I'd heard of the nightclub, but had never been there. It was supposed to be a high class striptease bar. I seriously didn't think Shaun wanted to get together tonight so we could hang out with a couple hot dancers and party, so I figured the lair he referred to had to be a vampire hangout. I drove past the club dozens of times and never did I think, "this is a great place for vampire."

Now that I stopped to think about it, it made perfect sense. A bunch of people drooling over vampire strippers, they could take the patrons into their private room for a little lap dance and some blood sucking. The name of the club even sounds like something a vampire would give it. Geez, I wonder if the Silver Moon Tavern down on B Street was a werewolf hangout. I don't think I will ever get used to the supernatural world.

I took the card even though I didn't want to go there and went inside. Everything looked the way I left it. The first thing I wanted was a shower. My skin smelled like medicine from all the crap they were injecting into me. I knew the shower wouldn't completely get rid of the smell, but anything was better.

After the shower I decided I should call Tom and get myself back on the schedule. Workman's compensation should cover most of the hospital bills, if not all of them. You never know though, so it was best to get back to work as soon as possible.

I called Tom on his cell phone and like usual he didn't answer, so I just left a message. I knew he would get back to me soon. When one of his drivers was out of commission for some reason or another he usually checks his messages regularly. The trick was to get him to call you back when it wasn't an emergency or work related. I started to think the only reason he even has a cell phone is to annoy me with a stupid radio commercial I hate. Tom likes to listen to talk radio, which I despise. He would listen to it for hours and every time a certain annoying commercial came on it would drive me nuts. Tom realized how much I hated it and ever since then he would call me when it was on and hold the phone up to the speaker. I probably hold the record for the number of times an employee has hung up on his boss. That's alright though. I found out he doesn't like a certain eighties rock band.

I spent the next hour looking up web sites on vampires, never thought I would be doing such a thing. I had just finished browsing through the fifth site when my cell phone rang. I checked to see who it was first because I really didn't want to talk to my mom. It was Tom so I answered.

"Monday morning at eleven," Tom said even before I had a chance to say hello.

"Ok," I said.

"See ya," Tom said.

I heard the click as he hung up. Unless he's being a pain or if it's an emergency, our phone conversations are relatively short.

I went back to my research on the computer. Most of the web sites agreed on the same stuff, crosses and holy water can hurt vampires. If you wanted to kill one you had to stake it through the heart or drag one out into the sunlight. I figured that a wooden stake through the heart would kill anyone, vampire or not. I didn't want to kill a normal human so I figured it was best to use sunlight. Now all I had to do was find a vampire and some way to contain it until morning without getting myself killed.

I made some dinner and watched an old vampire movie. It pretty much agreed with the internet on what to use on a vampire. I didn't have any crosses or holy water, but I was sure Shaun had plenty of both.

Half way through the movie my mom called. She asked how I was doing and wondered if Janet and Andrew called me yet. They hadn't. She started to tell me about what her neighbors did today and what she had for dinner so I decided to make up an excuse to hang up. I told her I was still extremely tired and needed some sleep. It worked, she hung up and I finished watching my movie.

After the movie I glanced outside and noticed it was dark. I looked at my watch and saw it was almost nine-o-clock, so I turned off the TV and headed for the door. As I stepped outside I noticed a black sedan parked behind my car. I walked down the sidewalk and saw a man dressed in a black dress shirt, black slacks and a blood red tie get out of the sedan. As he approached me I stopped dead in my tracks. My first thought was vampire, but I didn't see any red glowing eyes. The man walked up to me and extended his hand in greeting, and then he said, "Jack Holladay?" When I didn't respond he smiled and withdrew his hand. "My name is Sam Jones and you have been summoned."

"Summoned?" I asked as I stared at the man. He had brown eyes and neatly trimmed black hair that was parted to the side. "What do you mean summoned? Who the heck are you?"

"Like I said, I am Sam Jones," The man replied. "My employer has instructed me to bring you to her establishment. She would like to have an audience with you. Her name is Katrina De Luce."

"What does this Katrina want to talk to me about?" I asked with no intentions of going anywhere.

"I do not ask my employer what her intentions are," Sam replied still in a very calm voice. "She tells me what she wants and I see that it gets done. Now if you don't mind Katrina is waiting."

"I'm sorry," I said in a very determined voice. "I already have plans for tonight. You're employer is going to have to wait for another night."

"You don't seem to understand," Sam said and I heard a little bit of irritation in his voice. "Katrina doesn't take no for an answer. You will accompany us."

"Us?" I asked as I looked around for someone else, but there was no one to be seen. "Listen. This Katrina is going to have to learn some humility because I'm not going anywhere with you. Now get out of my way and don't ever try to tell me what I am going to do again."

"The hard way it is," Sam said and gestured to the sedan. As soon as he did the passenger door opened and a beautiful black haired woman stepped out. As she walked towards us I noticed that she moved very smoothly, especially since she was wearing the highest heelsI have ever seen. "Selene my dear, would you help me escort Jack to the car?"

Selene didn't say a word. She looked at me with her big green eyes and I saw that they were full of sorrow. I didn't let the sadness fool me. Selene's eyes revealed more than any words possibly could. Even though she looked at me with an innocent smile I could tell she was a predator.

Selene reached slowly for my arm, but I pulled away. The woman was very beautiful, but I could tell she was also very dangerous. Sam grew tired of the game. He grabbed at me with incredible speed and even though I tried to avoid him I wasn't fast enough.

Sam began to drag me towards the sedan and with little effort. I was amazed by his strength. He didn't look anywhere as strong as he led on, but this man was as powerful as an ox. Selene fell into suite as she began to follow us. I struggled with Sam to no avail, so I took a swing at him with my free arm. My fist connected with his jaw and his head cocked to the side. It felt like I hit a brick wall and my hand throbbed from the pain. When Sam looked back at me he had blood trailing down from his lip, but that wasn't what had my attention. His eyes were glowing red. Sam was a vampire.

There was no fear effect and I don't think Sam noticed or even cared if I was scared. I saw him clench his fist and swing at me. I got my arm up in time to block, but it didn't matter. The vampire's strength was so much more than mine that all I ended up doing was hurting my arm on his. I didn't even slow his motion. Sam hit me on the forehead and everything went black.

Chapter Four

I woke up with one heck of a headache. I tried to open my eyes, but the light just intensified the pain. I reached up to my forehead and cringed yet again. There was a bump the size of a mountain. Why couldn't he have hit me on the side of the head? Now I will be going around for days looking like a unicorn, if I live that long.

"Wait a second," I thought to myself. "I have just been hit in the head by a vampire."

I forced my eyes open through the pain and once they adjusted to the light I noticed I wasn't home. Who's ever home I was in they definitely had expensive taste. The bed was an antique canopy with a blood red curtain around it. It was the first thing I noticed for the simple fact I was laying on it.

The covers I was on were also blood red and when I got off the bed I saw the carpet was red as well. The walls were a glossy light gold color that somehow seemed to compliment the red in the room perfectly. The rest of the furnishings were also antique, everything from the wardrobe to the nightstand. Even the loveseat sitting to the right of the bed was an old Victorian style, but I was sure what was laying on it was even older yet.

A young woman that looked no older than eighteen was stretched across the loveseat. She wore a black form fitting dress with purple roses designed into it and black pumps. She had straight golden blond hair that was parted down the middle and she did nothing more than look at me with her big attractive piercing blue eyes. Her eyes alone told me she was much older than what she looked. She didn't move. She almost looked like a wax statue with her pale skin. She just lay on the loveseat and stared at me. It was weird how she stayed perfectly still, not even breathing. She showed no signs of life until I stood up, then she gracefully sat up on the loveseat. Her eyes never left me and the more creeped out I felt, the more content she seemed to be.

I had a sudden urge to run for the door, but I'd seen the speed of vampires. She would be there waiting for me before I even sprinted halfway. This game was getting old to me and I was already very late for my meeting with Shaun. Irritated because I was taken unwillingly from my home and placed in a room where nothing was less than a hundred years old, and not to mention assaulted. Now I have a young woman rudely staring at me and I was quite positive she wasn't this Katrina which wanted to see me. So I looked back at the woman and in a firm, but polite voice I said, "You can't possibly be Katrina."

"Why do you say that?" The young woman asked as a smile spread across her lips and when she did I saw the tips of her fangs. "Is it because I look so young?"

"Yes, I guess it is," I replied with a nod. The woman seemed to like my ignorance because she giggled. "How old are you?"

"Let's just say I am older than everything in this room," the vampire replied with a wide smile and this time I was able to clearly see her fangs.

"Then you are Katrina," I said assuming she was and very much to her amusement. The vampire laughed, almost hysterically.

"Mortals are so amusing when it comes to things they can't understand," the vampire said as she brought her laughter under control. "Katrina is even older than I am. The sheer sight of her can make mortals tremble with fear."

"I guess since I don't tremble with fear in you're presence you must be kind of weak," I said in a mocking voice.

It was probably a stupid thing to do, but the vampire was arrogant and one thing I couldn't stand was arrogant people, human or vampire.

"How dare you speak to me like that?" The vampire yelled as she jumped off the loveseat and cleared the distance between me and her in an instant. The vampire's eyes were glowing red as she grabbed my neck with one hand and pain surged throughout my body. I felt some of my stitches break under my bandages. She effortlessly lifted me off the floor even though she didn't look like it, she could possibly lift a car. All air flow had ceased and I couldn't breathe. "I should rip out you're throat and drain you off all you're blood!"

For a moment I actually thought she was going to follow through with her threat. Just when I thought I was going to lose consciousness I heard another woman's voice, "Jezebel! Put him down right now! He is worth nothing to us dead!"

I felt my air passage open freely and I gasped deeply as I fell to the ground. I felt a warm liquid begin to run down my neck. My wound had opened back up and blood slowly flowed from it, leaking out from under my bandages. As soon as my breathing became normal and the black spots vanished I looked up at the new woman. She was beautiful, even more so than Jezebel. She had long red hair and her eyes were emerald green. She wore a black evening dress slit up to the hip on the left side, exposing a generous amount of leg. A glossy black leather belt and red high heel shoes completed her outfit. She looked down at me with those green eyes and I saw years of wisdom in them. Years that far surpassed her apparent age.

"What do you mean I am worthless to you dead?" I asked as soon as I was able to talk. "Who are you?"

"I am Katrina De Luce and you, Jack Holladay, have been found responsible for the deaths of four vampires," Katrina said.

The vampire watched my expression when she said four vampires. I didn't know what she was looking for, but my guess was she wasn't disappointed because she smiled delightfully.

"What do you mean four vampires?" I asked.

I remembered they didn't know Shaun was involved in this and he was actually the one responsible. I could only count for two vampires that Shaun killed; for all I knew he could have killed others in the last few days.

"Are you saying you didn't kill them?" Katrina asked and I could tell she was anxious for my response. If I tell her no then she would know I had help and I would end up putting Shaun's life in jeopardy.

"I didn't say that," I replied as I tried to think up lies as I went. I was getting pretty good at making things up. "Ok, I was the one that killed them."

"Really?" Katrina asked and I could tell she was playing with me. She obviously knew something I didn't and I seriously doubted she bought my lie. How could a mortal possibly kill four vampires, especially with no weapons and in the hospital? "Tell me Mr. Jack Holladay, how did you go about doing so?"

"The one in the prairie I stabbed with an old dead branch," I replied as I struggled with what to say. "The one in the hospital I stabbed with a silver crucifix I found in the top drawer of the nightstand."

"A silver crucifix?" Katrina asked in an amused voice and this time she wasn't able to hide her smile. "Usually they keep those securely fastened on the wall above the bed. Did the crucifix work well?"

"Yup," I replied even though I knew she didn't believe me. Something I said gave me away so I didn't see anymore reasons to play her game. "Fried the bloodsucker, right before it imploded."

"What about the other two vampires?" Katrina asked in a mocking voice. She saw that I caught onto her game and I didn't want to pursue it any further.

"Cut the crap!" I yelled and I could see the anger in her face. In the corner of my eye I even saw Jezebel take a couple steps towards me, but Katrina stopped her with just a raise of her hand. "We both know I had nothing to do with the deaths of any of the vampires. I was a victim in both attacks. As for the death of the last two I don't know anything about them."

"I know," Katrina said in a calm voice. All traces of anger had vanished. "This time tell me the truth about the vampire deaths."

I thought about telling Katrina about Shaun. Maybe if I did she would let me live and take her revenge out on him instead. Not likely. Shaun saved my life twice and who's to say Katrina would let me go after I betray him. The most likely scenario is she would kill both of us, or worse, turn us into one of them to make up for lost minions.

"That's information I don't wish to reveal," I said and once again Katrina's anger flared up and I could feel the tension in the room.

"I could care less what you do or don't want," Katrina said as her eyes began to glow red. I could tell at once she was trying the fear effect on me and to her surprise as well as mine, it didn't work. The vampire master screamed as she glared at me and her face contorted with rage. "How is this possible?! Why aren't you trembling at my feet?!"

"Probably because I don't find you scary," I replied. When I did I knew it wasn't the best thing to say to something that could rip off my head.

"Let me punish him for you mistress," Jezebel said and she took a couple aggressive steps towards me. "I promise I won't kill him, just make him wish he was dead."

"No! I have killed and devoured mortals for far less than what you have done here tonight," Katrina replied as she showed me the full force of her anger. "Now you insolent dog, get down on you're knees and beg for my forgiveness!"

I could feel Katrina's power all around me and also in my head. It tore at me like a thousand hungry demons would an innocent soul. I tried to block her out, but her will was too strong. I felt I must drop to my knees or go insane. Katrina's power was above me, forcing me down. My legs trembled until they finally collapsed. I dropped to my knees and I could hear Katrina's voice in my head, telling me to beg for forgiveness. It was so compelling I found myself wanting to obey her. For all my will, for all my fighting effort, it was still all for nothing. In the end I still pleaded, "Please forgive me."

I looked up at Katrina as I felt her slowly leaving my head and I wanted to kill her. I wanted nothing more than her blood on my hands as I snuffed out whatever unholy spark that was sustaining her life force. I slowly tried to get to my feet, but my legs were still too wobbly. Then I heard a door open and I looked past Katrina to see who it was. Sam walked into the room with a body slung over his right shoulder, then moments later Selene gracefully entered behind him. From my position I couldn't see who the vampire was carrying, but my intuition told me it was someone I knew. Sam walked over to us and half laid, half dropped the body next to me. There was a grunt of pain as the body hit the floor. That is when I knew it was Shaun.

Shaun's hat was missing, but he wore an old western style duster. Selene walked up to us holding two .45 hand guns and a sawed off shotgun, which explained the duster that Shaun was wearing. He needed something long to conceal the shotgun. Shaun lay on the red carpet without moving. If it wasn't for his breathing I would have sworn he was dead.

"Don't worry," Katrina said as she smiled down at us. "He lives for now and he may just keep on living if you do what you're told."

"What do you want from me?" I asked as I finally found enough strength in my legs to stand. "What could I possibly do to earn our freedom?"

"The two vampires your friend killed were not from my coven," Katrina said as she walked over to the loveseat and sat down. Selene followed the master vampire and sat at her feet. "They belonged to another master named Boris Von Kruger. He is very powerful, almost equal to my own strength."

"Wait a second," I said as I moved a comfortable distance away from Sam, who showed no expression what so ever. "I know Shaun killed two vampires. Who killed the other two?"

"Those two vampires came to the hospital to kill you the night before you're release," Katrina replied, as she absent mindlessly stroked Selene's hair. "One of our human informants that works there told us about you're attack, you know her by the name Nurse Sutherland. I knew that Boris would have you killed, so I sent some of my servants to make sure they couldn't possibly succeed. If Boris was concentrating on his servants he could have been looking through their eyes. We attacked quickly from behind so Boris would not be able to see who attacked them. My plan was flawlessly executed."

"Why?" I asked because I was very confused about why Katrina wanted to keep me alive. "What importance could I possibly have for you?"

"Like I said, Boris thinks you killed all four of his servants," Katrina replied a little irritated by the interruption. "He planned to kill you tonight at you're home, but we contacted him first and told him we had you. After some negotiating we came to terms that you will be traded for an alliance against a much more powerful master vampire. One that is more powerful than both Boris and I put together. His name is Nathaniel Nevis."

"Give me one reason why I should assist you?" And don't say you will kill Shaun because he would rather die than help you," I said and I was determined to make Katrina kill me before I did her bidding. Boris was probably going to anyway, but if I played my cards right maybe I could get him to kill Katrina as well.

"That is very true," Katrina said as she smiled and I saw her fangs. "I could force you to do my will. The same way I made you beg for forgiveness, but where would the fun be in that? How about we all go out for pizza tonight before the meeting with Boris? I heard Aces Pizza is a great place to dine."

Katrina didn't need to say another word; I knew exactly what she meant. If I didn't willingly do what she wanted, then her entire entourage would visit Aces and kill everyone there. There were a couple employees I wasn't fond of and I wouldn't mind if they came up missing, but I would hate to see the same thing happen to the rest.

"You win Katrina," I reluctantly said. "I will do whatever you want on one condition. Shaun is released after the trade and I don't mean by killing or turning him."

"You are hardly in a position to negotiate," Katrina said with a very amused tone in her voice. I could tell that she was very surprised I was trying to bargain. "Fine, I agree. You do exactly what you're told and when I return I will release the fearless vampire slayer."

I really didn't believe Katrina. I was sure she meant to kill Shaun as soon as she returned, probably to make an example of him. Maybe by the time the bloodsuckers returned he will have awakened and found a way to escape. Katrina was sure to leave a guard or two, but from the sound of things she wanted to take as much muscle as possible with her. She would probably leave a couple newer recruits, which is still more than any weaponless mortal could handle.

I doubt she would leave Sam. He may not say much, but I could tell he was her champion and he is old. Not as old as Katrina, but definitely older than Jezebel. Selene also has a very old feeling about her, but I couldn't tell if she was older, or younger than Sam. By the looks of things one thing was for sure, Katrina seemed to favor her. She stood apart from the rest of the vampires in lots of ways. Vampires moved very smoothly, but her movements were even more so. Another thing I noticed was her skin wasn't pale like the others. As a matter of a fact if I stared closely enough I could see her breathing. I didn't know if it was because she was a newly turned vampire and breathing from force of habit or if she wasn't one at all.

"I see you staring at Selene," Katrina said and she smiled when she did. "Is there something wrong with her?"

"I don't know why, but she seems to be out of place here," I replied as I looked at Selene's perfectly shaped face and slim muscular body. "Is she newly turned?"

"No," Katrina replied as she burst out in laughter. I heard Jezebel also laugh and when I looked at Sam I actually saw the slightest smile appear on his face. "As a matter of fact Selene isn't a vampire at all, nor is she completely human."

"What is she then?" I asked and I could already tell that she wasn't completely human, even without Katrina confirming it for me.

"Selene is a lycanthrope," Katrina replied and she smiled when she saw me recoil a little. "What's the matter Jack? Don't you like lycanthropes?"

"Not really," I replied and I found I could no longer stare at Selene. "Why is she here with you? According to the movies vampires and werewolves were enemies."

"Those vile creatures are enemies with every living being," Katrina replied and I could hear the distaste in her voice. "Selene is not a werewolf though. Her lycanthropy comes from the cat family. They are called were-panthers."

I was confused and Katrina could see it. I was new to the supernatural world and unless I saw it on a movie I had no idea it existed. Lycanthropes were always savage bloodthirsty creatures, but then again I guess so were vampires. I wished Shaun was awake. I'm sure he'd heard of were-panthers and could explain them to me.

"Well that confirms she isn't a vampire," I said and I could feel Selene staring at me. I took a chance and glanced up at her and when I did our eyes locked. When I looked into those big green orbs I didn't see the inhumanity as when I looked at Katrina. There was sadness in her eyes, almost as if she felt pity for me. "It still doesn't explain why she is hanging out with a bunch of bloodsuckers."

Jezebel was instantly upon me; her clawed hand was wrapped around my neck. I never saw her move until I felt my air passage close and saw her red glowing eyes staring at me. I knew she didn't like being called a bloodsucker, no matter how true it was. This is one of the reasons why I kept using the term.

"Let him be Jezebel," Katrina said in calm, but commanding voice.

Once again the vampire released me and I was able to breathe. I heard a sucking sound and I saw Jezebel licking my blood from her hand. She smiled at me and made a yummy sound.

"Selene is with us because of an alliance she made with me," Katrina continued after the lively interruption. "Unlike werewolf packs there are few were-panthers in a Pride. The only time a human is ever turned into a were-panther is when they are willing. Like their cousins Selene and her kind can change at will, but when the moon is full werewolves lose all control of their humanity and become mindless bloodthirsty beasts. Even in their human form werewolves tend to be foul and full of hate. When they feed they prey upon humans, while Selene and her Pride prefer to feed upon livestock. For some reason the werewolves in this city have been attacking other lycanthropes. Selene needed our help to fight against the werewolf pack and with her power added to mine Boris has been inclined to keep things neutral between us."

I heard the door to the room open again, but this time I saw someone walk in I didn't recognize. The person that walked in looked like he was an average man in his forties. He had short black hair that was neatly combed back and dark blue eyes. He wore a dress shirt and pants that fit him perfectly. Just by the clumsy way he moved I could tell he was human, probably one of their contacts. He didn't have the vampire feel about him.

The man walked over to stand next to Sam, while all along never taking his eyes off Katrina. He never even looked at me and Shaun. I guess he considered us beneath him. Either that, or by not looking at the prisoners was like they were not there. One way or another he took Katrina's attention off me, for once she saw him she asked, "Yes, what is it Sebastian?"

"The limos await," Sebastian said in a very proper manner. "Boris said he will meet you at midnight in the Rosemont."

"What's the Rosemont?" I asked since I was a delivery driver and never heard of the place. "Is it some kind of vampire hangout?"

"Something like that," Katrina replied with an amused chuckle. I guess I must have said something funny again. Ok people, let's head out."

"What about Shaun," I said as I gestured to his motionless body. "We can't just leave him laying there."

"So be it," Katrina said with a sigh. I could tell she was getting frustrated with my human ways. "Sam, put the vampire slayer on the bed, gently this time. We seem to forget how fragile these mortals are."

Sam reached down and picked up Shaun. I saw that he was still breathing, at least for now. The vampire carried Shaun over to the bed and laid him gently on it. He still didn't show any signs of stirring. Whatever the vampires did to him they made sure he was out for the count.

"Happy?" Katrina asked in her sarcastic voice that in this short time I have really come to hate. I didn't say anything, a nod was sufficient. "Good, now let's go."

We left the red carpet room and entered another room. This room was big; at least five times the size of the bedroom. In this room there were several pieces of furniture which congregated around a seventy two inch big screen television. It sat against the farthest wall from the bedroom. I found it kind of ironic it was a plasma TV. There was a refrigerator and microwave and against one wall there were five arcade style pinball games. About fifteen feet in front of the bedroom stood a professional size pool table.

The walls were covered with wood paneling and the carpet on the floor was midnight black. I found this interesting since I've never seen a black carpet before. There was also three other doors in this room besides the bedroom. One was on the wall near the pool table and the other two were over by the television. All the doors were closed so I had no idea what was behind them.

Standing outside the red carpet room were two vampires. I figured they were standing guard just in case Shaun woke up. I only got a glimpse of them when we walked by. I did notice one had a crew cut and the other had a long ponytail. Both men wore jeans and T-shirts. The crew cut vampire's shirt was plain, but the other had a design on it. If I saw it right as I walked by it was a cross with wings. I didn't understand what a vampire was doing wearing a cross. I thought they were repelled by the religious symbol. At least that's what all the movies and web sites said.

We left this room through the door next to the pool table. Behind this door was a small room with a spiral metal staircase that went up. We ascended the stairs until coming to another door and on the other side I heard loud music. Sebastian opened the door and we walked out into what looked like a storage room of a bar. There were kegs of beer and lots of boxes filled with bottles of booze.

The music came from the door on the left and there was another door to the right. Sebastian started for the door on the right and when he opened it I saw it led outside. When we stepped out I saw two limos parked in the alley and standing next to them was three women and a man. All three women were dressed in evening gowns and the man wore ripped blue jeans and a plain white sleeveless t-shirt. He had long blond hair that was short and kind of spiky on top. Between his hair and the clothes he wore he looked like some kind of teenage rocker from the nineteen eighties generation. As soon as Katrina walked outside he walked over to her and said, "We're all here and accounted for."

"Good work Zack," Katrina said as she looked at the vampire. "When Boris arrives and begins displaying his power I need all of you to try to withstand it. Most of the burden will be upon me, but if Boris sees any of my servants falter he will think we have become weak."

"Well if lover boy here and his bimbo brigade don't screw things up, we should have no problem," Jezebel said as she gave Zack an icy look.

"What this all about?" Zack asked with a look of bewilderment on his face. "I'm feeling a real lack of love here."

"Please you two," Katrina said and by the looks of things this wasn't the first time these two tangled. "I grow tired of you're constant feuding."

"My apologies Katrina," Jezebel said and even though she apologized the tension between the two vampires was still evident.

"What's this displaying of power you were talking about?" I asked as I looked at Katrina.

"It is kind of how I entered you're mind to make you do my will," Katrina explained as she walked down to one of the limos. "Instead of focusing the power on one target a master vampire can open it up outward and let it touch everyone. If you are more powerful than you're challenger, then you will feel you're power above his. Some vampire masters have grown so strong they have a hard time finding a suitable challenger."

"How does a vampire gain power?" I asked again because I was trying to understand what I was up against. "Does it have to do with how many servants a master has?"

"Not at all," Katrina replied as she waited for the driver to open the door for her. "Most of a master vampire's power comes from how old they are. With age vampires gain more power, so the older they are, the more powerful they become. Master's can increase their power with minions and a human servant, but age is where the real power comes from."

"I guess that means the first vampire ever created must be extremely powerful," I said and I started to wonder if the legend of the first vampire was true or just another hoax. "So is it true Dracula was the first vampire?"

"Dracula, or should I say Vlad was a wimp," Sam said and you could hear the distaste in his voice. "He wasn't even a vampire. He was just another human that was fascinated with vampires and wanted to be one. He tried to persuade and at one time he even begged Katrina to make him an immortal. Personally I thought he was a shallow individual, not even worthy of being a human. When Katrina denied Vlad's request he took his fury out on the peasants. His name quickly became Vlad the Impaler and even though he wasn't a vampire he claimed to be one. He probably caused more bloodshed in the name of vampires than any vampire in the history of our world. Vlad drank the blood of his victims even though it didn't have any nutritional value for him. He was a cowardly dog that reveled in the power which was attained by his army, not by his own deeds."

"Vlad Dracula was born in the fourteen hundreds," I said and I couldn't hide how astonished I was. "That would mean you and Katrina are around six hundred years old."

"I am nearing it," Sam said and for the first time I saw him fully smile. "Katrina is even older than I am."

"How old are you?" I asked the vampire as the driver opened her door.

"A lady never tells her age," Katrina replied as she climbed into the limo, followed by Sebastian and Selene. "Besides, asking a ladies age is considered rude."

I apologized to Katrina as the driver came over to my door and held it open. I looked at the driver for a second and noticed that he was breathing. He was definitely human, so I just figured he was one of Katrina's human contacts.

I climbed into the limo first, followed by Sam and then Jezebel. I saw Zack and his four lady friends get into the other limo. I didn't know him anymore than I knew Katrina, but something told me I would enjoy the trip more if I was in his limo.

It was funny how things changed. Just a few days ago I was just another pizza delivery driver and now I find myself in a limo full of supernatural beings. I still had no idea how I got myself into this predicament. I wasn't even the one responsible for the vampire deaths. I guess in a way it was kind of ironic. I usually deliver people's dinner to them, but now I find myself being delivered to a master vampire as dinner.

Chapter Five

The trip to the Rosemont was mostly quiet. Katrina, Selene and Sebastian sat on one of the seats, while Sam, Jezebel and I sat on the other. There was a little table between the seats that had a built in bar. Sebastian fixed himself and Selene a drink, and then he offered me one, which I declined. I usually didn't drink anyway and with the predicament I was in I wanted to keep my senses sharp.

I watched Sebastian sip his drink and if he noticed he never led on. I wondered why a human would hang around a bunch of vampires. We were nothing more than cattle to them. Katrina noticed me looking at him and asked, "Is there a special reason why you are staring at Sebastian?"

"I was just wondering why a human would pick a bunch of vampires as a social group," I said as I watched Sebastian down the rest of his drink. "Is he one of your contacts?"

"Actually I am Katrina's human servant," Sebastian replied as he prepared himself another drink.

"Have you ever heard of a human servant?" Katrina asked as she stared at Sebastian and I swore I actually saw a fondness in her eyes.

"Shaun explained a little bit to me," I replied and I wondered if I should have revealed what knowledge he had. "I really don't understand it though."

"Let me enlighten you then," Katrina said as she reached over and stroked Sebastian's cheek. "Contacts are nothing like a human servant. Contacts are usually humans who want to be vampires. We use them to get information or to complete tasks for us during the daylight hours. Human servants are chosen by a master vampire to have a personal bond with. When the servant is close by, the master gains more power. The more powerful the servant becomes, the more powerful the master will be."

"I don't understand," I interrupted no matter how much it angered Katrina. "How does the human servant become more powerful?"

"When a master vampire bites a servant they can share some of their essence," Katrina replied as she pulled back Sebastian's shirt collar to reveal a series of fang marks. "When the essence is shared the servant can obtain immunities or certain vampire abilities. It doesn't happen all the time, but when it does the servant and the master become more powerful."

"You mean like the fear immunity I developed when I was bitten," I interrupted again and this time Katrina showed her anger.

"What happened to you is an abomination!" Katrina screamed and for a split second even the living quit breathing. "Only a master vampire is able to gift a mortal with immunities. The way you acquired the immunity to the fear and then retained it even after the vampire's death is impossible. Such a thing has never happened before."

I saw how upset the conversation was making Katrina so I decided to end it. I didn't mind getting her minions riled up because I knew she wouldn't let them hurt me. I was needed to complete her alliance and without me the deal was off.

Katrina on the other hand could do far worse things than physical damage. When she was inside my head it was the worst experience I think I've ever had. I was mentally present, but not in control whatsoever. To have someone else controlling your every thought and know they are doing it. I never wanted Katrina or any other vampire in my head ever again.

"Actually Jack," Katrina began to say and then she stopped in mid sentence. She looked like she was staring at something that wasn't there. Her eyes began to glow red and her face contorted with rage. After a moment she spoke again and when she did a chill went down my spine. "Blast it! Rocco and Leo are both dead! You're buddy Shaun just killed them! What do you know about that scum?! Where does he live?"

"I don't know anything personal about him," I said and even though I was immune to a vampire's fear, I was still frightened. "He's the one that does all the contacting."

"If I ever find him I will rip out his throat!" Katrina screamed and I could feel a form of energy leave her body. I assumed this was a mild sample of the power she talked about earlier.

After a few moments the feeling went away and Katrina became quiet. She looked out the window and was soon lost in her own thoughts.

I looked out the window Katrina was and saw a sign that read, "Rosemont Cemetery." Now I knew why Katrina laughed when I asked if the Rosemont was a vampire hangout. From what I saw so far, vampires really have a sick and twisted sense of humor.

As we drove through the cemetery, gravestones rose up out of the ground on both sides. Their shadows in the moonlight made it look like they were moving towards us. I knew it was just my eyes playing tricks on me, but with the things I have seen lately, maybe it was something more. Maybe the dead were actually reaching out at me through the shadows, reaching for the one thing they no longer posses and crave more than anything, life. I didn't even like visiting cemeteries during the day, visiting one at night was something I thought I would never see myself doing. Especially a cemetery full of vampires who wanted me as a midnight snack.

Soon after entering the cemetery the limo came to a stop. I looked out the window and saw we were parked under a huge oak tree. There were no gravestones near the tree so I figured this was their meeting spot. The driver got out of the limo and opened Katrina's door first, then he walked around the car and opened ours. As I stepped out the first thing I saw was a gravestone with a huge cross extending out of the top of it. I looked over at Katrina and asked, "Doesn't that bother you?"

"What?" Katrina asked as she looked in the direction I was looking. "Oh, you mean the cross. No it doesn't."

"So holy symbols and apparently holy ground doesn't have any effect on you?" I asked and I saw Katrina shake her head. "What about holy water?"

"You can't believe everything you see on television Jack," Katrina replied as she walked over to the tree. "Most things that are said to hurt or repel vampires is made up, some of it by us."

"What do you mean a lot of the superstitions were made up by vampires?" I asked while wondering why they would do such a thing.

"It's simple psychology actually," Katrina replied as the rest of her entourage joined us. "We spread the rumors on what can hurt a vampire. When a vampire slayer encounters us and pulls out a cross, we would laugh at him. That really terrifies them. We would feed off their fear until we become bored of them."

"Then what do you do?" I asked and I really didn't want to know the answer, even though I was sure I already did.

"What do you think?" Katrina asked and she began to laugh, followed by the rest of her vampires.

I didn't find it funny and by the looks of things neither did Selene and Sebastian. Apparently, Katrina's human servant might want to be a vampire, but he was still a human. As for Selene, she may only be half human, but she respected the human life enough to feed off livestock. At first, when I heard she was a lycanthrope I was frightened of her, but now when I look into her big green eyes I see a sadness there I didn't notice before.

I stared at Selene and she caught me doing so. When our eyes met I saw they were full of pity, and then she smiled at me. The lycanthrope moved towards me and at first I felt inclined to back away, but I didn't. Selene brushed up closely beside me and whispered softly into my ear, "I'm sorry this had to happen to you. If there was anyway to save you from this awful fate I would."

Before I could respond Katrina stared at us and before anything was questioned about what Selene whispered to me I said, "What about garlic and silver? Do they work?"

"Garlic essence if it is prepared properly could be quite unpleasant to us, but silver is actually one of our newer ruses and it was made up by my Jezebel," Katrina replied as she gestured towards the gloating vampire.

Even though Katrina messed with my head I liked Jezebel the least out of all the vampires. It was her arrogant attitude that turned me off. I didn't know what type of rank she held in Katrina's organization, but one thing was for sure, she really was conceited.

"That makes sense," I said and I was a little embarrassed about making the comment earlier about killing the second vampire with a silver crucifix. "In the old books and movies you never heard of silver hurting vampires, it only worked on werewolves. The first time I heard about silver being used against vampires was in a movie. It was about a character that was half vampire and he used silver as a weapon."

"I saw that one," Zack said in an amused voice. "I was laughing my butt off. He would step in a room full of vampires and spray off a clip of silver bullets. I love Hollywood."

I found myself laughing along with the vampire. The horrible reality of my situation was forgotten for a moment, and then I saw Zack become very serious. When I looked at the rest of the vampires I saw they were serious as well. Selene stepped in front of me as I noticed the shadows around us were starting to move, circling like a predator would its prey. Then, one by one, they stepped out of the shadows, glowing red eyes were everywhere. Closer and closer they came and even though the fear effect had no power over me I couldn't help being frightened. The closer they came the more I wanted to run and hide. I didn't try it. I stood my ground. Not that I wanted to, I just knew they were faster than me. I just stood there staring back at the red eyes, knowing each of them meant my death.

All of a sudden the vampires stopped circling and stood very still. I counted at least ten of them, they easily had us surrounded. Katrina didn't look alarmed; then again she wasn't the one being served up as dinner. I couldn't help but tremble, then I felt a hand on my shoulder and I saw it was Selene's. She squeezed my shoulder gently and smiled at me. I saw the calmness in her eyes and I felt her presence reach out to me. At first I wasn't sure what she was trying to do, then I realized. The vampires were trying to feed off my fear and even though their fear effect wasn't working I was still afraid. Selene was simply trying to calm me down. I took a deep breath and tried to relax the best I could. I guess it worked because some of the red eyes faded and I started to hear them talk among each other. I could tell it was about me. I guess they were wondering why the feast ended.

All the talking stopped when a bearded man stepped into the circle. He had black hair and eyes. He wore a white dress shirt and black pants. The shirt was unbuttoned half way so his muscular chest was visible. A woman with long black hair and a very enticing body that was scantily covered approached with him. She draped herself along his back and I could feel his power emanating outwards. Right away I could tell this vampire was a master and it could be no other than Boris.

I saw Sebastian move closer to Katrina, close enough that they touched, and then I felt Katrina's power emanate outwards as well. I didn't understand just how powerful Katrina was until I felt her power actually push me back. I had to firmly brace myself to avoid being pushed into the hands of the vampires behind me and even then I still wasn't strong enough. Selene had to reach out and steady me and for the first time I felt just how strong she was. She may have the curvy body of a supermodel, but this runway queen could bench press a car.

I felt Katrina's power begin to struggle as Boris seemed to be getting the upper hand. He was unquestionably the stronger of the two. Katrina began to sway and her legs wobbled even though Sebastian tried to hold her steady. Boris was winning their test of power.

I saw Selene reach forward with her free hand to support Katrina. As soon as contact was made I felt a surge of energy flow through me. For a moment I could feel the vampire and the lycanthrope's power as if they were a part of me. I felt like I could channel their power; control it to do my bidding. At first I felt Boris's strength weighing down on us, and then I pushed back. I felt part of me flow through Selene and Katrina and as it traveled through them I felt it grow stronger. By the looks on their faces they could feel the power grow stronger as well, until it erupted. I felt our power completely engulf Boris until he could no longer be felt at all. For a moment everything was completely silent, and then I heard an ear piercing sound like the sonic boom. Boris and his servant were violently repelled backwards in different directions. The vampire flew back into his minions and there was a sickly bone cracking sound as the human hit the tree.

Boris was lying on the ground, stunned. When I looked at Katrina I saw she was staring at me. Her eyes were wide and her mouth was open. The vampire looked down at Selene's hand touching her arm, then back at me. I could tell by the look on her face she could feel everything I did and like me she was also at a loss of words. I knew she wanted to figure out how it happened, but Boris recuperated quickly and was back on his feet.

Boris walked over to the tree where his human servant lay. He knelt down next to her and shook his head. He picked up the shattered body and buried his face in her hair. Boris's body trembled with grief. He pulled his head back and yelled into the night. When I saw his face bloody tears were running down his cheeks. Boris lowered the body of his human servant gently back on the ground and glared hatefully at Katrina. The vampire jumped to his feet and stormed towards her as he screamed, "You killed Amy!"

Sam and Jezebel stepped in front of Katrina, while Zack and the rest of her servants protected the rear from the enclosing vampires. I saw Sebastian step back behind Katrina, and then I heard a popping and snapping sound to my left. I looked in that direction and saw Selene was beginning her transformation. Her limbs began to bend in odd proportions and she fell to the ground on all fours. The whole transformation must have been extremely painful, because her muscles went into spasms and her face began contorting with pain until it was more catlike than human. Her clothes ripped and fell free, and then fur began to sprout from all parts of her newly shaped body. Her ears lengthened and the pupils of her eyes became slits like those of a feline. The whole transformation process was extremely quick and within a matter of seconds a large panther was standing next to me.

"What kind of trickery is this?" Boris screamed as he slammed into Sam. The younger vampire was forced back a couple of feet, but he quickly regained his footing.

A group of vampires attacked us from behind, but Zack and his three lady friends were there to stop them. One of the vampires took a swing at Zack and the young vampire skillfully ducked under it, and then retaliating with an uppercut of his own. The punch connected with his attacker's jaw and there was a cracking sound as the vampire flew backwards, slamming into one of the limos.

I heard a growl next to me and turned in time to see Selene leap at a vampire. The large cat latched onto the bloodsucker, biting at its face and raking with her hind claws. The vampire was able to throw the panther off, but not before the damage was done. Intestines, blood and body fluids oozed from the stomach wound and the vampire fell to the ground while trying to hold his organs in. Selene was back on her feet and apparently unharmed from the landing.

A couple more vampires tried to attack Katrina. Jezebel intercepted one of the attackers, but the other got through. The bloodsucker swung a clawed hand at Katrina's throat and she easily deflected it. The attack left the minion off balance. Katrina saw this and attacked with lightning speed, driving her clawed hand deep into her poser's chest. The vampire went limp and fell to the ground as Katrina ripped out its heart.

I turned as I heard a scream from behind. Another vampire had gotten the advantage over one of Zack's lady friends. The vampire stumbled off while holding her throat, blood gushing from the wound. Her assailant stared at me with red glowing eyes. The vampire charged me and I had no way to defend myself. I turned to run, but it was instantly upon me. I had just enough time to scream, "SELENE!!" before I was hoisted into the air. The panther looked in the direction of my voice in time to see the vampire pick me up over its head, but she was too far away to help. A moment later I found myself falling, the vampire dropped me. As I hit the ground I rolled with the impact and at the same time I tried to position myself so I was facing my attacker. I looked up at the vampire and saw it grasping at a wooden stake protruding from its chest. Zack was standing behind the vampire looking down at me with a big grin on his face. As the bloodsucker turned to dust and imploded into the little black marble Zack gave me a hand up and said, "Never come to a vampire brawl without a wooden stake."

Zack handed me a stake and protected me until I was able to stand on my own. He then stormed towards a group of vampires that had the advantage over his two lady friends and dove onto them, bringing the whole group crashing to the ground. I heard another scream behind me and when I turned I saw Jezebel had finished off her opponent, but not before taking a deep cut to her left arm that almost severed it from her body. The wound gushed blood and the vampire ignored it as she let it hang loosely at her side. She stood defensively in front of Katrina, putting her master's life before her own.

I saw Boris and Sam still struggling with each other until the older vampire finally got the upper hand. Boris slammed his fist into Sam's face and tossed him aside like a rag doll and continued towards Katrina. Jezebel quickly stepped between them while she favored her wounded arm. I knew even without the wound she wasn't a challenge for Boris and wouldn't be able to hold him long.

Katrina looked over to where Sam was struggling to get to his feet and then for the first time I swore I could see a worried look come across her face. At that time I knew for sure that Boris was stronger and even through her pride Katrina realized it as well.

"Why are we fighting?" Katrina said obviously trying to buy some time. "I thought we were here to make a trade."

"As did I until you started you're tricks," Boris said as he stopped his advance. All the vampires saw the master's stop fighting and followed suit. "If you still wish to trade then lets trade, but you had better sweeten the deal after this outrage. I have lost far too many minions and my human servant because of the sorry existence of this mortal."

"I have decided I would like to keep the human and would like to bargain for his life," Katrina said and I knew she wanted to know more about how I was able to channel and control her power.

"What?" Boris asked obviously suspicious of Katrina's intentions. "What's with the change of heart Katrina? What benefit could this human possibly contribute to you? What is so special about him that would make you want to spare his life?"

"I feel great potential in him," Katrina replied as she tried not to reveal too much about my ability to manipulate her power. Also this negotiation would allow her servants ample time to regroup just in case the negotiations failed. "I think he would be of great use to us if we should ever encounter Nathaniel."

"You already have a human servant. What other importance could this human have for you besides nourishment?" Boris asked and I saw him stare at me with the utmost hatred. "Bah, I could care less what you want him for. What is it you want to trade for him? Keep in mind before you answer that I have lost much."

"I offer five of my servants to you," Katrina replied and I could tell Boris wasn't satisfied with the offer. Katrina must have seen the vampire's displeasure as well because she instantly sweetened the pot. "Also, since you have lost you're human servant I will offer you mine to do with as you please."

"What?" Sebastian asked in an astonished voice and I could tell all of

48

Katrina's minions were surprised at the offer. "How can you do this to me? I have served you loyally for over a century."

"Quiet!" Katrina commanded and Sebastian instantly fell silent. "I chose you as my human servant all those years ago. Now I choose to offer you to Boris for whatever means he sees fit."

"This is your offer to me?" Boris asked and I saw Katrina nod her agreement. "It's not enough. I need more servants to make up for my losses and as for you're human servant I have no use for him. I do admit he would increase my power since I have lost Amy, but I prefer my human servant to be female."

"I have no more servants to spare," Katrina said. I looked around and saw Zack's lady friends had been all defeated.

"What about the lycanthrope?" Boris asked as he watched Selene lick the blood from her paws. "Give me her and you're five servants and I will let you keep both humans."

"Her loyalty is not mine to give," Katrina said and after the display of power between the three of us I knew there was no way Selene would be traded. "The were-panther does not serve me. We have an alliance with each other. The same kind of alliance I was trying to make with you tonight."

"Then besides the human you have nothing I want," Boris said and in a blink of an eye he covered the ground between us before anyone could react. "Then Katrina, I will take what is rightfully mine and if you try to stand in my way I will destroy you along with him."

Even Katrina wasn't fast enough to stop the vampire. He grabbed me by the neck and hoisted me off the ground. I tried to stab him with the wooden stake Zack gave me, but Boris simply knocked it out of my hand. Before anyone could stop him the master vampire sank his fangs into my neck and began to drain my life force. I kicked and lashed out at him, but my attacks were like a mosquito would be to an elephant. I knew there was nothing I could do. I stared at Katrina and she looked like she wanted to help, but Boris was more powerful than her and I knew she wouldn't risk everything, even for her new found power. The only one that even made an attempt to help me was Selene. The were-panther growled and got ready to pounce, but before she could do anything she was subdued by three of Boris's servants.

I felt my life begin to drift away and then I heard the sound of a gun shot in the distance and the vampire loosened his grip on me. Boris dropped me to the ground and when I looked up at him I saw he was holding his head. Blood streamed down his face from the bullet wound. All the vampires were stunned by what they saw. Boris had been shot. Lying next to me on the ground I saw the stake Zack gave me. I grabbed the weapon and before anyone could react I plunged it deeply into the vampire's chest, penetrating his heart. Boris screamed as he grasped the stake, but there was nothing he could do. The vampire burst into flames and within a few agonizing moments he turned to ash. The remains then imploded until all that remained was a little black marble.

I stumbled and fell to the ground, weakened by the loss of blood. I remained conscious, but unable to move. I heard Katrina yell something. All of a sudden there was a lot of movement around me, but I wasn't aware what was happening. As I laid there I saw a form above me and then I got the sensation I was being picked up. I felt the wind on my face and the world around me began to move in an incoherent blur. I tried to concentrate on what was going on and managed to focus on who was carrying me. I noticed I was in Zack's arms and he carried me across the graveyard at a remarkable speed.

A short time later we stopped moving, then I heard the popping and snapping sound again that could only be Selene's transformation. Zack set me down and I looked up at him and the lycanthrope. I saw Selene had transformed into a hybrid form which had both human and panther resemblance. She now had the body proportions of a human, but she was covered in fur. Her face was a mixture of the two. She had cat ears and eyes, but her mouth and nose was that of a human. I had one word for the way she looked, creepy.

"I can talk in this form," Selene said as she looked down at me with her cat eyes. "How are you doing? Can you sit up yet?"

"I think so," I replied as I tried to raise myself to a sitting position. I felt kind of queasy in the process, but I was able to. "What's going on?"

"You killed Boris," Zack replied and as he did I started to remember the fight. "Now that Boris's servants don't have a master, Katrina has decided to take over that role. She will try to dominate their will and make them part of her coven. She had to do it right away because a couple of the vampires were powerful enough to become masters. If Katrina waited to recruit them, one of them would have claimed dominance and we would have had a new master to deal with. By recruiting Boris's minions Katrina will increase her own power."

"What happens to the vampires that can't be dominated?" I asked as I looked at Zack.

"They are destroyed," Zack replied and he had a devious smile on his face when he did.

"Speaking of power," I said as I tried to clear the cobwebs from my head. "What was it that happened with Selene, me and Katrina? I felt both of their powers inside of me and I was able to control them."

"It is called a spirit bond," Selene replied and her voice had a sort of purr to it. "It's a special power that a master vampire shares with its human servant, but for some reason it channeled through the three of us. I have never heard of such a thing happening before. I guess Katrina never has either, which is the reason she wanted to save you."

"I need to get back to Katrina," Zack said as he looked off in the distance at something I couldn't see with my mortal sight. "Can you take care of him from here?"

"Yes," Selene replied as she knelt next to me. "I will make sure he gets away safely."

In a blink of the eye Zack was gone. I was confused on what was going on. It was obvious Katrina had Zack and Selene take me out of the carnage which was at hand and I was sure it was for her own personal needs. Whatever power the three of us shared, it was a triad I defiantly didn't want to be a part of.

"So who shot Boris?" I asked and I saw a confused look on Selene's face.

"What do you mean?" Selene asked and I could tell she didn't have the slightest idea what I was talking about. "I tried to save you and got shoulder deep in vampires. I didn't see anything until you staked Boris."

"I shot the bloodsucker," a voice said from behind a tree. The voice startled me and when I looked in the direction it came from I saw Shaun step out. "Now if you kindly move away from Jack we won't have to add lycanthrope to the list."

"It's ok Shaun," I said as I tried to move in front of Selene, but my maneuvering was still kind of limited. "She tried to save my life."

"I know," Shaun said as he kept an eye on Selene. "That is the reason why she is still alive. I saw everything from over here. I can't believe it, Boris is dead. I've been trying to get that bloodsucker for months."

"How did you escape?" I asked because the last time I saw him he was unconscious. "Katrina had two goons standing outside the room."

"That's kind of a long story and this isn't the safest place right now," Shaun replied as he came over to help me to my feet. "Let's just say that our lycanthrope friend here left one of my guns on my body when she searched me. I have always been really good at concealing weapons; just don't ask where I hide them. Besides the two vampires standing outside the door were a couple of idiots."

I laughed as I tried to get to my feet with Shaun's help, but everything started to spin and I almost vomited. It was no use; I wasn't getting out of here by walking. After a few moments I regained my focus and was about to try to get up again when I heard Selene say, "Hold on a second. I may be able to help you if you want me to."

"We need to get out of here before things start calming down over there," Shaun said and since Katrina wanted him dead I agreed with him. There were at least ten vampires in this cemetery right now and most of them without a master. "Go ahead and do whatever it is you can do to help Jack."

Selene nodded and then knelt next to me. I felt her nuzzle her face against my neck and she began to purr like a cat. She slowly began to lick my wound and at first I cringed from the pain, then my body started to tingle. My neck began to feel weird and I felt my strength return to me. After a few moments the puncture wounds began to heal and the pain disappeared. Whatever it was she was doing it was working. After the were-panther was finished she looked at me with her big green cat eyes. Even in her hybrid form Selene was still beautiful and any other time this would have been great, but right now she was covered with fur and our lives were in jeopardy.

"How do you feel?" Selene asked.

"Awesome," I replied as I felt my neck and it was completely healed. "How did you do that?"

It's an ability my kind shares," Selene replied as she stood up. Our saliva has the power to heal. I just sped up the process by using some of my energy. You should be able to walk now."

I tried to get up and found this time I had no problem doing so. I looked at Shaun and he had a disgusted look on his face. I guess he found the whole lick healing process pretty gross. I thanked Selene and trudged off after Shaun. I looked over my shoulder and saw her run towards the vampire meeting spot. I found it hard to take my eyes off her and almost ran into a tree by doing so. After a short walk we came to Shaun's truck. I got in and he took me home. Once again I was happy it was all over and like before

Shaun wasn't so sure it was. Anyway I was happy to see my house.

I thanked Shaun for everything and went inside. First thing I did was search the whole house for anything supernatural, especially closets. I hate the closet monster. All in all it was a very interesting night. I was abducted by a vampire and a hot were-panther. Hauled off to a master vampire's coven and got bit again. Killed the master vampire which wanted me dead and the best part of the night was that I made it to first base with the hot were-panther. My life was starting to get really weird. One thing was for sure. Things will never be the same again.

Chapter Six

I spent all the next day in bed. Shaun called to see how I was doing. I actually felt really good despite being used as a vampire buffet again. He told me how he escaped from Katrina's coven. Shaun said he pulled open the door to the red room and shot the crew cut vampire, and then while the other vampire was freaking out by his partner turning to ash and imploding, he shot that one as well. Shaun said vampires usually don't freak out, but then again people don't usually use wood tipped bullets. It's nearly impossible to do, but both vampires were caught totally off guard.

Shaun said he was also caught off guard for a second. He told me the vampire with the ponytail was wearing a t-shirt with a winged cross on it. I told him I saw it and what Katrina told me about holy items. Shaun laughed and said, "That explains why a vampire laughed at me once a long time ago. It quit laughing when I shot it."

Shaun told me I should find somewhere other than home to lay low for a while. We had escaped Katrina and know where her coven is, not to mention the two servants Shaun killed. Katrina knew my whole social life, with a little bit of detective work I was sure it was easy to find out. She knows where I work and has already used that information against me. I wouldn't doubt she already knows my mom and sister also live in Pueblo. If Katrina really wanted to find me she wouldn't have a very hard time doing so. I wasn't going to run from her. I was just going to make sure I was ready for her when she found me.

I asked Shaun if he had any spare guns and ammo, luckily he did. We made plans to meet each other later at the City Park near the new skate track. When I got there I saw his car, but I didn't see him. After looking around for a while I spotted him at the duck lake near the track. As I walked over to him I saw he was fishing and by the looks of it the fish were biting. Shaun handed me a spare rod and some worms. I haven't been fishing in years, not since my dad past away. I baited the hook and cast my line. Shaun handed me a small lock box and a long fishing pole bag.

"Don't open it here, but in the box is a .380 hand gun and two clips full of wood tipped bullets," Shaun said as he reeled in his line. "In the bag is a sixteen guage shotgun and a box of wood chip shells. They will scatter real easily so make sure you are up close when you fire it. There is also a box of ammo in the bag for the handgun. Wood tipped bullets aren't easy to come by so don't waste them."

I thanked Shaun for the weapons and after a few more casts I was on my way back home. Once there I called my sister and like usual the conversation was enjoyable. Janet just asked how I was doing and when I said I was recovering fine, she left it at that. We did talk about Andrew since we haven't seen him in a couple years. I talk to him from time to time, but not very often. I think the last time I heard from him was four months ago. I was the last one to call, so now it's his turn.

After hanging up with Janet I noticed it was getting kind of late and tomorrow I had to work a thirteen hour open to close shift. I hadn't eaten for several hours so I prepared a quick meal, then hit the shower. The hot water felt great and I almost didn't want to get out. After my shower fatigue took over so I decided to go to bed. I put a clip in the handgun and switched the safety on, and then I placed the gun under my pillow. The shotgun only held three shells so I loaded it and placed it on the floor next to my bed. I didn't know if the part about vampires not being able to enter your house without an invitation was accurate or not, so I decided not to take any chances. If any bloodsuckers came calling I was ready for them.

I didn't have any vampire visits that night, but I did have more weird dreams. In one dream, Katrina and Boris were clashed in mortal combat, while Shaun stood off to the side with a shotgun waiting to blow away the winner. I haven't had a normal dream since the first night I was bitten and I was actually very happy when my alarm clock went off.

I reached over and turned off the annoying buzzing sound, then sat up. I knew from experience if I didn't sit up right away I would end up falling back asleep, making myself late for work. Danny was the manager for the morning shift today so I wasn't worried if I was running behind, he was probably running behind also. Actually none of the managers at Aces say anything if you are late, except for Frank.

I work one morning shift a week with Frank. He is one of those people that can eat his body weight and never gain a pound. It is totally sick on how much he can eat at a sitting and in the ten years I knew him he never put on any weight. He was just the same old Frank. Kind of nerdy looking with his short black hair parted to the side and big framed glasses, but he was tall and kind of muscular. Anytime I would walk in late he would look at me and say, "Well, well, well, look who decided to show up." Then he would slug me in the arm or leg. He always was a little aggressive.

I got up and decided I needed some coffee. I got dressed in my Aces uniform and put the handgun Shaun gave me in my pocket. It fit great just as long as I didn't have to sit down or get up quickly. It wasn't the best place to put it, but until I was able to buy a holster it was the only place that I could keep it.

While I was out buying coffee I picked up a new cell phone. I don't know what happened to my old one, it got lost sometime last night. I drank my coffee on my way to work and when I pulled into the Midtown shopping center parking lot I saw the farmer's market was open. Twice a week they would set up the market in the parking lot. In a way it kind of sucked because it was hard to find a parking spot. After a few moments I was parked and walking towards Aces. As soon as I walked in Danny poked his head around the doorway of the back room to 'see who it was and once he saw me he said, "Daaaack."

"D-man," I replied, just like I'd never been gone.

"How are you feeling?" Danny asked as he walked out of the back room while rolling a dough ball. "You look a lot better than the last time I saw you."

"I feel a lot better," I replied as I went over to the computer and clocked in. "Where's Robert?"

"He's already on a delivery," Danny replied as he headed back to the dough room. "All the morning prep is finished so all that is left is folding boxes."

I didn't like folding boxes. It wasn't hard, just boring. I just finished my first bundle when I saw Robert Rodgers pull up. He was also one of the employees at Aces I would call a friend. If there was such a thing as a nice guy award he would be most likely to win it. Robert was always doing favors for other people. I guess his big heart came from being such a big guy. He stood about six foot and weighed roughly three hundred pounds. Like Frank, Robert also wore glasses. He had long brown hair he kept back in a tail and a full facial beard. I seen Robert once without his beard, he definitely looks better with it. Either that or I was just used to seeing him with it.

"What's up Robert?" I asked as soon as he walked in the door.

"Hey," Robert replied as he put his pizza bag away. "How are you feeling?"

"Much better," I replied as I opened another bundle of boxes. "So did I miss out on anything since I've been gone?"

"Nope," Robert replied, as he came over and started to help me fold boxes. "Just the same old drama that happens at Aces everyday. Hey, did I tell you what I was going as this year for Halloween?"

"Superdude?" I joked. I thought it would be funny seeing Robert run around in tights.

"No, Steve is thinking about dressing up as him," Robert replied and I could see him dressed up like Superdude. He had the build for it anyway. "If I dressed up like Superdude I would look more like that Nacho wrestler guy from that movie. I'm dressing up like a vigilante from one of the comics I read. He wears a happy face button. I have the button which I picked up at a comic convention and I'm buying a couple guns like the ones he used off the internet."

Robert loved Halloween. He said he and his wife are pagans so it was part of their religion. He celebrated Halloween like other people celebrated Christmas. One day he told me about Wicca. It was kind of weird, but I guess at least he's not running naked around Stonehenge while chasing a chicken with a dagger.

Three hours went by and the day-shift was turning out to be a sleeper. Two-o-clock and I'd been on three deliveries, which equaled to one an hour and that was horrible. All the work was done and we were just sitting around talking. I was listening to Robert and Danny talk about some up coming movies when I heard the door open. I got up to help the customer and when I walked out front I saw Selene standing at the counter. She was wearing tight blue jeans that fit her figure perfectly and a red t-shirt with "La Luna" printed on it. She looked fantastic and I had a really hard time keeping my concentration on her face. I was actually thrilled to see her and by the smile she wore I figured she was happy to see me also.

"Good afternoon Selene," I said and her smile widened as I approached. "Are you here to make an order or to just see me?"

"To see you, of course, but it smells good in here so I guess I will make an order as well," Selene replied and I was happy she was here to see me. Ever since last night she was constantly on my mind. I just hoped her reason for being here was for pleasure and not business. "I am in a bit of a hurry so I was wondering if we could talk while the pizza was being made."

"Sure, there's nothing going on around here right now," I said as I took her order and then walked around the counter to the sitting area. No one else was up front so I yelled back at Danny. "Hey D-man, there's a carry out order that needs to be made!"

Selene sat down at one of the five tables in the dining area and I joined her. She looked at me and smiled, but I could see the tension on her face. This wasn't a social call. I knew I wasn't going to like what she was about to say, but because it was Selene I decided to sit here and listen anyway. I could tell she didn't want to say anything, but she reluctantly did as if being forced.

"Sebastian has been missing for over a day and Katrina wants to see you," Selene said and I swore she let out a sigh of relief once she did. "Katrina has lost her link with Sebastian and she wants you to come to the Crimson Chateau tonight at first dark."

"What does Katrina want to see me for?" I asked not at all happy about seeing Katrina or any of her bloodsucking flunkies again. "I don't know anything about Sebastian's disappearance and I'm sure Shaun doesn't as well."

"We know that," Selene said and I knew this meeting went far deeper than what I was being told. "Katrina wants to discuss another matter with you."

"Like what?" I asked and I knew the answer before I did. "Wait, I know. Katrina says she wants something and everyone jumps to do her bidding without question. Well you can tell the bloodsucking princess I am working at that time and I won't be off until late. You can also tell her if she doesn't like it, too freaking bad. The world doesn't revolve around her."

Selene could see I was set on my answer and nothing was going to change it. She didn't even try to convince me otherwise. I just hope my decision doesn't get her into trouble. By the time our conversation was over Danny was pulling Selene's pizza out of the oven, talk about perfect timing. I handed the pizza to her and then she leaned forward and kissed me gently on the lips. I looked into her big green eyes and I could tell she was worried about me. No one, especially a mortal tells a master vampire "no." I was sure this was far from over.

I watched Selene walk out to her car and then I heard a noise behind me. When I turned I saw Robert and Danny staring at her as well. I don't blame them. Selene was defiantly top rank model material. The only thing about that is, I'm average in looks at best and she kissed me, which meant the heckling will now begin.

"Wow," Robert said in total astonishment. "I mean WOW as in capital W, O, W. Who was that and why was she kissing you?"

"Yea, exactly," Danny said with a laugh.

"Her name is Selene," I replied and I tried to act like her kissing me was no big deal. I walked back to the office as I hid the smile on my face. "She's a good friend of mine."

"Really good friend by the looks of things," Danny said as he and Robert followed me. "She's quite a hottie. Where did you meet her?"

"I actually met her outside my house two days ago," I replied and I could tell they were not going to let me out of this one without an explanation. "Come on guys, its no big deal. We met and she invited me out to the Crimson Chateau. There's not much to tell."

"Danny," Robert said in his logical voice. "The lady looks like she should be on the cover of a Sports Illustrated swimsuit edition and its no big deal. Woman like that just don't walk around outside you're house."

"Especially outside you're house," Danny said and I could tell they were not going to leave me alone until I answered all their questions. "Not only that, but isn't the Crimson Chateau a strip bar?"

"Yes it is and no she doesn't work there," I replied before they could ask if it was her place of employment. "Come on guys, it was a simple evening. We met while she was walking outside my house. We talked, and then we went to the Crimson Chateau. We went for a walk in a graveyard and talked some more. After our walk she gave me a kiss goodnight. If you want anymore details than that then you are going to have to ask her."

"You walked through a graveyard on you're first date?" Danny asked and I could tell he was definitely at a loss. "What type of woman wants to walk through a graveyard at night on her first date?"

"Obviously D-man," Robert said in his logical voice again. "If I weren't married it would be the type of woman I would like to meet."

Robert and Danny still pumped me for more details, but I refused to tell them any. The phone started ringing after that and I was happy we were getting too busy to talk about Selene. I needed something to take my mind off Katrina wanting to see me. I knew I couldn't dodge her forever, but if she wanted me then she was going to have to wait.

Pascal came in around four. The first thing he did was clock in and then looked in all the trash cans. I had just taken the trash out an hour before he arrived so they were all empty. Pascal looked a little disappointed and then said, "Is there a crew pie?"

"Sorry Pascal," Danny said as he pulled a pizza out of the oven. "We ate about three hours ago, so if there was any left overs we threw them out in the dumpster already."

"I need a driver's bank," Pascal said and it was obvious he was disappointed. Once he got the money he counted it out and when he was finished he said, "Hey this driver's bank is a penny short. There's supposed to be twenty dollars here, but it's a penny short. I don't want to start my day a penny in the hole."

Danny reached in his pocket and pulled out a penny. He gave the coin to Pascal and shook his head. Robert whispered the word "wow" to me and I tried my best not to laugh.

The day seemed like it was going to be a typical one from this point on, until I got a delivery to the south side of town, in an area called Bessemer. Like all my deliveries I walked up to the customer's door, knocked, and greeted her with a smile. My departure depends on if I get a tip or if I get stiffed. If I am tipped I would thank the customer for a highly appreciated tip and wish them a great day. If I am stiffed I would turn around and leave without saying a word. Some people may think I am rude for doing so, but a pizza delivery driver depends on tips to survive and a car doesn't repair itself. Today was a different matter. After the customer answered the door I greeted her and handed her the pizzas, then I said, "You're total comes to seventeen dollars and ninety nine cents."

The customer handed me eighteen dollars and with a big smile she told me to keep the penny. To me it was a typical stiff so I turned to leave without saying a word. The customer called after me and said, "Hey pizza man, how did you like you're tip?"

I didn't say anything. I just walked out of her yard and around the corner where my car was parked. The woman went to a window and opened it. She stuck her head out and with a big smile she yelled, "Hey pizza man, what do you think about that tip?"

Personally I thought she went a little too far and I lost my composure. I turned and looked at the woman and said, "I think that it is crap just like you."

The woman screamed some obscenities at me as I got into my car and drove away. I drove back to Aces and when I walked into the store I saw Tom was here. He was on the phone talking to a customer. Once he saw me walk in he waved me over. I had a feeling what it was about, but sometimes you just lose your cool, especially if the other person is a jerk.

"I have a customer on the phone that says you said she and her tip was crap," Tom said in a very calm manner.

We have been working together for ten years and he knows unless there was a good reason I wouldn't have said what I did. I told Tom what happened and that she pursued me asking what I thought. I merely answered her question. Tom nodded and got back on the phone with the irate customer.

"Ok, I talked to the driver," Tom said and something told me I was in the clear. "Apparently you asked him what he thought about the tip you gave him and he gave you an honest answer. So in the future if you don't want to know what one of my drivers thinks about you being a jerk, don't ask. Have a nice day and thank you for calling Aces pizza."

After Tom said that he hung up the phone. I'm sure the customer was mad and probably cussing him out over the dead line. Tom didn't say anything else; he just went back to the cut table and started to pull pizzas out of the oven. Did I mention that Tom was a good boss and sometimes it was very gratifying working at Aces?

The evening turned out to be a very busy shift and I was constantly in and out. On one of my returns I pulled up to the store and saw a familiar black sedan parked out front. At first I feared the worst, but then I saw drivers leaving the store on deliveries. If Katrina was inside she wasn't here to massacre everyone. I went in the shop and saw Tom standing at the counter talking to Sam and Selene. I ignored the vampire and gave the lycanthrope a pleasant smile. I looked at Tom and he had a goofy smile on his face, apparently Robert and Danny told him about earlier. I didn't want Tom to know he was talking to a blood thirsty killer so I put my pizza bags away and walked over to them.

"What's up guys?" I asked as I leaned over the counter and kissed Selene on the cheek.

"Katrina is displeased you turned down her invitation," Sam said and I could tell he was trying to reveal as little as possible about his visit. "She has sent us to get you."

"Like I told Selene earlier," I said and I gave Sam a very determined look. "I'm working right now. Katrina is going to have to wait until my shift ends at midnight."

"Katrina does not wait for anyone," Sam said and I could feel the persuasion in his voice.

My head began to tingle and I felt the effects of his mind control. It was strong, but just like the fear effect it to soon vanished. Sam was trying to control me with his vampire glamour, but for some reason it didn't work.

I have become immune to it. Boris's bite came with a gift and I couldn't help myself, I looked deviously at Sam and smiled.

Sam saw his mind control had no effect on me and he became furious. The vampire lunged over the counter and grabbed me by the neck. My air passage was instantly closed. Sam pulled my face close and his eyes turned red as he stared into mine. I glanced out of the corner of my eye and saw Tom's face was full of horror. I knew even though he was staring at the vampire, fangs and all, he still had no idea what he was looking at.

No sooner did Sam grab my neck my hand went to the gun in my pocket. I pulled it out and placed the barrel to the vampire's head. Sam felt the pressure from the weapon and hesitated for a moment. He looked at me and smiled and for a moment I thought I was going to have to shoot him. My finger began to twitch and a moment before I pulled the trigger Sam released his grip.

I gasped for air and Sam's eyes returned to normal. I saw Tom had taken several steps back and the store had become completely quiet, except for the ringing phones. Everyone stared at me and Sam. The vampire put his hands up and took a step back. I stared at the vampire and in a voice I hope sounded confident I said, "Get the heck out of here and tell Katrina I will be there as soon as my shift ends."

Sam backed away. I knew he could take the gun from me in the blink of an eye, but then he would have to kill everyone here and that would be hard to explain. Halfway to the door Sam turned and said, "Let's go Selene."

I could tell Selene was here against her will and when she looked at me I felt her concern. She reached out and ran her hand gently down my cheek, then followed the vampire out. I smiled at her as she walked out the door, then I heard Tom ask, "Jack, can I see you in the office for a moment?"

I put the handgun back in my pocket and followed Tom into the office. All the way there I felt everyone's eyes upon me and when I looked at Robert and Danny I could tell from their wide eyed expressions they were shocked. Needless to say they now knew there was more to my story than what I was revealing.

Luckily I don't think anyone, except for Tom saw Sam's red glowing eyes when he vamped out. The vampire's face was up in mine and only Mr. Dillon was close enough to see them. As soon as I entered the office Tom shut the door behind me. I've seen driver's go into the office before with Tom and I think only once had one ever been terminated. That was for having an extremely bad attitude, not pulling a deadly weapon out and putting it to someone's head. Personally I think my situation was a little more extreme. As soon as the office door was shut Tom looked at me and said, "Give me the gun."

I pulled it out of my pocket and handed it to him. Tom took the gun and laid it on the desk and then he asked, "What the heck happened out there? Why was that guys eyes glowing red? What have you gotten yourself into?"

I took his questions one at a time, but not in order. I didn't know if this was the right thing to do, but I started with the night of the attack and I told him the truth. Tom was the type of person that didn't believe in the supernatural, he didn't even watch the type of movies with monsters in them. The thought of lycanthropes and vampires was pure nonsense to Tom, but now I saw the fear in his eyes. I told him the truth about Katrina, the second bite by Boris and what happened after. I told Tom the truth in it's entirety.

Tom was shocked and taken aback by what I told him. He picked up the handgun and popped out the clip, sure enough there were wood tipped bullets. Tom put the clip back in and handed me the gun. I took the weapon and put it back in my pocket. Tom looked at me and in a shaky voice he said, "You always seem to get yourself in the worst predicaments. This is hard to believe, even after witnessing some of it. I know you are in need of hours, but I think you had better take care of this situation before you come back to work."

I agreed with Tom. My working at Aces would not only jeopardize his life, but the lives of all his employees. I told him it was probably best if he kept what he saw and what I told him a secret. The last thing I wanted was for my boss to be locked up in the State Hospital.

I told Tom I would call to be put back on the schedule once everything was worked out. I opened the office door and walked out to see that a group of drivers had congregated. They were trying to catch what little tidbits they could about what was going on behind the closed door. Everyone stared at me with eyes as big as saucers. I didn't know what to say so I just headed for the door. I walked out into the parking lot and got in my car. I headed off down the road towards the Crimson Chateau. Once again I had to deal with the devil, but my names not Johnny and something tells me this isn't going to be a fiddle grudge match.

Chapter Seven

I parked in a lot across the street from the Crimson Chateau. The strip club looked lively tonight; most of the parking spaces were full. I wondered if I should take the back entrance, but decided to just go in through the front instead. I wanted to see what it looked like in the club anyway. I walked up to the door and opened it. Loud dance music blared from inside. The first thing I saw was a brute of a bouncer. He was tall, at least six foot six and he was extremely muscular. His skin was very dark to the point I almost didn't see him in the dim light. His head was shaved and when he spoke he had a very low voice.

"Welcome to the Crimson Chateau sir, there is a five dollar cover charge," the bouncer said as he looked down at me. "There's also a two drink minimum."

"I'm here to see Katrina," I said as I met the big guy's gaze.

I was in no mood to be given the run around and wanted to get this meeting over with as quick as possible. My life as I knew it was destroyed and all I wanted to do was to get these vampires out of it. I didn't think things would ever be the same at Aces again, providing Tom even lets me have my job back. How do you hire back an employee that brandished a firearm in you're business, not to mention one that has a mob of vampires after him.

"Katrina is a very busy lady," the bouncer said as he let a little smile spread across his face. "Who should I say wants to see her?"

"Tell her Jack Holladay is here," I said as I looked into the bouncer's eyes. He didn't look more than thirty, but for some reason I could tell he was far older. "Tell Katrina to keep her lapdogs Sam and Jezebel on their leashes. I'm sick of having my neck grabbed and hoisted into the air like a rag doll."

"Jacky boy, I heard a lot about you. Wait right here," the bouncer said as he laughed and walked off into the crowd.

A few moments later another goon in a suit came to stand in the same spot the previous bouncer was in. I assumed he was a vampire as well. Geez, how many servants does Katrina have? This guy didn't look at or talk to me; he just stood there like a statue.

After about five minutes the first bouncer came back and told me to follow him. When I entered the club I saw it was definitely packed. There were people from every social pattern in here. I guess Katrina wasn't picky on whose money and blood she let into her establishment. The first room we came to was big and housed a couple hundred people. Tables were everywhere surrounding a stage with a catwalk. On the stage was a couple dancing poles with dancers wrapped around them. Both the entertainers were already half undressed and I was kind of surprised to see one was a male. The audience was filled with men and woman who didn't seem to care, they applauded and hooted for both dancers.

As I followed the bouncer around the club to a couple swinging doors, I was forced to dodge waiters and waitresses that were carrying plates full of delicious smelling food. I found it kind of odd the servers were almost as scantly dressed as the dancers. I guess it was easier to get a tip that way. Maybe I should try it on one of my pizza deliveries.

We went through the double doors and into the kitchen. There were several chefs in here and I was extremely happy to see they had clothes on. Each one wore a full chef's uniform and just by watching them I could tell these guys knew their jobs well.

We walked through the kitchen to another swinging door. Through this door we came to a storage room, and then I knew where I was. I saw the back door which led out to the alley and the stairs that went down to Katrina's coven. As we approached the descending winding stairs the bouncer gestured politely towards them and said, "After you Jack."

I walked down the stairs with the bouncer in tow until we came to the small room at the bottom. I knew Katrina and her entourage were just behind the door and I could already see their smug smiling faces.

I opened the door and walked into the large room. The first thing I saw was Zack playing one of the pinball games. He noticed me right away and gave me a big smile. Out of all the vampires I have met so far, Zack and possibly the bouncer are the only ones I didn't want to stake.

I saw Katrina over by the big screen TV sitting comfortably on a loveseat and Selene was curled up next to her. Jezebel sat on a chair to her left, the vampire glared at me as I walked towards them. I could tell she didn't like me one little bit, but that was ok, the feelings were mutual. Sam stood to Katrina's right and even though he didn't show any emotion I knew what happened at Aces wasn't over between us. There were two other vampires here as well I haven't met before and that was the way I wanted to keep it.

One of the two new vampires was a man and the other was a woman, both looked to be in their mid-twenties. Their eyes implied they were much older. The male had long straight blond hair and a neatly trimmed goatee to match. The female had long hair as well, but it was black and naturally curly. Like all vampires I have seen so far they were very appealing to the eyes. The woman was beautiful with a luscious slim body. She wore a tight red mini skirt that left little to the imagination. The man was handsomely muscular and he wore leather pants and a vest.

As I approached all eyes were on me. Some with hatred and some were neutral, but with the exception of Selene they all saw me as prey. I knew Katrina was the only thing which was holding Sam and Jezebel back, otherwise the smorgasbord would begin. I stopped a few feet from the sitting area and Katrina smiled at me, then with a pleasant voice she said, "Jack, how nice of you to join us. Thank you Tyrone, you can return to your job."

"As you wish Katrina," Tyrone said with a great deal of respect, and then he turned and left the room.

I thought it was kind of funny how the big bouncer's personality changed while in the presence of Katrina. Personally I liked him better with the attitude he had upstairs.

"Before we begin I would like to introduce you to the two new members of our family," Katrina said as she gestured towards the two vampires. "This charming individuals name is Jean Luke and his lady friend is Elizabeth. They were both Boris's servants until his demise, now they have decided to follow me."

"Providin' dat de terms are met," Jean Luke said with a Cajun accent and just by the way that he said it I could tell he wasn't happy about the arrangement. "Don forget chere, Boris did not die by yer hand. Either Elizabeth or m'self can still claim de right to become a master and start our own coven. Isn't that right mon amie?"

"Yes it is," Elizabeth said and the bad vibes were strong in the room. "The only reason why we decided to accept you're offer was because of the potential we saw."

"Not ta mention dat you threatened ta kill us like you did ta de rest of Boris's servants if we didn't, right chere," Jean Luke said and there was a sarcastic smirk on his face when he did.

"Do not worry yourself Jean Luke," Katrina said as she looked at me. "Jack will not say no. Together we will be as strong, if not even stronger than Nathaniel Nevis."

I didn't want to make Katrina mad with all these vampires around. I didn't think she would let them kill me, but the human body can take a lot before it dies and I for one was not up for a night of torture. On the other hand, I did have my gun and I could probably take out a couple of them before they even knew it. I was sure Katrina would have me killed if I did, but sometimes even death was better than the alternative.

"What do you want Katrina?" I asked in a tone of voice that was less polite and respectful than what she was accustomed to. I saw her smile quiver, but she was able to hold her facade. "Thanks to you're peon here I'm now without a job."

"How dare you speak to Katrina like this?" Sam yelled as he lunged towards me with breath taking speed.

Before he could rip out my throat Katrina intervened. Instantly the older vampire was between us. Her speed was so uncanny I didn't even see her move. With one swift backhand Katrina sent Sam flying into the wall. The younger vampire slumped to the ground as blood began to flow from his lower lip.

"You fool!" Katrina screamed and I saw her eyes turn red as she looked at Sam. "I gave no order to kill him. You know of his importance to me. Jack is not to be harmed unless I desire so."

"Yes my mistress," Sam said as he stood up and returned to his place. "You have my deepest apologies. I did not mean to disobey you."

"You are forgiven old friend. Just don't forget your place again," Katrina said and then she turned her attention to me. "As for you Jack, you will learn respect for me if you plan to keep breathing."

"Respect is earned not given," I said and I could tell when I did I may have overstepped my boundaries. "All I see is a tyrant that keeps her servants under control through fear. Well Katrina, I do not fear you."

This time Katrina lost control and when she hit me I felt my body go numb. I had the feeling I was flying and when I crashed into the wall I knew I was. Pain spasmodically ran through my body and I tried my best to cling to consciousness. I probably had a concussion. I saw Katrina standing above me, and then she reached down and picked me up by the throat. Unable to breathe I stared at her and I remembered thinking to myself, "Why does it always have to be the throat?"

Darkness was quickly taking me and I saw the vampire lean in to feed. I reached into my pocket and pulled out the handgun. I jabbed the barrel of the gun into Katrina's chest and the vampire looked down. Once she saw the gun she laughed and with the last of my breath I said, "Wooden bullets."

Katrina's face became solemn and for a moment I swore I saw fear. I felt her try to enter my mind, but like Sam I closed her out. She slowly loosened her grip and I took a deep gasping breath. Most of the vampires in the room, including Jezebel stood from their seats and Sam took several large steps forward.

"Tell him to stop or I will pull the trigger," I said and Katrina did as I bid. For a moment I forgot about Zack and when I looked at him I saw him edging towards me. "Back off Zack, all I have to do is squeeze and you will need another master."

The only person in the room that didn't move was Selene. The lycanthrope stared at me with her big green eyes and I saw she was concerned. Selene shook her head at me and whispered the word, "Don't."

"If you kill me you won't make it out of here alive," Katrina said and I knew she was telling the truth. "Then once you are dead everyone you know will follow."

"What do you want from me Katrina?" I asked as I tried to concentrate on staying conscious and looking intimidating at the same time.

"I want you to be my human servant," Katrina replied and at that time I didn't know if I should laugh or just pull the trigger. "Sebastian had disappeared and my bond with him has been severed. I can no longer feel him, which means he is dead. Someone has killed him and I have need of the power we shared."

"After the misery you put me through you actually have the nerve to ask me to be one of you're pawns," I said and I didn't bother trying to hide my distaste.

"He doesn't want to be you're human servant Katrina," Elizabeth said and I could hear the sarcasm in her voice. By the looks of things I was the only thing that stood in the way of Jean Luke and Elizabeth's plans of becoming masters of their own coven.

"He will or his world as he knows it will be ripped apart," Katrina said and I knew what she meant.

It was the same old threat, do as she says or she will kill everyone I know. If I thought for a moment that killing her right now would save everyone from this insanity I would do it, even at the risk of my own life.

"Fine Katrina," I said as I lowered my gun. "You win as always, but I have terms that I want met as well."

"Let's hear them," Katrina said and I knew this whole conversation was amusing her.

Katrina knew I was in no position to make deals. I had to try something though. Until I could find a way to destroy her and all her followers I had to do whatever it took to save the people I cared about.

"I will become you're human servant and do what you want within reason if you agree not to harm my family and friends in any way," I said and I hoped the negotiations would at least buy everyone the time I needed to end this. "Also, I want you to stay away from Aces. All of these conditions go for your minions as well."

"Agreed, but remember this," Katrina said and what she said next made a chill go down my spine. "If at anytime you break our agreement or fail to fulfill your part, I will make sure that death would be a welcome release for everyone you know. Sam, get everything ready for the anointment ceremony."

"As you wish Katrina," Sam said and I could hear the distaste in his voice. I knew he was against me becoming a human servant, probably even more so than myself. Sam was a good little pawn though and he did as his master commanded.

Sam and Jezebel walked through the door behind the loveseat Katrina had been sitting on. I was at a bad angle so I couldn't see what was in there. A few minutes later they came back out. Sam had a plain gold goblet clenched in one hand and a jeweled dagger in the other, while Jezebel had two arms full of candles. I didn't know what the dagger was going to be used for, but something told me I wasn't going to like it.

Selene gracefully slid off the loveseat and walked over to me. She started to take off my shirt and I wondered what this had to do with becoming a vampire's human servant. Selene ran her hand gently over my chest and when I looked into her eyes I saw sorrow. Selene didn't say a word. She just folded my shirt and kissed me gently. She started to return to her spot on the loveseat, but I grabbed her arm and pulled her close. Her body touched mine and I felt her shiver. I embraced Selene around the waist with my left arm and with my right hand I ran my fingers through her hair. This time I leaned forward and Selene met me half way. I passionately kissed her and she pulled me closer. Our bodies melded together like one and I felt her firmness against me.

After what seemed like eternity Selene gently withdrew her body from mine and stepped back. Our eyes still lingered upon each other and I could contently gaze into those mesmerizing green orbs all day, but Zack had to go and ruin the moment by saying, "You know what guys? That was really gross."

Jezebel slapped Zack in the back of the head and the vampire turned to face her. At first I thought that they were going to fight until Zack said, "Why did you hit me? It hurt."

"Because I don't like you," Jezebel replied and her eyes slightly glowed red when she did.

"You don't even know me," Zack said and Jezebel took another swing at him, but this time the vampire saw it coming and dodged.

"That's more than enough you two," Katrina said and when she did the two vampires separated.

Sam walked over to his master with the goblet and dagger. Katrina held out her hand to him and the vampire slit her palm with the dagger. Blood ran freely from the wound and into the goblet. Once he was finished Sam began chanting in a language I didn't recognize.

Jezebel began to place the candles in a circle around her master. Once she was finished Katrina held out her hand to me and said, "Come to me Jack."

Selene turned away from me and walked back to her spot on the loveseat. I walked slowly over to Katrina, regretting every step. Jean Luke and Elizabeth watched quietly, while Selene just stared down at my shirt in her hands. I could tell she didn't want this ceremony to continue, but we both knew there was no other way.

I met Jezebel's gaze and the hatred was still there. I guess there will always be bad blood between us. Lastly, I walked by Sam and his chanting came to an end. The vampire showed no emotion, but as I passed by I felt vibes of resentment. Out of everyone here, including myself, I think he wanted me as Katrina's human servant the least.

I passed through the circle of candles and stood in front of Katrina. She took the goblet from Sam and handed it to me. I looked at the contents inside the cup and immediately felt ill. I didn't like the sight of blood. I guess being a vampire's human servant was a mistake since this was their diet of choice. I knew what she wanted me to do with the goblet, but from all the stories I read drinking a vampire's blood makes you one of them. I looked at Katrina questioning and said, "I thought drinking a vampire's blood will make me into a vampire. The deal was human servant, not full fledged bloodsucker."

"There is more to becoming a vampire than just drinking blood," Katrina explained as she stared at the goblet in my hands. "You must first be drained to near death, and then you must drink from my body, not from a cup. You're body will then die and you must be buried for three days. On the third night you would awaken as one of us. Drinking a vampire master's blood will just give a mortal a kind of intoxicated feeling. Now, bottoms up so we can complete the ceremony."

I did as Katrina wanted and chugged the contents of the goblet. I didn't think of what was inside; I just poured it down my throat. It was cold from being outside the body for too long and had a coppery taste. I ignored it the best I could and drained the goblet. I remembered reading a scripture in the Bible about not eating blood. I just hoped God would forgive me for the sacrifice I was making.

Once the contents of the goblet were gone Katrina didn't waste a moment. Before I could object she was instantly upon me, her fangs sinking deeply into my neck. I felt her presence inside me, bonding her to me. I started to read her thoughts and I knew she could read mine. I wanted to go for my gun, but I knew that would be a fatal mistake for everyone. It was over almost as quickly as it began. Katrina drew back from me, my blood oozing down from the corners of her mouth. I felt dizzy and my vision blurred. A feeling of comfort and bliss came over me and I felt as if I was flying. I had the sensation of hands upon me. I tried to concentrate on who it was, but the room circled around me. I closed my eyes and the full effects hit me. My skin felt like it was burning, but there was no pain. The hands lowered me down and I felt like I was lying on a cloud. As I laid there I felt a presence close by, then I heard a voice inside my head saying, "Sleep."

My head clouded and everything started to go black. There was no fighting it. Soon I drifted off and remembered no more.

Chapter Eight

My head throbbed and my stomach felt nauseous. The last time I had this feeling I graduated from high school and stayed up all night partying. I drank anything that came my way, big mistake. The next morning I had the worst headache and I thought I was going to vomit. From that day on I never drank alcohol again.

I tried to open my eyes, but the lights were too bright, making my head throb even more. I tried again a little later and even though it hurt I succeeded. I saw the light was coming from the lamp on a nightstand and I was lying on the bed in the red room. I looked around and noticed I was alone. I looked at my watch and saw it was twelve-o-clock, but was it afternoon or midnight? There weren't any windows in this room so I had no clue.

I sat up and a dizzy spell came over me. I closed my eyes until it dissipated and then I tried again, this time with success. I saw my handgun and cell phone laying on the nightstand. I retrieved them and put one in each pocket. I also saw a business card laying on the stand. The name of the business is La Luna and according to the address it was just a few blocks from the Crimson Chateau. I remembered Selene wore a red t-shirt with the name La Luna on it when she came to visit me at Aces. I turned the card over and saw some writing on it. It read, "Meet me here at three... Selene."

I put the card in my back pocket, then walked over to the bedroom door and opened it. There weren't any goons standing outside this time. As a matter of fact I looked around the big room and didn't see anyone at all. I walked down to the door I saw Sam and Jezebel go into earlier and when I was there I had a strange feeling. It was coming from the other side of the door and when I tried to open it I found it was locked. I didn't know why, but for some reason I felt Katrina and her servants were asleep on the other side. I didn't know how to pick locks and unless I spontaneously learned how, there was no way for me to open the door. I checked the only other door in the room I hadn't been through and saw it was a bathroom. I didn't think vampires needed to use the bathroom so I figured it was for the human servants.

I saw the refrigerator standing up against the opposite wall and curiosity took over. I had to have a look. I walked over to the refrigerator and opened it. The contents inside would make a blood bank manager happy enough to dance a jig. There were several vials and plastic containers full of blood. Each container was labeled with what blood type it held. I felt sick. I don't like the look of blood so I quickly shut the refrigerator door.

After seeing the blood I didn't want to stay here any longer. There wasn't anyone around anyway, at least not awake, so I didn't see any reason for me to stay here. I went out the door and climbed to the top. All the lights were turned off and there wasn't any music so I figured the club was closed

I opened the door that led to the alley and walked out into the sunlight, it was definitely noon. I started to walk down the alley and then I heard a woman's voice behind me say, "Hey you. Wait right there a second."

I turned and saw a rather good looking woman in her late twenties with long black curly hair. She wore a red skirt that went down to her knees and it matched the dress jacket she wore over a white blouse. She topped off her outfit with red high heel shoes.

The woman walked down the alley towards me and when she got close enough she pulled back the bottom of her jacket to reveal a police badge and then she said, "I'm Detective Sharon Oswald, and you are?"

"Jack Holladay," I replied as I wondered what this was all about. "How can I help you Detective?"

"Did you just come out of that door?" Detective Oswald asked as she pointed at the door I exited.

"Yes," I replied and I wondered what she wanted with the club. "Is there a problem?"

"I'm investigating a homicide that occurred sometime last night," Detective Oswald replied as she looked at me. "The body of a young woman named Julie Simpson was found a block away. She was last seen in the Crimson Chateau. I've been trying to get inside to talk to the owner, but it seems the club is only open at night. Would you happen to know the name of the owner?"

"Yeah," I replied and I wondered if I should turn in the bloodsucker brigade downstairs. I decided against it. I'm not really fond of padded rooms. "I don't recognize the name of the girl, but the owner's name is Katrina."

"Do you know her last name?" Detective Oswald asked as she pried for more information.

"Sorry Detective," I replied and wanted to get this conversation over with. I really didn't like discussing matters about Katrina, especially matters on a homicide. "I've only known Katrina for a few days. I'm sure I was told her last name at sometime, but I am really bad with names and most likely forgot."

"You don't work for Katrina?" Detective Oswald asked and I knew I just opened a new door for a whole bunch of questions.

"No," I replied and I was starting to get impatient. I was feeling grimy and wanted to go home to take a shower before my meeting with Selene at three. "I came here after work last night."

"Where do you work?" Detective Oswald asked and I really didn't want to tell her. I didn't want to get Tom involved in any of this.

"I work for Tom Dillon over at Aces Pizza," I replied. I mentioned Tom's name anyway because I knew she was going to ask for it. "I got off early so I decided to come here."

"If you don't work here and there's no one inside, then why are you here all alone?" Detective Oswald asked and I had to think of a lie fast.

"That's a good question," I replied and luckily I thought of an answer for it. "I guess I had too much to drink last night and passed out. I woke up with a note saying to let myself out."

"This Katrina must be a very trusting person to let someone she only knew for three days sleep it off at her club," Detective Oswald said and then I noticed her looking at my neck. "What happened to you?"

"I was attacked by a mountain lion about a week ago," I replied and the Detective looked a little surprised for a moment.

"I remember you," Detective Oswald said as she stared at the bite marks. "You're the pizza delivery person that got attacked by the mountain lion while changing a flat tire. I read the report, but the bite looks a little fresh to be from a week ago. Also, what about those bruises on you're jaw?"

"The bite wound seems to keep opening back up," I replied as I reached up and felt the minor swelling in my jaw. I figured the bruise was from when Katrina hit me last night. As a matter of fact it didn't even hurt until the Detective mentioned it. "I don't know where the bruise came from. I guess it could have happened last night, but I don't have any memory of it."

"If the neck wound keeps opening up then you had better have it looked at again," Detective Oswald said and I wasn't sure she entirely bought my story. "I'm finished with my questions, but if I have anymore can I call upon you again?"

"Sure," I replied even though I wanted to say no. The detective handed me her card just in case I remembered anything else and then we went our separate ways.

I walked around the building to the front and saw my car still parked where I left it. I got in and drove home. Once there I got out of the car and walked up to my house. I saw the newspaper on the porch so I picked it up. I listened at the front door before I opened it. I don't know what I was expecting. It was in the middle of the afternoon and as far as I knew all vampires were tucked away in their coffins or whatever it was they slept in. If the legends were true anyway vampires couldn't enter someone's house unless invited. Then again vampires do have human servants and contacts to take care of their business during the day.

I opened the door and walked in. Everything looked the same and after searching around the house I was convinced no one was here. I put the newspaper on the kitchen table and then went into my bedroom. I picked out an outfit for the day. I wore blue jeans and a t-shirt, same as every other day. I jumped in the shower and washed away all the grime. The hot water felt so good and it helped sooth my aching muscles from when I crashed into the wall after Katrina backhanded me. Even though I wanted to, I knew I couldn't stay in here all day. As soon as I got out of the shower I had enough time to wrap a towel around myself before the phone rang. I got to the phone on the forth ring and when I picked it up I heard Shaun's voice on the other end.

"Jack," Shaun said and he sounded excited. "Did you see the front cover of today's paper?"

"No," I replied as I wondered what had Shaun so excited. "I haven't had a chance to look at it yet."

"Go grab it and have a look at the cover," Shaun said and I walked into the kitchen to get it.

I picked up the paper and opened it. At the top of the page in big bold letter I read, **VAMPIRE VICTIM FOUND IN DOWNTOWN ALLEY**. I kept reading and found what I was looking for, the victims name and how she was killed. Julie Simpson, the same woman that Detective Oswald was investigating. The only wounds found were two puncture wounds on her neck.

"The newspaper said the victim was completely drained of all her blood," Shaun said and he almost sounded happy when he did. "Those bloodsuckers really screwed up this time. They left some evidence behind to prove they actually exist."

"I'm not so sure it was Katrina's bunch that did the killing," I said and Shaun became real quiet.

"What makes you think that?" Shaun asked and he sounded suspicious. The body was found a block away from the Crimson Chateau and the victim was last seen at the club. It's a dead ringer on who sucked the girl dry."

"I was with Katrina all last night," I said and I heard Shaun choke on whatever it was that he was drinking. "Katrina doesn't strike me as someone that would make a mistake like that. Nor do I think she would allow any of her minions to feed that close to the club."

"What the heck do you mean? Why were you with Katrina all last night?!" Shaun yelled after he was finished choking. "We escaped from the devil only for you to go back into her clutches?"

I told Shaun everything and he wasn't at all happy. I explained if I didn't do what Katrina wanted all my family and friends would be killed. Shaun wasn't convinced they would be safe even with the deal I made. I knew I couldn't truly trust Katrina, but if she feared losing me as her human servant, just maybe everyone I knew was safe for now.

Something real bad must have happened to Shaun to make him distrust and hate vampires so much. Maybe one of these days he will share it with me. Shaun hung up after I told him what happened last night, but not before telling me, "Watch you're back."

My stomach began to rumble and I realized I hadn't eaten since early yesterday. It was almost three-o-clock and I was supposed to meet Selene at Le Luna. It sounded like the name to a restaurant so I decided I would grab a bite there. If they didn't have a menu then we could always walk a couple blocks down to a Chinese restaurant.

I walked out to my car and drove off. I knew exactly where La Luna was, I remembered seeing it once on a delivery. I drove down fourth street and over a bridge that led downtown. I looked over the railing of the bridge and saw the Fountain River below. There hasn't been much rain lately so the river was low. I went down to Grand street and turned left. Towards the end of the street I turned left again and came to La Luna.

I parked my car and walked up to the door. An open sign was in the window so I went on in. As soon as I entered I saw I was in some sort of fine dining restaurant. The room I was standing in was big and very well lit by the light coming in through the windows. The atmosphere had a high society feel about it. There were several tables in the room. Each of them had white table cloths and a light was hanging above each table. The scent of fine spices and grilled meat hung in the air. My stomach growled reminding me that I was terribly hungry and my mouth began to water.

I saw the hostess standing in front of me. She was average looking with her black hair tied up into a tight bun on top of her head. She wore stylish glasses that magnified her stunning blue eyes. As I stared at her I noticed she had very sharp features and if she let her hair down and maybe put on some makeup she could be a very striking individual. As I walked up to her she looked at me and said, "Good afternoon sir. Will there only be you today?"

"I'm actually here to see Selene," I said and at once she went from being professional to extremely professional.

"Yes sir," the hostess said and her posture went from slightly relaxed to perfect. "Who should I say is here to see her?"

"Just tell her that Jack is here as requested," I said with a smile that I was trying very hard not to turn into a laugh.

The hostess was wearing a very nice black skirt with a dress jacket over a white blouse. I on the other hand had on blue jeans and a wrinkled t-shirt, but yet she treated me as professional as she would a person with a thousand dollar suit.

"I will tell Selene you are here at once," the hostess said and she quickly walked off towards the kitchen.

I wondered if Selene was the owner of this establishment. I couldn't picture her owning it because it just didn't feel like her. Then again I've only known Selene for a couple days so how much could I possibly really know about her.

After a few minutes the hostess came back out and said, "Selene will be with you in a moment. Would you like to have a seat?"

"Sure," I replied and I followed the hostess to a cozy little table in a corner. The table had just two chairs and there was a candle on it. All it was missing was a rose in a vase and I would say that it was romantic.

"Could I get you something to drink while you wait?" the hostess said.

"Thank you, but I'm fine," I said and the hostess dismissed herself and went back to her podium to wait on another customer.

About five minutes later I began to get that strange feeling I felt back at the Crimson Chateau. Selene came out from the back and the feeling was coming from her. She was dressed in a very professional looking red skirt and dress jacket. Under the jacket she wore a white blouse that had ruffles going down the center. She topped off the outfit with a pair of red high heals.

As soon as Selene saw me she smiled and gracefully walked over to my table and sat down. She looked at my face and saw that I had a puzzled look. Once she saw the look she frowned and asked, "What's wrong?"

"I guess it's nothing to be concerned with," I said and I wondered if Selene would have any idea what the weird feeling was. "It's just ever since I woke up today I keep getting this weird feeling."

"What kind of feeling?" Selene asked looking into my eyes, she looked concerned.

"I'm not sure how to explain it," I said and I wondered if it was another side effect from being bitten. "I first felt it at the Crimson Chateau when I was standing outside the door next to the big screen. I felt it again when you walked out from the back. I can't explain the feeling. It was almost like I felt you're presence before I even knew you where there."

"It sounds like you acquired some type of supernatural sense," Selene said and she smiled when she did. "It's nothing to be concerned about. It can actually be a very handy gift. With the ability to sense the supernatural you will always know when a vampire is near."

"Or other things," I said and Selene nodded. "So does that mean there were vampires behind the door this afternoon?"

"Yes," Selene said with another nod. "That's where Katrina and her minions sleep."

"Why do you have dealings with her?" I asked and Selene frowned.

"I don't like conspiring with Katrina," Selene said and her beautiful green eyes became moist with sadness." I am the alpha leader of my Pride and as the alpha I must do whatever it takes to see to the Prides survival. Even if it means I must do the bidding of a vampire."

"I thought the males were the alpha leaders of a Pride," I said and when I did I wished I had not.

Selene became extremely quiet and a tear rolled slowly down her cheek. I felt like an idiot. If Selene was the alpha then that means something happened to the alpha male, which meant the alpha male was her mate.

"I'm so sorry Selene," I said as I handed her a napkin. "I didn't know."

"Its ok," Selene said as she took the napkin and dabbed at her eyes. "It happened about a year ago. I guess I haven't put him behind me yet."

I kind of knew what Selene meant. I lost my dad a few years back and even though it was a bad comparison it takes a lot of time for the numb feeling to go away. I reached forward and took Selene's hand in mine. Her skin was smooth to the touch and when she looked into my eyes she began to cry. I got up from my seat and knelt down in front of her. Selene leaned forward and wrapped her arms around me; she buried her face in my shoulder and wept. I continued to hold her hand and with my free one I rubbed her back. For several moments we stayed like this until the crying stopped and Selene gently withdrew from me.

Selene dried her eyes on the napkin and when she was finished it was covered with eyeliner. Her makeup ran from the tears and smudged her face. I personally didn't know why she wore makeup, she definitely didn't need it. Selene looked at the napkin in her hand and saw the stains. She laughed through the tears, then looked at me and said, "I must be a mess."

I started to say no, but in truth she was. Her mascara ran down her face and mixed in with her blush. I guess if we were in a Goth nightclub she would fit right in, but since this was a fine dining restaurant I figured a little touch up wouldn't hurt.

I returned to my seat while Selene excused herself and disappeared into the back room. She was gone for just a few minutes and then I felt the weird supernatural sense again. I expected to see Selene walking out of the back, but instead I saw a slim figured man dressed in a chef's uniform. He had wavy shoulder length black hair and green eyes. The man looked in my direction and without saying a word he stormed aggressively towards me.

His speed was uncanny and the next thing I knew he lifted me from my seat and slammed my body against the wall. Even though the man did not look it, he was extremely strong. All the air was knocked from my lungs and I gasped as I tried to catch my breath. The man stuck his face in mine and in a deep voice he growled, "What did you do to Selene?"

I tried to answer, but I didn't have any air in my lungs. All I was able to do was gasp as I shook my head. The man slammed me against the wall again and I felt it give way a little. I saw the hostess run into the back as I reached into my pocket and pulled out my gun. I jabbed the weapon into the man's stomach and he looked down. When he saw the gun he smiled and said, "If you pull the trigger I will rip off you're head."

"If I pull the trigger you will be dead," I managed to say in a raspy voice.

"Hardly," the man said and for a moment I swore I saw his eyes slit like those of a cat.

I don't know if the man purposely allowed his eyes to change or if he momentarily lost control of his humanity. One thing was for sure; even if I didn't have a supernatural sense I could defiantly tell this man wasn't completely human.

I looked over the man's shoulder and saw Selene run out of the back room. As soon as she saw me pinned up against the wall she yelled, "Xylon, let him go!"

The man glanced back at Selene, but he did not release me. Selene took a few steps forward and this time she spoke in her normal tone, "What's the meaning of this Xylon?"

"I saw you crying when you came into the kitchen," Xylon replied, but he did not release me. "What did he do to you?"

"Jack did nothing to me," Selene replied and I felt Xylon relax just a little. "We were talking about Dante and I guess the memories of losing him are still more than I can bear."

Xylon finally released me and I felt my legs wobble. I slumped back down in my chair and Selene saw the gun in my hand. I looked up at her and saw she was staring at the weapon and then at me. I put the gun back in my pocket and then Selene said, "Please Xylon, return to the kitchen and we will talk later."

Xylon glanced one more time at me and then lowered his head. Without saying a word he walked past Selene and into the back room. Once he was out of sight Selene looked at me and asked, "Were you going to shoot him?"

"The man slammed me against the wall," I replied and when I did I saw the fault in my actions.

Xylon is Selene's friend and all he was doing was protecting her. It was a minor misunderstanding, but I was willing to shoot him for it. I lowered my eyes to the table. I was extremely embarrassed for what I almost did and couldn't meet Selene's gaze. The were-panther returned to her seat and put her hand on mine. I lifted my eyes to her's and she smiled at me. I tried to smile back, but it came out as a twisted frown.

"I'm sorry Selene," I managed to say. "I have been through a lot over the past week."

"Xylon had no reason to act the way that he did," Selene said and I was relieved that she wasn't mad at me. "He shouldn't have attacked you, especially in public. If someone would have seen him it could have caused problems for the whole Pride."

"Especially if I shot him," I said and my face blushed from embarrassment.

"I'm afraid if you shot him it would have just made him mad," Selene said and it dawned on me that Xylon could be a were-panther as well. I did sense supernatural off him when he came out of the back. "Unless you have silver bullets in you're gun Xylon would have healed way too fast for you to have done any serious damage to him."

"So he's a were-panther like you," I said and Selene nodded. All of a sudden I felt very foolish and then chuckled. "When I shoved the gun in his gut I was trying to act tough, but all along he knew I couldn't hurt him."

"I doubt he was completely sure," Selene said and I knew she did so for my benefit. "The chance was slim, but you could have had silver bullets. That thought is always in the back of every lycanthrope's mind."

For a few moments we sat in total silence and as if I wasn't already embarrassed enough my stomach growled. Selene looked at me and with a little laugh she said, "Was that your stomach?"

"Yeah," I replied and the smell of grilled meat that lingered in the air didn't help the matter out any. "I haven't eaten since yesterday morning."

"Would you like me to have Xylon fix you a plate?" Selene asked and when she did my mouth began to water.

"Please," I replied with a nod.

I didn't know if Xylon held any grudges against me and I doubt he would put any type of foreign substance in my food. As hungry as I was I really didn't care, just as long as I didn't come across any hairballs.

Selene got up from her chair and went into the back again. She was only gone for a few minutes and when she came back out she had a couple drinks. Selene set one of the glasses down in front of me and then took a sip from the other. I knew she didn't want to talk about Dante, but I felt if we were going to have any kind of relationship it was something she was going to have to share with me. It might be hard for her, but maybe with my help she could find a way to get through it.

"So is this you're restaurant?" I asked and Selene nodded. "Its nice, do you run it by yourself?"

"Every since Dante's death the Pride has helped me keep it going," Selene replied and I saw her eyes begin to moist over, but she blinked it away.

"Was Dante you're husband?" I asked and Selene nodded again. "Would you mind if I asked what happened to him?"

For a moment Selene didn't respond. She just stared down at her drink, her mind lost in some distant memory. I didn't push the matter. If she didn't want to tell me then I would just have to wait until she was ready. She has only known me for a few days. In the short amount of time we've been together, how could she possibly trust me enough to share her feelings? Selene looked up from her drink and our eyes connected again. She stared deeply into me and I don't know what she saw, but she opened up to me like a book without a cover.

"It was a little over a year ago," Selene said as she began her story. "We were celebrating our wedding anniversary and Dante decided to take me dancing after dinner. The night was magical and even though we had been married for many years we were still very much in love. We danced until the club closed and when we left it was very late. We walked out to our car and saw a group of six people standing around it. Apparently, sometime in the night we drew the attention of some vampires. I don't know why they picked us over everyone else in the club, maybe it was because we were so happy."

Selene paused for a moment as she took a sip from her drink. She swallowed a couple times and then continued.

"We didn't know they were vampires at the time. I tried to get Dante to go back into the club and call for help, but even though he was a wonderful man he was kind of arrogant. I guess he decided to impress his wife by standing down a bunch of drunken humans. Once he approached them Dante saw what they were and realized his mistake. All but two of them fell upon him like a rabid pack of dogs. The two that didn't attack came after me. I was able to transform in time, but Dante never had a chance."

Selene paused again and this time I saw tears gather in her eyes. I saw how much pain the story was putting her through and I was just about to stop her when she blinked the tears away again and continued.

"I had little trouble disposing of my two assailants and when I looked at Dante I saw even though he was bleeding badly from many bite and claw wounds he managed to complete his transformation. I joined the fight and helped Dante. With both of us fighting side by side we were able to defeat our attackers. When there was only one vampire left the coward tried to run away. Weakened from the loss of blood Dante turned back to his human form as I chased down the last vampire. Once I disposed of it I returned to see another vampire lifting Dante into the air by his throat."

Selene paused again and I could tell by where she left off she was coming to the climax of her story. She took another sip of her drink and dabbed at her eyes with a napkin. She took a deep breath and let it out slowly and then continued.

"I leaped at the vampire, aiming to rip out his throat. I didn't know at the time, but he wasn't an ordinary vampire. Our victory attracted the attention of a master that was seeking retribution for the deaths of his servants. The master back handed me and I flew back the way I came. The hit was so hard that when I landed I was dazed. By the time I got back up the master had latched onto Dante and was draining his life away. I tried my best to save my husband's life, but I couldn't think or even walk straight. The vampire finished with Dante and started towards me."

Selene stopped again when Xylon walked out of the back room with a plate of food. He looked like he was about to say something when he saw Selene crying, but before he could she smiled at him and patted his arm. The were-panther gave me a bitter stare and returned to the kitchen.

"I think someone must have drove by and seen the fight because the police arrived before the master could reach me. I transformed back to my human form and waited for them to find me. Since I was naked from the transformation and we both know that dead vampires don't leave bodies behind I told the police that we were attacked. I told them Dante was killed while trying to stop the muggers. Once they were finished with him they tried to rape me, but were unsuccessful because of the timely appearance of the police. They wanted me to go to the hospital, but I refused. My healing ability would suffice more than adequate for the wounds I sustained. Later I told the Pride what happened and after some detective work we found out the master was Nathaniel. The Pride proclaimed me as their new alpha and they wanted to seek revenge for the death of Dante, but I forbid it. The vampire was way too strong and our numbers were too few. Since we were weakened by the loss our alpha male a werewolf pack decided we would be easy targets. They continually attacked us until I was desperate enough to seek the help of Katrina. She and her vampires aided us and in time the werewolf attacks lessened."

Selene took another drink as she unconsciously watched me gulped down my food. I looked up at her with my mouth full and then she smiled at me and said, "Now you know my story and why I am with Katrina."

I was speechless. Selene's story was so dramatic and the ending was horrifically sad. I didn't know what to say. I was sorry she had to relive that horrible night again to satisfy my curiosity. My appetite was suddenly gone and I pushed the plate away. Selene saw I had finished eating and there was still some food on the plate.

"Is there something wrong with the food?" Selene asked as she looked at the plate.

"No," I replied as I took a sip of my drink. "I just wasn't as hungry as I thought."

It wasn't the truth, but the answer was good enough for her because Selene didn't question it. The were-panther just excused herself again and disappeared into the back room. A few minutes later Selene came back out and when I looked at her I saw she had removed her makeup. She walked back over to our table, but she didn't sit down. Instead Selene looked down at me and said, "Could you give me a ride?"

"Sure," I replied as I pushed away from the table and stood up. "Where are we going?"

"To make a visit that is long overdue," Selene replied and I didn't ask who. I bugged her already too much today about her personal life.

We went outside and got into my car. I didn't know where we were going, but Selene gave me directions and I drove. Once we were sitting outside the Hillview Cemetery I realized why we were here, Selene wanted to visit her husband's grave. I drove through the graveyard until she told me to stop. I parked the car and Selene got out. She walked past a few gravestones until she stopped at one. I stayed in the car. I didn't feel right visiting Dante's grave, not to mention I was sure that Selene wanted a few minutes alone. I waited patiently until she was finished and when she returned I wasn't surprised when she asked me to take her home.

I drove Selene home and when we arrived at her house she thanked me for listening to her story, even though I felt like I pried it out of her. She leaned over and kissed me on the cheek and then got out and walked up to her house. I watched her until she went inside and then I drove home.

By the time I got to my house it was after seven. I didn't feel like doing anything so I turned on the TV and surfed through the channels for a while. I didn't want to watch anything with drama in it since my whole day was full of nothing else. While I surfed I came across a comedy so I lay down on the couch and watched it. I don't know when I fell asleep, but one thing was for sure, I didn't get to watch the whole movie.

When I slept it was sound and very peaceful. I don't know why, but for the first time in days my dreams were not haunted by nightmares. Even though I didn't dream about vampires, I did dream. I didn't understand the dream, but for some reason it didn't matter.

In the dream I walked through a valley of white flowers and the sun shone brightly down upon me. On the other side of the valley I saw Selene standing there waiting for me. I walked up to her and she embraced me with a kiss. At that time the dream ended and I remembered no more.

Chapter Nine

I woke late the next morning with a ravishing hunger. There wasn't much to eat in the house so I decided to pour myself a big bowl of cereal. I no sooner finished preparing it and stuffed one spoonful in my mouth when my cell phone rang. I looked at the number on the screen and saw it was Tom. I answered the phone and said, "What's up Kaun?"

"Did you get everything worked out?" Tom asked.

"More or less," I replied between mouth fulls. "I made a deal with Katrina that will keep her and her servants out of Aces and also leave everyone alone."

"That's good to hear," Tom said and he had a slightly stressed tone in his voice. "Did you read yesterday's paper?"

"Yeah," I replied and I knew that was one of the reasons why he was upset. "Katrina's vampires didn't have anything to do with it, at least I don't think."

"What do you mean you don't think?" Tom said and I understood his suspicions. Even though I didn't think Katrina was careless enough to let such a thing happen I didn't know for sure.

"Katrina's servants seem to be extremely loyal to her," I replied and I didn't even know why I was defending the bloodsucker. I really hoped it had nothing to do with being her human servant. "I seriously don't think Katrina would allow her servants to feed that close to her club, especially if the victim was seen there."

"Whatever," Tom said and I knew he didn't like his involvement in the supernatural world anymore than I did. Maybe it was better off not knowing. Like a wise man once said, ignorance is bliss. "I didn't call about the murder anyway. The reason I called is because Pascal's car broke down and I was wondering if you could cover."

"Sure," I replied and I was happy to be back on the schedule. "When do you want me to show up?"

"As soon as you can get there," Tom replied and I could hear some of the tension fade from his voice. "Robert and Frank are handling it right now, but I'm sure if you were there it would take some of the stress off."

"Ok," I said as I took a bite of cereal. "I'll be there as soon as I finish scarfing down some food."

"See ya," Tom said and he hung up the phone before I could say anything.

I quickly finished the bowl of cereal and got changed into my Aces uniform. I honestly didn't think I would be wearing it again anytime soon, but I was happy I was. I brought a change of clothes just in case Katrina wanted me to make another visit.

Fifteen minutes later I was pulling into the Aces parking lot. I got out of my car and walked up to the store. As soon as I stepped inside I saw Robert leaving with a delivery. When he saw me he said, "I want details about what happened the other night and don't leave anything out."

"When we have time," I said because I really didn't know what to tell Robert and I needed time to make up a story. "When there are no deliveries I'll fill you in."

Robert went out the door with his delivery and I looked around the shop for Frank. I found him in the back rolling up some dough balls. As soon as I stepped into the backroom he said, "Well, well, well. Look at who decided to come back to work, as if you ever did any work around here anyway."

"Whatever," I said because it was the same old thing every time I worked with Frank. I would come in and he would bash me for the first ten minutes and then we could get on with our day. "What prep needs to be done?"

"Robert already did most of it," Frank replied as he finished cutting up a batch of dough. "Go ahead and fold some boxes until your delivery is ready."

I folded about half a bundle and then I bagged up my delivery and headed out the door. It was a long delivery to Fortino Boulevard on the North side of town. Doctor Smith is one of our regular customers. He orders once or twice a week. Funny thing is I have delivered to him countless number of times and have never seen him. I walk into the doctor's office and the receptionist pays for the pizza, then I leave. It was the same process every time.

Once I delivered the pizza I stopped off for gas and a coffee. They were both essential items to complete the day. I filled up and grabbed my coffee, and then I headed back to the shop. Once I was there I saw Robert's car. I was sure he would want to hear the details about the other night. Funny thing is I was the one telling the story and I also couldn't wait to hear it.

I walked into Aces and saw Robert folding the boxes I left. He looked up at me and before he could ask I said, "The guy from the other night was Selene's ex-boyfriend."

"If he is her ex, then why was she here with him?" Robert asked as he finished off the bundle he was folding and started on another. "To top it off, why did she leave with him?"

"The guys a jerk," I replied and I wished that Robert wasn't so observant. "Even though Selene said it was over between them, he still wants to go out. The reason why she came with him is to make sure he didn't start anything while he was here. The reason why she left with him is because she still sees him as a friend, not to mention he was her ride."

"What's with the gun?" Frank asked after he finished making a pizza. "Something like that should be left out in your car, or better yet, at your house."

"How about never bought in the first place," Robert added and I heard a serious, but sad tone to his voice. "I had a friend die from a gunshot wound. Ever since then I think the illegal carrying of firearms should have stricter penalties."

"I'm not a big gun fan either." I said and I meant it. In the past I always saw guns as a coward's way of settling things. When I was growing up if you had a problem with somebody you slugged it out. These days people just drive by and gun down whomever they're after. "Ever since that pizza driver got pulled over and robbed I decided it was safer to carry a gun."

"I'm still against them," Robert said and I didn't hold it against him, but I was sure that if he saw the things I did he would be packing as well. "So what's with the bruise on you're jaw. It wasn't there the other night when you left."

"After Tom sent me home I met Selene at a club," I replied as I did my best to make things up. "Her ex must have followed her there because he walked in and hit me from behind. Let's just say he only landed one punch. The bouncers kicked us out and we left before the cops arrived."

"Wow," Robert said and I saw the astonished look on his face. Something told me he bought my story and I was very happy he did. "I still can't believe a woman as beautiful as Selene could ever fall for a guy like you. You have to tell me what you're spiking her drink with."

I could tell that Robert was a little envious. I couldn't blame him; Selene is a very beautiful woman. I just didn't know how serious of a relationship this was. She seems to like me, but how much? Maybe the next time I saw her I would try to find out.

The day shift turned out to be a dud. Frank and Robert could have handled the business without me, but I did get back on the schedule. I also made up some lost hours, so I wasn't complaining. Tom came in around five, and then Danny and Alan arrived just after dark.

Alan Shoemaker is Steve's older brother and everyone just calls him Shoe. Quite often he talks in a monotone, but I think he does it on purpose when he is feeling playful. He's quite sarcastic, but it's just part of his playfulness as well. Alan is going bald at the young age of twenty five, so he just shaves his head. His ears are pierced, well kind of anyway. The earring that he wears is inserted into a big hole in his earlobes. When he takes the earrings out there are holes in both earlobes big enough to put an index finger through. Alan does that once in a while to gross me out. As soon as he walked in the door I looked at him and yelled, "Shoooe!"

"Oh no, it's Holladay," Alan said in his playful monotone voice. "I thought you were out of here for good. What's up with that?"

"Jack's like one of those bad pennies," Frank said with a big grin. "He's worthless and always shows up when he's not wanted."

"I'm afraid Jack has sprouted roots here," Tom said as he cut a pizza into slices. "He's going to be here forever."

"Sprouted roots?" Frank asked in a playful manner. "I guess that explains why he's so slow all the time."

"Jack isn't slow," Danny said with a smile. "He's as fast as needed to be for the situation at hand, just as long as the situation at hand doesn't involve moving."

Like most nights the Jack bashing had begun. I was so happy when my delivery was ready. I quickly bagged up the pizza and headed for the door. I walked out to the parking lot and within moments I was in my car driving up the fourth street bridge. I was headed for Corona Avenue, which was on the other side of the bridge. I turned left on Corona and entered an area pizza driver's call the Blocks. The reasoning behind this is because it is a little community made up of lots of small streets about a block long each.

Corona is the only long street in the Blocks that stretches from one side to the other. There are few street lights in this area and the houses are very close together. It can be a very dark and scary part of the city at night.

Since I made many deliveries in the Blocks during the day, I had little problems locating the residence I was looking for. I pulled up in front of the house and looked around before I got out of the car. There were lots of dark areas where someone could be hiding, but after what I've been through for the last week the common thug didn't sound so threatening anymore.

Once I was satisfied and sure no one was lurking in the shadows I got out of my car and walked up to the house. The night air smelt like rain and before I reached the porch I got hit by a couple rain drops. I knocked on the door and a few moments later a young semi-attractive woman in her early twenties answered. As soon as she opened the door I said, "Hi, how are you tonight?"

"Fine," she replied with a southern accent. "What about yourself?"

"I'm great," I replied as I handed her the pizza. "You're not from around here are you?"

The young woman giggled and told me she just moved here from Alabama. There's not many jobs down there I guess, not many here either. She paid for the pizza and then scrounged enough change together for a dollar tip. I was happy about that. A dollar tip was better than no tip at all.

I thanked the young lady and head back to the car. The rain was coming down steady now and it made an eerie sound as it pattered on the street. Once I got to the car I was just about to get in when I got the supernatural feeling again. I put my pizza bag in the car and followed the feeling until I came to the entrance of an alley. I peered down the alley and it was almost pitch dark. I didn't like the idea of walking down an alley at night, especially one I sensed supernatural in. I was just about to head back to the car when lightning struck overhead and in the flashing light I saw movement. I wasn't sure, but it looked like a mugging and then I heard the muffled cry of a man calling for help, followed by a thunderclap.

"Hey!" I screamed as I pulled my gun out and ran down the alley towards the apparent mugging. "Leave him alone!"

The closer I came to the struggle the stronger the supernatural feeling became, until I was sure the feeling was coming from the mugger. As soon as I was within ten feet of the struggle I saw red glowing eyes and at that time I knew this wasn't a mugging, but a feeding.

The vampire withdrew and I saw blood flowing freely from the victim's neck. A low growl started in the vampire's throat and it let out a hiss. I saw its fangs and knew it was trying to use the fear effect on me. The vampire looked bewildered for a moment when I didn't succumb to the fear, and then I felt a tingle in my head and knew it was trying to use its mind glamour. The vampire hissed again and I could tell by the look in its eyes that it was furious. The fear and mind control had no effect. I looked deep into the vampire's eyes and swore I saw a faint sign of fear, then it asked, "Who's you're master?"

"I have no master," I replied and it hissed again.

Standing in the rain I stared the bloodsucker down, almost as if it was a test of power. I didn't know for sure, but I think I may have won because the vampire charged me. I didn't know if it was using super speed or not, but I saw it move clearly. I raised my gun and pulled the trigger. The wood tipped bullet struck the vampire in the chest, stopping its momentum and knocking it back a couple feet. The vampire clenched at the wound and screamed. It looked at me as it turned to ash and with its final breath it said, "What are you?"

"Death," I replied and before the vampire imploded it screamed one last time.

After the vampire imploded the little black marble fell to the ground next to the victim. As I bent over to pick it up the man looked at me and with a quivering voice he said, "What was that thing?"

"You can believe me or not," I replied as I looked down at the middle aged man. "I could care less either way, but that was a vampire."

The man looked at me; his blue eyes were as big as saucers. His black hair was soaked from the rain and it hung loosely in his face. Another victim had been pulled into the world of the supernatural, now only time will tell if it consumes him or if he learns to embrace it.

I held my hand out to the man and offered my help, but he quickly scuttled away. I could tell he was in shock, but that was to be expected. The rain was coming down harder and I was getting soaked. I didn't want to stand here in the alley any longer, but I really couldn't leave this man laying here in the mud. I was sure someone heard the gunshot and probably called the police. I took a step towards the man and said, "Is there anything I can do for you? Do you need help getting home?"

The man looked at me and then to his surroundings. He put his hand to the bite on his neck and I saw him wince in pain. He withdrew his hand

and looked at it. Blood, mixed with rain covered his hand. He quickly wiped the blood on his pants and rose to his feet. I stared at him and when he saw me he acted like he just noticed me for the first time.

"Who are you?!" The man screamed as he stared at me. Then all of a sudden he burst into a full sprint. He ran past me and when he did he screamed, "Leave me alone!"

I watched the man run down the alley and out into the street. He ran to a house across the way, opened the door and went inside. There was a loud slamming sound as the door flew shut and then all was quiet except for the patter of the falling rain.

I quickly walked back to my car and got in. I was completely soaked. I noticed I still had the gun in my hand so I put it back in my pocket. I started the car and drove back to Aces. Once I got there I saw a familiar black sedan sitting in the parking lot. I became angry, Katrina had broken her promise. I got out of my car and immediately felt supernatural coming from the sedan. I noticed the driver side door open and Selene stepped out; Katrina had kept her promise after all. I was relieved and happy at the same time. The lycanthrope walked up to me and smiled, but before she could say anything I pulled her close and embraced her with a kiss. At first Selene shared my embrace and then she gently pushed me away and said, "You're soaked."

"Well it is raining," I said with a laugh. "I see you have the sedan. So is this visit pleasure or business?"

"It's always a pleasure to see you Jack," Selene said and I could have sworn I heard her purr. "But Katrina does want to see you."

"I take it she knows about her servant I killed," I said and when I saw the confused look on Selene's face I could tell she didn't know anything.

"What servant?" Selene asked and I was starting to wonder if it really was one of Katrina's servants or the servant of another master.

"Just less than thirty minutes ago," I replied and Selene still looked completely confused. "I ran into a vampire while it was feeding. It attacked me and I killed it."

"None of Katrina's servants have been killed," Selene said and she sounded a little worried. "It could have been a rogue vampire, one of Boris's servants Katrina missed when she was recruiting. At least I hope it was anyway."

"Why does it matter?" I asked as I wondered what had Selene

worried.

"Nathaniel Nevus and Katrina are the only two master vampires left in the city," Selene explained and I was starting to see where she was going with this. "If the vampire that you killed wasn't one of Katrina's or a rogue, then it was likely a servant of Nathaniel."

"If it was a servant of Nathaniel, then he will hold Katrina responsible for his servant's death," I said as I finished Selene's thoughts for her. "Great. We better hurry up and get over there then. Katrina has to be told."

"Ok," Selene said as she began to walk back to the sedan. "Let's go."

"First I need to go inside and let my boss know what is going on," I said as I started for the store. "I'll meet you in the parking lot across from the Crimson Chateau."

Selene agreed and drove away as I ran towards Aces. I went inside and explained the situation to Tom. Business had died down and he was about to send me home anyway, so it really didn't matter. I cashed out and changed from my soaked uniform into the clothes I brought with me. I ran back out to my car and within moments I was on my way to a place I didn't want to be, but seemed to be spending a lot of time at. A week ago my life was kind of dull and ordinary, but now it was supernatural.

Chapter Ten

I pulled up to the parking lot across the street from the Crimson Chateau. I didn't see the black sedan, but I did see Selene standing on the sidewalk waiting for me. I parked and got out. I met her on the sidewalk and we both walked across the street to the club.

Before we entered I got the supernatural feeling again. It was coming from the other side of the entrance. This time I concentrated on the feeling and I'm not sure how I did it, but I sensed Tyrone standing on the other side of the door. I was really starting to like this new gift. I'm not sure if I acquired this new ability when Katrina bit me or if it was a special ability from being a vampire's human servant. One thing was for sure it was a real handy thing to have when supernatural was around.

As soon as we entered the club I knew Tyrone was there even though I couldn't see him standing in the shadows. With his dark skin he was hard to see so it was something he liked to do. I'm not sure why. Maybe it was to frighten the customers as soon as they walked in, that way he could get a quick feeding off their fear. He tried the same tactic on us as soon as we walked in by stepping out of the shadows and saying, "Good evening and welcome to the Crimson Chateau."

"Thank you Tyrone," Selene said not at all frightened. She walked past the big bouncer and into the club.

"Selene and Jacky boy," Tyrone said as soon as he realized it was us. "I hope I didn't scare you. I wasn't expecting the two of you to come in through the front."

"No, you didn't frighten us," I said and I was sure Tyrone knew since he wouldn't have been able to feed off us. "I knew you were there even before we entered."

"Just how did you know that?" Tyrone asked with a little bit of suspicion in his voice.

"I sensed you standing there," I replied as I followed Selene. "Not only that, but you're always there. I know how you like to get that quick feast."

Tyrone let out a hardy laugh and then said, "You two love birds have fun tonight."

We both shot Tyrone an embarrassing glance and I swore I saw Selene blush. Tyrone laughed again and returned to his spot as I followed Selene through the club. The place was packed and as I waded through the crowds I got the supernatural sense from most of the waiters and waitresses that walked by. I guess most of Katrina's hired help were also her servants.

We went through the swinging double doors and into the kitchen. The food smelled divine and I saw the chefs working hard at their stations as we walked by. I did catch supernatural off a couple of them as well. I guess they must have gone to night school to learn their trade.

Selene led the way to get to the storage room and we descended down the spiral staircase. As soon as we reached the bottom I sensed supernatural coming from the big room on the other side of the door.

Selene opened the door and we walked in. The first thing I heard was the unmistakable sound of a cue ball cracking into another ball. I looked in that direction and saw Zack shooting pool with Jean Luke. The younger of the two vampires looked up at us when we entered and said, "What's up Jack? Want to play me once I finish whooping Jean Luke?"

"De game isn't over yet mon ami," Jean Luke said as he prepared to take a shot. I looked at the table and saw Zack definitely had the advantage.

"Maybe," I replied and I really didn't think we would have a chance. "I need to speak to Katrina first."

"Kool," Zack said as Jean Luke took his turn. Two balls were sunk with his shot. Zack's eyes grew as large as saucers and I swore that his pale complexion got some color to it. "How the heck did you do that? You must have cheated when I was talking to Jack."

"Wen you have skill t'ere is no reason ta cheat," Jean Luke said and he smiled at Zack as he prepared to take another shot.

I followed Selene over to the sitting area by the big screen. Elizabeth was sitting on the recliner with her legs propped up, while Sam sat on one of the loveseats and Jezebel lounged on the chair to his left. The only place left to sit was a loveseat. I didn't want to sit next to Sam so I chose the loveseat across from him. Selene slid next to me and sort of curled up into a ball. She tucked her legs behind her and rested her head on my shoulder.

Everyone was silent except for the occasional aggravated yell from Zack every time Jean Luke took a shot. After a few moments of sitting in silence I heard the door to the red room shut. I looked up to see Katrina standing there, while dabbing at the corners of her mouth with a red silk handkerchief. She started to walk in our direction and when she saw me she said, "Jack, how nice of you to join us."

Katrina sat down on the loveseat next to Sam. Her skin had a little more color than usual so I figured she had fed recently. Once Katrina was comfortable she looked at Sam and said, "Would you be a dear and take care of that little mess in the bedroom?"

"As you wish Katrina," Sam replied and he immediately excused himself and headed for the bedroom.

"I'm happy to see you came as soon as I beckoned," Katrina said as she looked at me. "Nathaniel Nevus has asked for an audience with me. I assume the recent fall of Boris has gotten him concerned. He wants to meet with me and make sure I don't have any plans of deception."

"But you do," I said and when I did I saw everyone stare at me. "At least you did until I killed Boris."

"Which is something we will keep a secret," Katrina said and I knew that little piece of information could put the vampire mistress in a heap of trouble with Nathaniel. "This meeting isn't just to see if I have any deceptive intentions. I also want to know if it was one of his servants that fed upon the woman last night. It's against our law for a vampire of another master to hunt so close to their rivals coven."

"Law?" I asked and once again I didn't have any idea what Katrina was talking about. "Vampires have a law they follow?"

"Of course," Katrina replied and I couldn't believe how serious she was. "We vampires have very strict laws we must follow. Without them the stronger masters will over power the weak and we would have countless vampire wars. It would be impossible for us to remain hidden if we continued to war with each other. There would be total chaos and the death toll of vampire and human's alike would be astronomical."

"Who makes up the laws?" I asked with extreme curiosity. "Do you have some type of vampire governing body?"

"The vampire council made up the laws and we all abide by them," Katrina replied and I could tell from the tone in her voice she didn't like certain restrictions of their law. "The council is made up of the five oldest and wisest of our kind. They formed the council and created the laws after the great Vampire War that left thousands of vampires and tens of thousands of humans dead. The wars brought almost total destruction to their lands.

Since then they have learned to live and work with each other. They have prospered from it and any vampire that breaks their laws must face them. The accused is judged and the sentence is carried out swiftly."

"What gives them the right to enforce their rules?" I asked and I could tell I may have stepped over the boundaries of what questions to ask.

"They are the oldest and strongest of our kind," Katrina replied in a stern tone. She may not like their laws, but it was obvious she respected the council members. "You ask what right does the council members have. I can ask you the same question about the nations of you're world. They rule because it is their right to rule and out of the rest of us only Nathaniel has the power to challenge the weakest of them for a seat on the council."

"How does one challenge a council member?" I asked because I found the subject interesting.

"To make a challenge all one has to do is proclaim it," Katrina explained and I could tell she had seen it happen before. "It's a test of power, similar to what you saw happen between me and Boris in the cemetery. The stronger of the two will take the council seat and the loser is destroyed. This is why challenges to become a council member don't happen very often."

"What about human servants?" I asked and I couldn't hide the concern in my voice. "What happens if a human servant kills a vampire of another master?"

"It could be seen as an act of war," Katrina replied as she looked at me with a great amount of suspicion in her eyes. "The master whose servant was slain could retaliate with no consequences to their self or they could just bring it in front of the council. Why do you ask? What has happened?"

"During one of my deliveries I happen upon a vampire feeding on a human," I replied and I hoped Katrina didn't hit me again. My jaw was still very sore from the last time. "I didn't know it was feeding at the time. I just thought someone was getting mugged. When I intervened I saw it was a vampire and when it saw me it attacked. I defended myself the only way I could. I pulled out my gun and shot it."

"That's not good," Katrina said as she shook her head and sighed. "If the vampire you killed was one of Nathaniel's servants then that would add to his suspicions and he might call upon the council or even take matters into his own hands. If we go in front of the council we could at least plead a self defense case, but if Nathaniel decides to go to war I'm afraid we may not win."

For a moment there was complete silence in the room. Even Zack and Jean Luke quit shooting pool to listen in on our conversation. The silence was interrupted when the door to the red room closed again. When I looked in that direction I saw Sam standing there with a rolled up red blanket over his shoulder. Something the size of a body was rolled up inside of it. The vampire carried the load out the door to the spiral staircase like someone would a pile of trash. I didn't think anything of it at first, then I looked at Katrina and asked, "Is there a body in that blanket?"

"Yes," Katrina said without a care. "Not to worry. Sam will dispose of it."

"Who was he?" I asked and I couldn't believe just how calm and cold she was acting about the situation.

"Just someone I picked up off the streets to fulfill my needs," Katrina said as she watched my reaction.

"You brought some strange guy here so you can kill him?" I asked and I couldn't hide my anger.

"I didn't bring the human here to kill him," Katrina replied with a slight smile. "I brought him here to feed and fulfill other needs as well. Normally it is the human servant that fulfills this role, but I doubt you would offer yourself to me. Not to mention it may make Selene jealous. As of late the two of you seem to be getting very much acquainted. Anyway, if it makes the matter of the human's death any better, he did die with a smile on his face."

"You're a monster," I said and I wanted to pull out my gun and shoot her, ending the nightmare.

"Well, I am a vampire," Katrina said and her smile grew wider until I could see her fangs. "Most of us try not to kill when we feed, but sometimes we get carried away and accidents happen. You are going to have to understand we see humans as you would see cows or chickens. Humans are our nourishment and we must feed on them to survive. At least we don't line humans up in a slaughter house and bash their heads in with a sledge hammer. Most of the time humans find great enjoyment when we are feeding on them. If they do die they usually don't even know it, like the young man Sam just carried out."

I was just about to tell Katrina what I thought of her and other vampires, when the door leading out to the spiral staircase opened and Sam returned. Behind him was Tyrone. The big vampire walked across the room to Katrina and in his most obedient voice he said, "Nathaniel Nevus and company are here to see you."

"Show them in," Katrina commanded and Tyrone bowed. I smiled and when I did the big bouncer looked at me. I almost laughed when he did. The way he acted when he was around Katrina compared to the way he was upstairs was like two entirely different people. I made a kissing sound with my lips and Tyrone knew I was calling him a butt kisser. The big vampire laughed and then turned and walked back the way he came.

Tyrone opened the door as Sam returned to his perch next to Katrina. In single file the guests began to enter. First was a middle aged man. He stood six feet tall and had an athletic build. He had long black hair that was braided into a tail and also a neatly trimmed goatee. He had an air of importance about him, so I figured right away this must be Nathaniel Nevus.

As soon as Selene saw the master vampire I felt her tense up. I wasn't sure, but I may have heard her growl like a cat. I saw her body begin to shake and her fingernails lengthened into claws. I heard Selene growl again and this time I wasn't the only one. Katrina also heard her and looked at the lycanthrope. Selene began to move her legs into a position that enabled her to spring. Both Katrina and I knew she was going to attack Nathaniel as soon as he was close enough.

"Selene, calm yourself!" Katrina screamed and her command did little to persuade the lycanthrope from her intentions, but it did catch the attention of Nathaniel.

The master stopped in his tracks as he stared at Selene. His eyes began to glow red and the first thing that came to my mind was I may have to save my girlfriend from a master vampire. I knew both of us combined weren't a challenge for Nathaniel and Selene was about to spring. I didn't know what to do, so I just did the first thing that came to mind. Quickly I moved so I was in front of the lycanthrope and then I positioned my face directly in her line of vision. Our eyes met and I could tell Selene had almost completely given over to her bestial side. I looked into her cat like eyes and knew she wasn't looking at me, but through me to the one she wanted to destroy. If Selene was still in there I needed to find her quickly.

I stroked Selene's soft black hair with one hand and with the other I cupped her chin in my palm. The lycanthrope seemed to relax a little, but she was still extremely tense. I leaned forward slowly and gently kissed her on the lips. This time she did stare at me, but her pupils were still slitted like a cat and I knew she still meant to attack Nathaniel.

After what the vampire did I couldn't blame her for wanting him dead. I felt the same way about Katrina for much less. I smiled at Selene as she stared at me and then I whispered to her, "Do what you need to do, but know this, I won't be stuck in this supernatural world without you. If you attack him here today I will be by you're side, with or without Katrina's help. I really don't know how serious our relationship is, but I am willing to risk my life to save yours so we can find out."

I gently kissed Selene again and this time when I pulled away I looked into her eyes and saw the beautiful green orbs I have passionately come to love. Selene was herself again and she began to cry. I pulled her close and held her to me. Her body trembled and I couldn't help but feel her pain. I cradled her in my arms as we sat back down on the loveseat. I looked over at Nathaniel and the vampire's eyes have also gone back to normal, but a sadistic smirk remained on his face.

Nathaniel continued to walk across the room towards us. As he did I noticed that he was looking at Selene with a smile. Apparently he remembered Selene from that night a year ago, the night he murdered her husband.

Nathaniel's clothing was made out of the finest silk and he adorned with many rich trinkets. Each of his hands sported two rings embedded with jewels. He wore a gold necklace around his neck and on the end of it was a pendant with engraved arcane markings. Nathaniel was an amazing sight and I could tell he was a man of amazing power.

Behind Nathaniel was a hooded black robed woman. Her head was so drawn back into the hood that no features of her face could be seen. She kept her head down and walked closely to Nathaniel. She wasn't graceful like the other vampires I have seen, so I figured she was his human servant.

Behind the lady in black was another woman. She was definitely a vampire, but unlike the robed figure before her, covering her body wasn't a concern. Like pretty much every vampire I have seen she was appealing to the eyes. She had blond hair that was tied up into piggy tails. It made her look girlish and innocent, until you looked into her eyes or saw the way she dressed. The vampire wore a tight pink halter top that left little to the imagination and a short, short mini skirt. She topped off her outfit with spiked high heeled leather boots that came up to the top of her calves. I didn't know how she managed to walk in those boots, but she moved gracefully and with no difficultly.

Next was a teenager. The young man didn't look more than sixteen, but when it came to vampires looks were very deceiving. He had short black hair and when he was closer I noticed a lot of his features were similar to Nathaniel's. The young looking man also wore rich silk clothing and adorned trinkets made from gold and jewels.

The last vampire to enter the room had blond hair that was parted down the middle and feathered back on the sides. He wore a t-shirt and blue jeans. The shirt had a sadistic looking happy face on it. His choice of footwear were sneakers. Out of all the vampires that entered the room, he is probably the only one that would come close to passing off as a human.

As Nathaniel approached us I saw the robed woman behind him reach forward and touch the master. Immediately the vampire's power filled the room. It was breathtaking and I felt it begin to overcome me, forcing me down. I tried to fight back with all my will, but I never felt anything like it before. I looked around the room and saw Katrina and all of her servants were suffering the same effects. I had a feeling of helplessness come over me and I felt like there wasn't any way of fighting back.

I fell to the floor while holding my head. The pain was almost more than what I could bear. The feeling of helplessness had almost completely overcome me, until I felt someone grab my hand. I looked up through tear filled eyes and saw Selene kneeling next to me. She was holding her head with one hand and with great difficultly she said, "Nathaniel is testing Katrina's power. We have to try to reach her and help fight back."

With Selene's help I struggled to my feet and then she half pulled, half dragged me over to Katrina. Nathaniel's power was so awesome I could hardly stand, moreover walk. I didn't know how Selene was able to endure the strain. Maybe her hatred for Nathaniel gave her the strength to withstand his power, I didn't know for sure, but the lycanthrope seemed to fare the best out of all of us.

Selene reached out and grabbed Katrina by the arm and I immediately felt both the vampire and the lycanthrope's power as it soared through me. The effects of Nathaniel's power instantly left me and my mind was clear. I absorbed all of the energy from Katrina and Selene I could until I thought my body was about to explode. This time instead of forcing the power back like I did against Boris, I let it gradually flow to Selene and then into Katrina. As soon as the immense amount of supernatural energy touched the master vampire, she released the power, not being able to contain it.

At first, even though I could no longer feel the effects of Nathaniel's power, I could still feel his energy in the room. Once Katrina started to push back I felt her power begin grow and the other vampire's power dwindle. I looked around the room and noticed Katrina's minions were also beginning to recover. I felt her power grow until it matched Nathaniel's. I glanced in his direction and saw he had an astonished expression on his face. The show of power continued, each master not giving an inch, until Nathaniel said, "That's enough Katrina. You're power has grown greatly since the death of Boris."

I felt Katrina relax as everything in the room returned to normal. My body felt drained of energy and even Katrina had lost the newly acquired color to her skin.

"I would like to begin by introducing myself and also my servants to all who do not know," Nathaniel said and I figured he was talking about me. "If you didn't know before I am sure you do now. I am Nathaniel Nevus and this lovely robed lady is my human servant Sarah. This young looking couple behind us is my son Joseph and his lady friend Kiki. Finally, lurking in the back is Eddie."

At that time Katrina started to introduce all of us. When she got to me I didn't care for the way the vampires looked at me. It was almost like they had plans that involved me, dark and evil plans that I didn't want to be a part of.

"Now that the formalities are over it is time we start our discussion," Nathaniel said as he walked over to the loveseat I had been sitting on and sat down. Sarah sat down next to her master. She still kept her head down and drawn back into her hood. Joseph walked over to stand behind his father, while Kiki sat on the arm of the loveseat. Last of all Eddie walked over to stand behind the recliner Elizabeth was sitting on. If she noticed he was behind her the vampire never showed she cared.

"I agree," Katrina said and I thought she looked a little nervous. "What would you like to discuss first?"

"I would like to know how you acquired so much power in such a short amount of time." Nathaniel asked as he looked around the room. "Not to mention you nearly rivaled me without you're human servant. Tell me Katrina. Where is you're human servant? Where is Sebastian?"

"I'm afraid Sebastian is dead," Katrina replied with the same emotional tone in her voice she got when she talked about her old human servant. "I honestly do not know what happened to him. He disappeared the day after Boris's death. Jack here has taken his place."

"You took the human who killed Boris as you're servant?" Nathaniel asked and he sounded surprised. "By our law his life should have been forfeited, not taken as a human servant."

"You can try if you like fang face," I said as I looked at Nathaniel.

I saw the master vampire's face contort with anger and he stood up from his seat. I went for my gun, but before I could get it out Katrina back handed me and sent me stumbling back a few feet. I knew it wasn't anywhere near as hard as she could hit, but it still hurt all the same.

"Be quiet you fool!" Katrina snapped at me and I wanted nothing more than to shoot her, even though I knew the reason why she hit me was to stop Nathaniel from doing so. "How dare you speak to Nathaniel like that."

"It's too late for that Katrina," Nathaniel said and this time all eyes were upon him. "I know you are conspiring against me and you're human servant has just proved it by killing one of my minions."

"Jack killed you're servant in self defense," Katrina said before I had a chance to do so myself. "He was attacked by you're minion and forced to protect himself in the only way he could. He didn't even know the vampire was one of your servants and by our law it was your servant who acted out of line. No vampire may attack a master's human servant. In doing so is an act of war and charges can be brought up against the vampire or his master."

"Preposterous," Nathaniel said and his anger flared up again. "This human should have been drained of his life the moment he killed Boris."

"I tried to bargain with Boris to spare Jack's life," Katrina said and I was impressed on how she turned the tables on Nathaniel. "The fool wouldn't have it and attacked Jack."

"What were you bargaining for, Katrina?" Nathaniel asked and I saw the vampire smile. "You took the human to the graveyard so you could trade him. What did you want to trade him for?"

"How did you know that?" Katrina asked as she looked at me.

"Tell me Katrina," Nathaniel said and the vampire looked like he was excited. "Even with Boris at you're side, do you really think you had a chance to defeat me?"

"That's impossible," Katrina said and her face became even paler. "How could you know all of this?"

"Let me show you," Nathaniel replied as he looked at the door they entered through. "I know how much you miss him so let me reacquaint you with you're old human servant. You may come in now Sebastian."

The door leading out to the spiral staircase opened and Sebastian walked in. Everybody's jaw dropped and I have to admit, mine did as well.

Katrina stood when she saw her old human servant and she couldn't hide the bewildered look on her face. Sebastian walked over to where everyone was and Katrina took a few steps towards him.

"How is this possible? Katrina asked as she stared at Sebastian. "You were dead. I lost all connection with you. You had to have been dead."

"I'm sure you liked believing that," Sebastian said in a cold voice. "With me gone you were free to take Jack as you're human servant."

"How did you break our bond?" Katrina asked and Sebastian smiled wickedly.

"The morning after our meeting with Boris I sought out Nathaniel and when I found him I told him you're plans of conspiracy," Sebastian replied as he stared coldly at Katrina. "I asked him if there was anyway I could break the bond between you and me and he said Sarah was a witch and if there was any way of doing so she would know how."

Everybody turned their gaze towards Sarah. Little could still be seen of her face because of the black hood, but her mouth was visible and she smiled wickedly. Nathaniel also seemed to be enjoying the event at hand, because his smile matched his servants.

"It was a very old spell, but I found it in one of my ancient tomes," Sarah said and her voice was dark and raspy. "The spell of separation came with a price, but Sebastian didn't care, he was more than willing to pay for it."

"What was the price?" Zack asked and everyone looked at him. "What? I'm just curious."

"Just my humanity," Sebastian said and he let out a sinister laugh when he did. "The woman in the paper that is said to have been killed by vampires was my sacrifice to the dark powers. That sacrifice freed me from Katrina's hold. From the moment I accepted the dark powers gift I was cursed. For the rest of my days I must feed on the life blood of humans, but with all the years I have been socializing with you bloodsuckers I have grown accustomed to it."

"Why would you turn against me Sebastian?" Katrina asked and I swore I saw a small amount of remorse in her eyes.

"It was you who turned on me!" Sebastian yelled and his face contorted with rage. "For over a century I did as you bid and you offered me to Boris to save the life of Jack. All you ever had to do was ask me and I would do it for you. I loved you and you betrayed me. Why?"

"For power," Katrina replied and her expression became cold and stern. "You saw what happened the night Boris tested my power. He was stronger than us, but when Selene and Jack touched me, my power greatly increased. You know my whole life has been devoted to the power I seek. I will not let anything stand in my way from attaining it, not even you."

"Then that is where you're wrong Katrina," Sebastian said and the wicked smile returned. "I am here to take away from you what you have taken away from me. I challenge Jack for the right to be you're human servant."

"Challenge me?" I asked as I looked at Sebastian in total astonishment. "What the heck are you talking about? What's he talking about Katrina?"

"Sebastian is challenging you to a fight to the death," Katrina replied and it actually looked like she was amused by the idea. "If you win then you remain my human servant, but if Sebastian wins he will become my servant again."

"Screw that," I said as I looked back and forth between Katrina and Sebastian. "I'm not going to fight him. I don't even want to be you're servant."

"Too late for that, Jack," Sebastian said as he pulled a long knife out of a sheath he had strapped to his back. The sheath was under his shirt and unless you were really looking it was almost impossible to see. "I'm going to carve you into little pieces and then I will drink you're blood to quench my hunger."

"This is crazy," I said as I looked at Selene and saw she had a very worried expression on her face.

"She can't help you Jack," Katrina said and even though she didn't want to lose me as her servant I could tell she was enjoying this. "This is an honor fight. No one can interfere."

"That's right Jack," Sebastian said and he smiled as he waved the knife back and forth in front of him. "No one is going to help you."

"Wait, what's the rules and where is my weapon?" I asked as I took a step back from Sebastian.

"There are no rules Jack and you have to bring you're own weapon," Sebastian replied as he took a jab at me and I just barely jumped back out of the way.

"We don't have to do this Sebastian," I said as my hand went to the pocket where I keep my gun. "Please call this off. I don't want to kill you."

"Oh, but I do want to kill you," Sebastian said as he lunged at me and I dodged out of the way again.

"Fine, so be it," I said as I pulled out my gun and pointed it at him.

Sebastian lost all color in his face and his eyes grew as big as saucers. He looked at the gun which was pointed at his heart and asked, "Where did he get a gun? You can't use guns."

"No rules," I said and I pulled the trigger.

The wood bullet hit Sebastian in the chest, penetrating his heart. He screamed once and then fell lifelessly to the ground. Everyone stared at me, but before anyone could say a word the door leading to the spiral stairs flew open and Detective Oswald burst in, gun in hand and screaming, "Freeze!! Nobody move!!"

Detective Oswald looked around the room and everyone stared at her. She saw Sebastian's lifeless body lying on the ground and then she noticed the smoking gun in my hand. She pointed her .45 revolver at me and yelled, "Drop the gun Jack and lye down on the floor with you're hands on you're head!"

"Who's this and how does she know you?" Katrina asked as she looked at the detective.

"Her name is Detective Sharon Oswald," I replied and I wasn't sure if I was glad to see her or not. It was nice to have a police officer here if Nathaniel tried something, but there was a dead body on the floor and I was the one holding the gun. "She's the detective that wanted to speak with you yesterday morning."

"Darn it Jack!" Detective Oswald yelled at me again. "Drop the gun and get on the floor now!"

I dropped my gun and was just about to do what Detective Oswald said when I noticed Sam begin to move towards her. Out of the corner of my eye I saw Joseph start to move towards the detective as well and when he did Sam stopped and looked back at Katrina. The master vampire shook her head and Sam took a step back.

Detective Oswald noticed Joseph moving towards her and while she kept the gun trained on me she yelled, "Stop right there buddy! Jack, I said get down on the floor and put you're hands behind you're head!"

Joseph ignored the detective's command and continued towards her. This time Detective Oswald took her gun off me and pointed it at the advancing vampire. She threatening pulled the hammer back on her gun and chambered a bullet.

"I said stop right where you are or I will shoot!" Detective Oswald yelled at Joseph, but he still continued towards her. "Oh God, will someone please make this boy stop?"

"I'm sorry detective," Nathaniel said and I saw the concern in the detective's eyes. She saw Joseph as a boy and didn't want to kill someone so young. "You have seen too much and we can't allow you to leave."

I knew Joseph could have cleared the distance between him and the detective instantly, but he was playing with her, feeding on her fear. The vampire came within three steps of Detective Oswald and want to or not the detective shot two rounds point blank into Joseph's chest. The vampire stumbled back a couple feet and then continued towards her again. The detective fired another round with the same results.

Joseph looked down at the three bullet holes in his chest and then back at Detective Oswald. I don't know if she expected to see him drop mortally wounded to the floor, but one thing was for sure she definitely wasn't expecting what happened next.

Joseph smiled at the detective, showing his fangs. Instantly he covered the last few feet between them before she could react. Joseph grabbed Detective Oswald by the throat and looked deeply into her eyes. His own eyes began to glow red as he started to use the fear effect. The detective shoved her gun into Joseph's gut and fired the rest of her bullets into the vampire as she screamed, "Get him off me!"

Joseph leaned forward to feed on the detective as I stooped down and retrieved my gun. I pointed the weapon at Joseph and said "Let her go.

Everyone was staring at me, even Joseph. My voice stopped the vampire before he was able to penetrate the detective's neck. Once Joseph saw me pointing the gun at him he smiled and said, "You fool, didn't you just see how futile this mortal's weapon was. What makes you think yours will fare any better?"

"Because I use wood bullets," I replied and when I did Joseph looked stunned for an instant. "Now let the detective go or I will see how many bloodsuckers I can turn into little black marbles before you finally get me."

At that time I saw Eddie look at Nathaniel and then with lightning speed the vampire charged me. I don't know if it was another ability I received from being a human servant or from Katrina's bite, but I saw the vampire sprint towards me. I turned the gun on Eddie and pulled the trigger. The bullet hit him in the chest, stopping his momentum. The vampire never even knew he was shot until he began to turn to ash, but at that time it was too late. Eddie opened his mouth to scream, but nothing came out. The vampire began to crumble and his remains imploded into the little black marble. Nathaniel stood up from his seat and I pointed the gun at him. For a moment he looked like he was about to attack me, but for some reason he didn't. I don't know if it was because I had wood bullets or if Katrina had the upper advantage over him with all her servants present. I didn't care, just as long as I didn't have to tangle with a vampire as old as him.

I looked again at Joseph and this time I screamed, "Let the detective go!"

Joseph released Detective Oswald as they both looked at the spot where Eddie once was. Nathaniel glared at me and there was death in his eyes and then he said, "You will pay for that mortal."

"We shall see," I said and then I looked at the detective. "Get out of here."

"Holy crap Jack," Detective Oswald said as she looked at the black marble which was once Eddie. "What just happened?"

"I'll explain later," I said as I kept an eye on Nathaniel and his servants. Just get out of here, now!"

I didn't have to tell Detective Oswald again. She turned and ran for the door. I saw Kiki begin to follow, but I targeted her and she stopped. Nathaniel stared at me and the tension was thick.

"You're a dead man Jack," Nathaniel threatened and I just shrugged. "That is the second servant of mine you killed. The council will hear about this. They will not stand for a human that has killed three vampires, especially with one of them being a master."

"You know as well as I Nathaniel, Jack was merely defending himself," Katrina said and her words only angered the vampire more.

"This meeting is over Katrina," Nathaniel said and he started for the door followed by his servants. "I found out everything I came here for. You were conspiring against me. We shall see what the council has to say about this."

All of us just watched Nathaniel leave and once he and his servants were gone Katrina turned on me and said, "Are you crazy? You just killed another one of Nathaniel's servants and this time right in front of him."

"The bloodsucker attacked me," I said and I was really tired of being caught up in all of this. "What did you expect me to do, turn my head to the side so it had a better target?"

"I expected you to let them have the detective," Katrina replied and then she looked down at Sebastian's body.

"I'm sorry Katrina if I still care for human life," I said and I didn't think it was possible, but I may hate Katrina even more now than before.

"Sam, could you please get this out of here before it begins to stink?" Katrina asked as she gestured towards Sebastian's body.

Sam walked over to the body and carefully picked it up so he didn't get blood on his clothes. I watched him carry it across the room and out the door that led to the spiral stairs.

"My God, you make me sick," I said as I stared at Katrina. "He was you're human servant for over a hundred years and you just had Sam carry him out like a bundle of trash."

"What do you expect me to do?" Katrina asked and she looked like she was getting irritated. "He betrayed me. Besides what do I care? He was only a human."

"I'm out of here," I said and I headed for the door before I said something I would really regret. "I need to get some sleep. Some of us need to function during the day as well as night."

I walked over to the door that led out to the spiral staircase and I knew everyone was staring at my back. I opened the door and felt a hand on my shoulder. I turned and saw Selene. She looked at me with a deep amount of concern in her eyes. One thing was for sure. No matter what happened at least I knew I wouldn't be alone.

We walked out of the big room and started to ascend the spiral staircase, and then I heard the door below us open. I looked down and saw Zack and Tyrone. They began climbing the stairs behind us and then I heard Zack say, "Hey Jack, just to get the record straight, we're buds, right? I mean, you wouldn't shoot me, would you?"

"I don't know," I said and I couldn't hide my grin.

"I know I would," Tyrone said and I heard the big vampire chuckle. "I bet Katrina would thank me for it. Then again maybe it would be better to just keep you around for the amusement value. I'm sure Katrina could use another stripper, even though I can't think of any woman who would like to look at you."

The two vampires traded insults until we reached the club's entrance. As soon as we entered, Zack walked over to a table with a couple attractive ladies sitting at it and introduced himself. Tyrone followed us to the door and positioned himself in his favorite spot. I opened the door and we walked out into the evening, then I heard Tyrone say, "Hey Jacky boy. Don't do anything I would do."

Before I could respond Selene pulled me away. We walked across the street to my car. I opened the driver's side and got in. I saw Selene standing at the passenger door so I reached over and unlocked it for her. The werepanther opened the door and slid into the passenger seat. I looked at her and asked, "Where to?"

"You're place," Selene replied and when she said those two words they came out sounding like a purr.

Even though I hated the supernatural world, there was at least one part of it I loved. I guess even in a field of weeds, a rose can bloom.

Chapter Eleven

I awoke the next morning on the couch with someone knocking on my front door. I sat up and rubbed my eyes. I slept on the couch last night, while Selene took the bed. Our intimate relation was delayed. The werepanther was not able to take our relationship into the next stage until she had some closure on her husband's death. She wants to move on with her life, but as long as Nathaniel still lives it just couldn't happen. I want my life with Selene to work out so I did not press the matter. I understood how things were for her right now and if making her happy meant we had to wait, and then I would.

Another knock came from the door and I sat up. I tried to clear the sleep out of my head and then I groggily got to my feet and stumbled to the door, almost stubbing my toe on the chair in the process. I opened the door and saw Detective Oswald standing there. As soon as she saw me she said, "Good morning Jack.

"Kind of early for house calls, isn't it Detective?" I asked in a sarcastic tone. I was still half asleep and my head had that fuzzy feeling in it.

"I guess it is," Detective Oswald replied as she looked at her watch. "I wasn't able to sleep last night. I was up the entire night trying to figure out what happened."

I yawned and ran my fingers through my matted hair. I was still very sleepy and at six in the morning I really didn't care about much. I looked at her with my bloodshot eyes and asked, "What can I do for you detective?"

"Would you mind if I came in?" Detective Oswald asked as she took a step towards me. "I have a couple questions I would like to ask you."

Detective Oswald seemed determined so I stepped aside and let her in. The detective walked past me and into my front room. As she did I finally noticed she was wearing jeans and a red t-shirt instead of the skirt and blouse she wore the last couple times I saw her.

"Dressing kind of down today aren't you detective?" I asked as I looked at her choice in clothing.

I wasn't complaining. One thing was for sure, the jeans and shirt sure portrayed the detective's figure. She looked great before in a skirt and blouse, but now with tight form fitting clothing, I couldn't avoid staring.

Detective Oswald looked down at her choice in clothing and then back at me. I tried not to stare, but I guess it was obvious. For a moment I saw the detective blush and then she asked, "Are you checking me out?"

"He better not be," I heard Selene say from the doorway to the bedroom.

I looked in the direction of Selene's voice and saw her standing in the doorway of my bedroom. All she was wearing was one of my t-shirts and when I saw her in it I wondered why I bothered checking out Detective Oswald at all. The detective had a really nice figure, but it wasn't anywhere compared to Selene's. I don't know if it had anything to do with her being a were-panther, but to tell the truth I really didn't care.

I put my hand out to Selene and she walked over to me. I slid my arm around her waist and pulled her close. Her body felt good next to mine and when Detective Oswald saw Selene she blushed again and said, "I guess I must have been mistaken. I don't want to take much of you're time. I'm sure you two have... um... other things you want to do."

"Have a seat detective," I said with a smile and I almost laughed when the detective paused.

I didn't have much in the way of furniture, just a chair and a very comfortable couch. I would have to say I slept more on the couch than my own bed. I would come home late at night from work and turn on the TV to wind down. I lay on the couch and the next thing I knew it was morning.

Detective Oswald sat down on the chair and I took the couch. Selene slid next to me, resting her head on my shoulder and staring at the detective. It took her a couple moments to get started, but she took a deep breath and began.

"What happened last night?" Detective Oswald asked and I recognized the confusion in her eyes. It was the look I had for a while after being pulled into the supernatural world.

"You were there detective," I replied and I wasn't really sure how to tell her that she was almost an appetizer for a vampire. "You saw everything I did."

"Don't play games with me Jack," Detective Oswald said and I saw she was extremely on edge. Seeing a supernatural creature for the first time will do that to you. "The only reason why I'm not arresting you right now for murder is because I'm not sure what I saw last night. People don't have red glowing eyes and sprout fangs. People don't turn to ash and implode when you shoot them. What happened last night Jack?"

I debated if I should tell Detective Oswald the truth. I looked at Selene and when our eyes met she somehow knew what I was thinking. The were-panther shook her head ever so slightly.

"What?" Detective Oswald asked and we both looked at her. "You looked at her and she shook her head. I have a keen sense of observation; now tell me what you're hiding."

"We're not hiding anything detective," I said and I was really impressed with the detective's awareness. "You already know what it is you saw last night. You just choose not to believe it. I know I was once in the same spot you are right now. It's hard when you realize all the horror stories; all your nightmares are true. It's hard to believe the supernatural actually exist."

Detective Oswald just stared at us with confusion on her face. I looked at Selene again and she just shrugged, this time not trying to hide it. I didn't know how well the detective was going to take the truth, but I was tired of making up lies. Maybe it was better if people actually knew monsters existed. I took a deep breath and let it out slowly. I looked the detective in her eyes and said, "Everybody in that room last night, with the exception of the three of us and the man I shot just before you walked in are vampires."

Detective Oswald's jaw dropped when she heard what I said. I didn't know if she was going to laugh, cry, or just scream. She just sat there, staring at me with a lot of mixed emotions showing on her face. The detective shook her head as she looked for the words to say, but in the end all that came out was, "What?"

"Believe it or not detective, but it is true," I said and just by the way she looked at me I could tell she didn't believe me.

"It's not true," Detective Oswald said and she shook her head when she did. "It's not possible. Tell me the truth Jack or I swear I will put both of you under arrest right now."

"Show her," I said to Selene as I looked into her beautiful green eyes.

The lycanthrope stared back at me and I knew she didn't want to reveal what she was. I knew Selene wanted to keep her supernatural side a secret, but for me she began the transformation.

Bones popped and reshaped themselves, while ligaments tore and mended. The whole process sounded and looked painful. After countless transformations I was sure Selene was used to the procedure.

This was my first time actually watching Selene transform and I found it kind of creepy and unnerving. I knew what to expect though. Detective Oswald, on the other hand, was not ready for such an event. Her eyes grew wide and her hand went to her gaping mouth. All color left the detective's face and her body trembled with fear, but all in all I would say that she handled the plunge into the supernatural world better than expected.

"Wh-- Wh-- What the heck is that?!" Detective Oswald asked when she was able.

Selene crouched on the couch next to me in her half panther, half human form. She explained to me before that this was her hybrid form. She looked much like she did when she transformed in the cemetery. Her body looked human except it was covered with a thin layer of black fur. Her face was a mixture of cat and human. Selene's eyes were still shaped the same, but the pupils were slitted like cat's eyes. Her mouth was normal besides the fangs and her nose became more round shaped.

"Do not be afraid of me," Selene said and I saw the detective mouth the words, "Oh my God."

"It... She talks?" Detective Oswald asked and I guess the realization was too much for her to handle.

The detective withdrew as deep into the chair as she could and pulled her knees up to her chin. She sat like that, staring at Selene and all the while her hand was just inches from her gun.

"You might want to transform back before Detective Oswald becomes one with the chair," I said to Selene and she did as I requested.

Certain parts of the transformation I didn't like to watch, but the detective never took her eyes off Selene. She just sat there wide eyed and trembling.

"Ok, so everyone in the basement of the club were vampires and Selene is a furry cat thing," Detective Oswald said and I could tell Selene didn't like being referred to as a furry cat thing. "So what the heck are you Jack, Frankenstein?"

"Actually, I'm the only full human of the bunch," I said and when I did I wasn't sure on how true it was anymore. "At least I think I still am."

"What's that supposed to mean?" Detective Oswald asked and I could only imagine what was going through her head right now.

"Let me explain everything to you," I said and even though the detective was scared of Selene I saw her edge just the slightest bit forward.

I started my tale from the first night I was attacked and filled Detective Oswald in on all the events up until last night. By the time I finished my story the detective had her feet back on the ground and the color had returned to her face.

"I can see why you stuck with the mountain lion story," Detective Oswald said. "They would have definitely locked you up and thrown away the key. I watched Selene transform and I'm still having a hard time believing it. At least the murder of Julie Simpson is solved. I just have to think of something to tell everyone down at the precinct. I don't think they would buy your story without the kind of proof I got."

"I'm sorry that you had to be dragged into the supernatural world," I said and I truly meant it. I was plunged into it and I probably would always despise the day it happened. "Your life will never be the same again."

"That's ok," Detective Oswald said and in a way I could tell she was kind of relieved. "I'm actually happy I found out. At least I know the supernatural exists and now I can prepare for it. It could have been disastrous if I tried to face down a vampire with a gun full of worthless bullets."

"I would get you some wood bullets, but I'm not sure on how to contact Shaun," I said. I really wished Shaun would have left his number with me. I could use his help right now, but I'm afraid he doesn't like the fact I am conversing with the enemy. Heck, I practically joined their ranks.

"That's ok," Detective Oswald said as she stood up from her seat. "I think I may know where I can have some made. It will take a few days though. Hey, I need to get going and tend to a few matters."

Detective Oswald started for the front door and when she reached it I said, "Wait a second detective. What type of gun do you use?"

"I use a .45" Detective Oswald replied as her hand unconsciously went down to the firearm strapped to her hip. "Why?"

"I have some extra wood bullets if you have a .380," I replied because I figured if I needed more than one clip of bullets I would probably be dead before I popped the old clip out and put the new one in.

"I have a .380 at home, but I haven't used it in a while," Detective

Oswald replied, then she became quiet for a moment like she was lost in thought. "I guess having some bullets right now would be better than not having any at all."

I went into my bedroom to get the bullets. I glanced at the shotgun Shaun gave me and wondered if there was a way I could conceal it in public. I decided to put a little more thought into it later. I grabbed the bullets and headed back to the front room. I handed the bullets to Detective Oswald. She looked at them and said, "I still can't believe its all true. I mean, I saw Selene transform, but it seems more like a nightmare instead of reality."

"Believe me detective," I said, as I watched her put the bullets in her pocket. "Even though you're awake and all of this is true, it's still a nightmare."

Detective Oswald opened the door and walked out. She started down the sidewalk to her car, and then I heard her say, "You have my card Jack. Give me a call if you need me."

I watched her get in the car and drive away. I shut the door and went to my bedroom. Once there I saw Selene getting dressed. As soon as I walked in she looked at me and said, "I have a few things I need to take care of over at La Luna. I'll give you a call later on."

"Do you need a ride?" I asked as Selene walked past me and into the bathroom.

"I already called Xylon," Selene replied as she took out a brush from her purse and brushed the tangles out from her hair. "He will be here in a few minutes. I would invite you along, but it will be extremely boring just sitting there waiting for me all day."

I did have a few things I wanted to do today, like figure out how to conceal the shotgun. I heard a car horn honk outside and figured it was Xylon. I saw Selene grab her purse and head for the door. I met her there and asked, "How can I reach you if I need you?"

"What's your cell phone number?" Selene asked and I told her. She took out her phone and called my number. My phone rang in the other room and once Selene heard it she hung up. "There you go. It should be on your phone now. If anything else you can just look up La Luna in the phone book. Give me a call if you need me."

Selene leaned forward and kissed me gently on the lips, then opened the door and walked out to the car. I stood in the doorway, watching Selene depart. Once they were out of sight I went back in and took a quick shower. As soon as I stepped out I heard my home phone ringing. I grabbed a towel and ran for it. I picked up the phone on the fifth ring and when I answered it I heard Shaun's voice say, "Good morning Jack. I hope I didn't wake you."

"Nope," I said as I wrapped the towel around me. "I was in the shower. What's up?"

"I just heard from one of my contacts that you killed two of Nathaniel's servants last night," Shaun said and he sounded excited.

"You heard right," I said. I wondered who these contacts were and how they had heard about it. "I don't know how your contact found out though."

"Nathaniel had been raging about it ever since the meeting he had last night with Katrina," Shaun said and that explained how the contact heard about everything, but not who the contact is.

"So who's this contact you're talking about?" I asked even though I didn't think Shaun would tell me.

"Don't worry about it," Shaun replied and I could tell by the tone of his voice he didn't like me asking. "The person I get my information from doesn't want to be revealed. I wouldn't worry about who it is anyway because you have something bigger to worry about."

"What's that?" I asked as I wondered what else could happen to me.

"You ticked off an ancient vampire," Shaun replied, but I already knew that. "Nathaniel wants you dead and since you went against everything I told you not to do, you may have started a vampire war. Congratulations! You did the one thing I could never get to happen. You got the bloodsuckers feuding with each other. From what my contact told me Nathaniel has sent word to the council, asking for permission to go to war with Katrina."

"Great," I sighed. "I never wanted any part of this. The only reason I became a human servant is because Katrina threatened the lives of everyone I knew. I don't care if the vampire's wipe each other out. I just wanted to make sure everyone I care about was safe."

"I don't know how this is going to play out," Shaun said. "One thing is for sure though; if there is anything I can do to help just let me know."

"What's a number I can contact you at?" I asked and Shaun told me. "By the way, do you have any bullets for a .45?"

"What did you do, buy a gun?" Shaun asked and he sounded amused.

"No," I replied even though the thought did cross my mind. "The bullets are for a cop named Detective Oswald. She got herself mixed up in this as well."

"My contact told me about her and that reminds me," Shaun said and there was a sound of urgency in his voice. "If you know how to contact this Detective Oswald you had better warn her. Nathaniel's son was talking about doing some real horrible things to her and I don't just mean ripping her apart."

"I'll let her know, but I don't know how much good it will do," I said and I was sorry the detective had to be dragged into all of this.

"Hey, I got to go," Shaun said and he hung up without saying another word.

Once I hung up with Shaun I called Detective Oswald. She answered after the third ring and it sounded like she was in her car. As soon as she answered I said, "Detective, its Jack."

"What's up Jack?" Detective Oswald asked. I could barely hear her with all the noise in the background.

"Pull over and roll up your window," I said and after she did I continued. "First of all the vampire that tried to bite you last night wants you dead in a really bad way. If you see him I would advise you shoot first and hope you don't miss."

"Understood," Detective Oswald said and even though she was good at masking it I still heard the fear in her voice. "Is there anyone that can help us?"

"Besides Selene the only other person I can trust is Shaun," I replied since I doubt Katrina would do anything to help Detective Oswald or anyone in my social circle. "I already enlisted his help. Are there any other cops you can get to help?"

"None that would believe me," Detective Oswald replied after a moment. "What about Katrina and her vampires. You're her human servant. Will she help?"

"Katrina doesn't care about humans for anything else than a meal," I replied. "She won't do anything to help you, but if Nathaniel attacks me or any of her servants then she will step in."

"I guess we're on our own then," Detective Oswald said. I could tell she wasn't any more happy about it than I was. "Keep me posted if you hear anything and watch your back."

I stood in my front room with the telephone receiver in my hand and a towel around my waist. In all the excitement I forgot to get dressed. I hung up the phone and went into my bedroom. I heard my cell phone beep; reminding me I had a missed call. I picked it up and saved Selene's number to the memory.

I got dressed and headed to my car. My first stop was a leather clothing store inside the shopping mall. I bought a black trench coat. then made my way to a hardware store. I bought a hacksaw, then headed home.

Once I was there I sawed off the barrel of the shotgun Shaun gave me. It made the weapon illegal, but it wouldn't fit under the trench coat otherwise. I rigged up the coat so it had an inner pocket deep enough to put the shotgun in. I also rigged the shotgun with a strap to hold it in place. That way it wouldn't bounce around or fall out. Once I was finished I put the coat on and checked it out in the mirror. The shotgun was invisible. As soon as I finished the project my cell phone rang. I answered the phone and saw it was Tom.

"What's up Kaun?" I asked.

"Pascal's still down and his car won't be fixed until late this afternoon," Tom replied and I knew he was going to want me to cover the shift. "He was supposed to be here from eleven to rush. Can you work it?"

I thought about it for a moment. I did have a master vampire after me and whoever I was around. At least if I was at Aces I could try to protect them if any decided to have a pizza employee for dinner tonight. Yeah, right, a human versus a horde of vampires. All I would be is one more shrimp on the barbie.

"No problem, I'll be there shortly," I finally replied after a brief moment of thought.

"Sweet, See ya tonight," Tom said and he hung up.

I looked at my watch and saw it was ten thirty so I quickly changed and headed for Aces. I arrived ten minutes later. I saw Robert and Frank's cars in the parking lot. I got out of my car and walked to the shop. I was just about ready to go in when I heard a car door shut behind me. I turned around and saw Steve walking across the parking lot. As soon as he reached me I said, "What's up Scooter?"

"Nothing much," Steve replied as I opened the door for him. "How are you doing?"

"Great," I lied. I seemed to be doing that more and more over the past week.

We went inside and Robert greeted us. He was standing behind the counter folding boxes. Frank came out of the back room when he heard us and said, "Well Steve, I don't know what Tom was smoking, but with the business we've had so far today, I don't think we are going to need two pizza makers."

"That's what we thought last week and we ended up with a solid day," Steve said as the two of us walked over to the computer and clocked in.

"I quit judging what a day is going to be like until after I leave," Robert said. He put away the boxes he was folding and grabbed another bundle. "Whenever I think its going to be dead, the calls start coming in."

All the prep work was done so I helped Frank make dough. Luckily we only had two batches left to do so it only took about a half hour. I went back out front when we were done and saw Robert was finished folding boxes. It looked like all the day prep duties were finished, so all there was left to do was stand around until some deliveries came in.

"Hey Jack," Robert said as soon as he saw me come out from the back. "I got some of my Halloween costume in the mail yesterday."

Robert worked fast when it came to his Halloween costumes. It was still over three months away and he was already ordering things. Robert went into the office and came back out carrying two guns and holsters. He handed them to me and said, "Check out the weight on them. Those things are heavy for being plastic BB guns. They even have a removable bullet clip. I picked them up online for twenty dollars each."

Robert was notorious for spending a lot of money on his Halloween costumes. I think it was last year he dressed up as a Spartan warrior. He said the whole costume cost him around three hundred dollars.

Robert invited me over to watch a movie once. He had the movie room upstairs. When you entered it was almost like walking into a movie rental store. There were autographed movie posters plastered on the wall. He had props from movies and hundreds upon hundreds of DVD's and blue rays. I couldn't believe how many movies he had. I think he said he had over two hundred blue rays alone.

As I inspected Robert's toy guns the phone rang and he went over to answer it. Another call came in, so I put the guns back in the office and answered the phone. It was another delivery order. I guess today wasn't going to be a sleeper after all.

Business stayed relatively busy during the day. Towards evening Tom and Danny came in. At that time we were in a full blown rush. Tom took control of the ovens so Frank could concentrate on making pizzas. Robert was out on the road and I was getting ready to leave. Besides the three orders I was taking, there were still five left and more coming in. There wasn't much time for chit chat, but I did manage the usual greeting when I saw Danny.

"D-Man," I said while I was bagging up the pizzas.

"Daaaack," Danny said heartily. "What's up?"

"Just getting our butts kicked," I replied while laughing and rolling my eyes for effect.

"I see that," Danny said as he clocked in. "Looks like I came in at the right time."

"Yup," I said as I started walking for the door. "See ya in a few."

As I reached the door, I saw Alan coming in. I laughed and yelled, "Shoooe!"

"Get out of my way Holladay," Alan said in his usual monotone voice. "Don't tell me I have to close with you tonight."

"Nope," I said as I walked out the door. "I'm only here through rush."

"Good," Alan said in his playful, monotone voice. "At least I'll have some help tonight."

I chuckled and walked out to my car with an arm full of deliveries. By the time I returned to the store it was completely dark out. I pulled into the parking lot and saw Pascal's car. Apparently he got it fixed. I parked my car and walked up to the store. I got within ten feet of the entrance and that's when I felt it. Somewhere nearby was definitely something supernatural. I looked in the front window of Aces and saw Pascal standing at the counter. He had a young lady with pig tails hanging on his arm and she was laughing. The supernatural feeling I got was coming from her, then she sensed me and turned around. When our eyes met she smiled at me and bared her fangs. I recognized her as Nathaniel's servant Kiki.

I opened the door and went in. Pascal turned around and said, "Hey

Jack, I want you to meet my new girlfriend. Her name is Kiki."

"We've met before," I said and Kiki just smiled a fangless, but evil smile.

"Kiki's taking me home for dinner," Pascal said and he had a big smile on his face. "She wants to introduce me to her father."

She was talking about Nathaniel. I was sure he would love to have Pascal for dinner. I didn't like Pascal, but I didn't want to see him end up as a vampire snack. I didn't want to tell Pascal that Kiki was a vampire. He wouldn't have believed me anyway, but I had to try something.

"Hey Pascal," I said and I was really getting tired of Kiki smiling at me. "I need to talk to you alone for a second. Can we step outside?"

Pascal stared at me suspiciously for a moment and then nodded. The old man told Kiki he would be right back and then followed. Once we were outside Pascal looked at me and asked, "We don't have much time so what do you want?"

"I met Kiki last night at the Crimson Chateau," I replied and Pascal just crossed his arms. "Did you know that place is a strip club?"

"Yes," Pascal said irritated. He was getting impatient. "Why should I care? It's not as if she works there."

"I know, but she was there with some real nasty people," I said and I wasn't sure he cared. "If she hangs around with a rough crowd, it could cause problems for you."

"Whatever, Jack," Pascal said angrily. "I know what it is. You like her and you don't like the fact that she picked me over you. The way I see it is you're jealous."

"That's not it Pascal," I said and he just shook his head.

"Shut up Jack," Pascal said and he shoved me in the chest. "I don't want to hear it. None of this is any of your business anyway. Just shut up and keep out of my way."

Pascal walked back over to the door, opened it and said, "Let's go Kiki."

The vampire smiled at Pascal as she joined him. I saw her look at me from the corner of her eye and I knew unless I knocked Pascal out or shot Kiki where she stood, there was nothing I could do. I don't even know why I cared. Pascal was right, it wasn't any of my business.

"Hey Kiki," I said as they strolled out towards Pascal's car. They both turned and stared at me. "Bon appetite."

The vampire smiled and Pascal just looked confused. I watched them get into his car and drive away. I went back into the shop and saw Tom standing there waiting for me.

"What was that all about?" Tom asked with suspicion in his voice.

"She's a vampire," I replied. My response shocked him.

"What?" Tom asked and he lost the rest of the color to his already pale complexion. "You're telling me I was standing in there talking to another vampire."

"Yup," I said. Tom looked like he was losing it. "Come on Tom, why else would a beautiful young lady even remotely want to be with Pascal."

"I thought you said all the vampires were going to stay out of Aces," Tom said in a frustrated voice.

"I told you Katrina's vampires will stay away from Aces," I replied. I figured it was best to tell him about the other vampires. "Remember, I told you there were three master vampires, Katrina, Boris and Nathaniel. I killed Boris, but Nathaniel and his minions are still out there. I met him and Kiki last night and I ticked Nathaniel off."

"What do you mean you ticked him off?" Tom asked and his voice sounded stressed again.

"You tell me what you would have done Kaun," I replied as I looked at Tom with a very serious expression. "Nathaniel's son was about to kill a police officer. I pulled out my gun and threatened to kill him if he hurt her."

"I guess I would have done the same thing," Tom said after a moment of thought.

"Exactly," I said. I was happy Tom saw things my way.

"It looks like they need help making pizzas so we can talk about this later," Tom said and I agreed. "I didn't know vampires could have kids."

"Actually they can't," I said as we went back on the floor. "Joseph was Nathaniel's biological son before he became a vampire. Selene told me Joseph was the first person Nathaniel turned into a vampire."

Tom stared at me for a moment and then just shook his head. He returned to the ovens and I waited for another delivery. It was getting late and Robert was cashing out to go home, which meant I was next. As he was leaving Robert walked up to me and asked, "What do you think about Pascal's new girlfriend? She's young enough to be his grand daughter."

"I know," I replied even though I was sure Kiki was far older than Pascal. "It's really sick. One of these days that old man will get what's coming to him."

"Maybe her father will see how old Pascal is and pepper his back side with some buckshot," Robert said with a laugh. "I'm out of here. Have a goodnight everyone."

I told Robert bye and watched him walk out the door. I turned my attention back to the bagging area once Tom handed me a couple pizzas and said, "Rush is about over so enjoy this delivery because you are probably going home afterward."

I bagged up the pizzas and headed out to my car. The address was on the Northern part of the East side near the highway, so I decided the highway was the best route to take. I was lucky enough to hit all the green lights and within ten minutes I was there. Like always, before I got out of my car I looked around until I was satisfied. I got out of the car and walked up to the customer's door. On my way there I heard a loud noise that sounded like honking. It was coming from my right in the neighbor's yard. I noticed a man opening the door to the house I was delivering to, so I looked at him and said, "What the heck is that? It sounds like a goose."

"It is," the man said as he looked in the area where the honking was coming from. "It belongs to my neighbors. They call it goose goose. That stupid son of a gun just walks around the yard honking. It was the nosiest darn thing I ever heard. You hear me goose goose, you stinking feathered freak!"

At that time I saw the goose. It came walking around the corner of the neighbor's house, honking as it did. I couldn't help myself, I laughed. The goose had every dog in the neighborhood barking.

"Thanksgiving is in a few months," I said chuckling. "They're probably just fattening the goose up for Thanksgiving dinner."

"No, that stupid honker has been around for years," the man said and the honking became louder. "Once that darn thing starts up every stupid dog in the neighborhood starts in. The barking goes on all night because of that stupid son of a gun. You hear me goose goose. One of these days you're going to be my dinner."

I laughed again as the man handed me some money and told me to keep the change. He grumbled to himself some more and then took his pizzas inside. I laughed all the way back to my car. I thought it was nice to end my night with a smile for a change.

I got in my car and head back the way I came. I was on the highway when I noticed a big diesel pulling up next to me. I didn't like driving next to those big trucks. They were loud and if the driver doesn't see you when he changes lanes, it could be disastrous.

We drove side by side down the highway until I happened to have that supernatural feeling. I looked in the direction it was coming from, but didn't see anything until somebody ran out onto the highway. I slammed on my brakes and screeched to a halt. The truck next to me was weighed down. I heard the air brakes lock up, whistling the same time mine did, but it couldn't stop fast enough. The truck rammed into the figure on the road, dragging the body for almost a hundred feet before it came to a halt.

I pulled up next to the truck and got out of my car. I looked at the body on the ground and my heart skipped a beat. Laying on the road in a bloody mess was a man in an Aces pizza uniform. His hat was missing and I could tell the man was bald. I knew right away who it was and my heart was full of sorrow. I ran over to Alan's mutilated body and saw he was gasping for breath. I pulled out my phone and dialed nine one one. I told the operator what happened and an ambulance was dispatched before I hung up. I looked down at Alan and said, "Hold on Shoe, the ambulance is coming."

I wanted to help Alan, but I didn't know what to do. There were too many wounds and he was losing too much blood. I knelt next to his body as the trucker came over. The man was shaking and I could tell he was in shock. The trucker began mumbling to himself and I managed to make out the words, "I couldn't stop. I couldn't stop. He came out of no where. I just couldn't stop."

Kneeling next to Alan I got the supernatural feeling again. I looked in the direction it was coming from and saw two pairs of glowing red eyes staring at me. Then I knew why Alan ran out onto the highway. He was being chased.

The two vampires came a little closer and I saw their faces. One I didn't recognize, but the other was Joseph. The vampire just smiled satanically at me, showing a lot of fang. The trucker never saw the vampires. His attention was fully on Alan. Off in the distance I heard the ambulance coming, then I saw the two vampires step into the shadows. The supernatural feeling faded as they disappeared into the night.

Alan's body begin to convulse and moisture began to build up in my eyes. Tears streamed down my cheeks. I wanted to do something, anything to help him, but all I was able to do was lie to him and tell him everything was going to be alright.

I saw the lights from the ambulance in the distance, speeding down the highway towards us. Alan's body convulsed some more and then stopped. His breathing became shallower and occasionally he gasped for air. The ambulance was a hundred feet away when I noticed Alan had quit breathing. I ran to the ambulance and yelled, "Hurry! He just quit breathing!"

The paramedics grabbed their medical kit and ran to where Alan lay. There was blood everywhere and they quickly cleaned out his air way. One of the paramedics started CPR as the other did his best to start an IV and radio the hospital. More emergency crews showed up and the police. They loaded Alan on the gurney, loaded him in the ambulance, and sped away with lights and sirens blaring.

A police officer came over to me and my cell phone rang as he began to ask questions. It was Tom. He was most likely wondering where I was. I couldn't answer the phone right now, so I let the call go to my voice mail. I really didn't want to talk to Tom right now anyway. I didn't want to be the one to break the news to him and Steve about Alan.

I answered the police officer's questions as truthfully as possible, while leaving out the part about the vampires. Both mine and the trucker's stories checked out and since I wasn't the one that hit Alan they told me I could leave.

I got back in my car and headed to Aces. I was just about to call Tom when my cell phone rang again. I answered it and I was totally surprised to hear Nathaniel's voice on the other end.

"How's you're friend?" Nathaniel asked and his voice had a mocking sound to it.

"You bloodsucking piece of crap,\!" I yelled as I heard Nathaniel laugh. "Your beef is with me. Leave my friends out of this."

"What are you talking about?" Nathaniel asked feigning innocence. "Your friend was killed by a truck, not by us."

"You know darn well your son was chasing him when it happened," I replied angrily. "Just stay away from me and everyone I know."

"Does that mean you won't be joining us for dinner tonight?" Nathaniel asked and he laughed again. "You're friend Danny will be very disappointed."

"What are you talking about?" I asked and I felt dread whelm up inside of me. "You better not have touched him."

"What are you going to do about it if we did?" Nathaniel asked and I knew by myself there wasn't much I could do. "Your friend is still among the living, but if you are not here within one hour I will feed him to my servants."

"Where do you want me to meet you?" I asked and I knew I was playing directly into the vampire's hands.

"In the county off Thirty Second road," Nathaniel instructed. I knew the area he spoke of. "You can't miss it. Just look for an old mansion with an iron gates around it. Oh, and one more thing Jack. Come alone."

Nathaniel hung up. I looked at my watch and saw I only had forty five minutes to get there. It was possible to get to Nathaniel's on time if I headed straight there, but I didn't have any plans of showing up alone. That would be suicide. I called up Shaun and he answered on the third ring.

"Hello," Shaun said breathing heavy.

"Shaun, it's Jack," I said as I turned off the highway and started down Sixth Street towards the Midtown Shopping Center. "Are you ok?"

"Yup," Shaun replied between breaths. "I'm just catching my breath."

"What were you doing?" I asked because he had me curious.

"Let's just say there is one less vampire to worry about," Shaun said and when he did I smiled. "Don't worry, it wasn't one of Katrina's. So what's up?"

I told Shaun what happened and where I was going. He knew where the place was and offered his services without being asked.

"Don't worry Jack," Shaun said excitedly. "I've been searching for this bloodsucker's hideout for a while now. I'll be there. You may not see me, but I'll have your back covered."

I hung up with Shaun and called Selene. I told her to meet me at the Crimson Chateau and, not surprisingly, she was already there. She wanted to know what was going on and I told her I would explain when I got there.

I hung up with Selene as I was pulling into the Aces parking lot. I went inside and saw Tom standing by the ovens. As soon as he saw me he said, "Dang Jack, where have you been? I tried calling your cell phone, but you didn't answer. I'm missing two other drivers right now and I had to stick Steve and Frank out on the road."

"Tom, we have to talk," I said and when he looked at me he saw it couldn't wait.

"What's up Jack?" Tom asked and I heard the worried tone in his voice.

"I think Alan's dead," I replied and I saw the color drain from Tom's face.

"How?" Tom croaked. He looked dazed.

"He was hit by a truck on the highway," I replied and Tom's mouth opened to say something, but nothing came out. "I saw it happen."

Tom walked away from the ovens and went into the office. I followed him and watched him sit down at his desk. I could tell he was shocked by the news, then he asked me for details. I didn't have much time, but I told him what happened. I told him everything except for the part about the vampires.

"I need to go," I said and Tom just looked at me with tears in his eyes.

"I need you here," Tom said. His voice was a mix of stress and sorrow. "I don't know where Danny is. He isn't answering his cell phone."

"I'm afraid Danny is the reason I have to go," I said and I didn't know how Tom was going to take the news about him.

"What aren't you telling me Jack?" Tom asked and when I told him everything he said, "Get you're money and get out."

I had a feeling I wasn't welcome at Aces any longer. All this happened because I was at the wrong place at the wrong time. I never wanted anyone to get hurt. I became Katrina's human servant to save everyone, not to have them killed by another master. I just hope one day everyone would be able to forgive me.

Chapter Twelve

I parked in the lot across the street from the Crimson Chateau like I have many times before. I ran up to the club's entrance. I sensed Tyrone on the other side of the door as I flung it open. I blazed past the big bouncer. On my way past I think I actually startled Tyrone instead of the other way around. As I ran out into the club I heard the big vampire holler, "Hey Jacky boy, where's the fire?"

I went through the kitchen to the storage room. I saw the stairs going down and quickly descended them. At the bottom I came to the door leading to the big room. I sensed supernatural on the other side just before I opened it.

Inside the only people I saw were Katrina and Selene. I saw them by the big screen and went over to join them. Once I was there they both looked up at me and then Katrina said, "Hello Jack. Selene said you were coming by. To what do we deserve such an honor?"

"Nathaniel kidnapped a friend of mine and is holding him hostage until I get there," I said. I saw the concerned look on Selene's face, but Katrina just looked blankly at me. Apparently she didn't care. "He told me to come alone, but it would be great if I had some help."

"It sounds like a trap, Jack," Selene said fearfully.

"It is," Katrina said and she sounded very sure about it. "I have an easier solution than going there and facing a master vampire. Just don't go."

"What?" I asked incredulously. I seriously didn't think Nathaniel was bluffing. "If I don't show up he will kill my friend."

"And the reason why I should care is?" Katrina asked and I wondered how someone could be so heartless. But then she was, after all, a vampire. She had no heart.

"If you want to keep me as your human servant you will help me save him," I replied hotly. I was ready to tell Katrina to stick it where the sun don't shine.

"My dear Jack, I'm afraid you don't have a choice in that matter," Katrina laughed and a chill went down my spine.

"If I go to Nathaniel and he kills me, then you will be without a human servant," I said, hoping I could convince Katrina to help.

"Which is why I forbid you to go there, "Katrina said and I couldn't believe she had actually had the nerve to say I couldn't go. "Think about it. If I go over there Nathaniel will see it as an act of war. I really don't think we are strong enough to face him, especially in his territory."

"Fine," I said, frustrated. "I'll go alone."

"If you fight Nathaniel in any way, other than self defense, he will hold me responsible," Katrina said pointedly. I understood what she meant. Nathaniel wanted me to start a fight so he could go to war with Katrina "If you want to fall victim to Nathaniel's trap, I won't do anything to stop you, only if you promise not to attack first. The whole reason Nathaniel wants you to go over there is so he can goad you into a fight by killing your friend while you watch."

"I know why he wants me to come," I said exasperated. I didn't care anymore, I just wanted to get away from Katrina before I ended up shooting her. "Danny is one of my best friends. I can't just turn my back on him. And, I swear, I won't fight unless attacked."

What I really meant was I wouldn't fight unless I was attacked or if Nathaniel tries to harm Danny, but I didn't tell Katrina that. I just hoped being her human servant didn't clue her into what I was thinking. I turned to leave and got a few steps before Katrina said, "I meant what I said, Jack. I don't want to go to war with Nathaniel, not yet. I don't want to deal with the council either. If you bring any of this down on me, I will make sure you suffer. I don't care if you are my human servant."

Ignoring Katrina's threat I kept walking. I thought it was going to be just me and Shaun until I felt a hand on my shoulder. I knew it was Selene before I looked. I should have known she wouldn't let me do this without her. Even if it meant breaking her alliance with Katrina. I took her hand and together we left the big room and climbed the winding stairs. We walked through the club, dodging customers as we went, until we were stopped by Sam. He just stepped out in front of us and at that moment I wondered if Katrina could read my mind. Sam glared at me for a second and said, "If you do anything tonight to cause problems for Katrina I will beg her to let me carry out your punishment."

"Don't worry Sam," I said calmly. I wasn't intimidated by the vampire in the slightest. "One of these days we will find out who's the best between us. I already have three black marbles. I wouldn't mind adding a fourth to my collection."

I knew I hit a sore spot. Sam's eyes flashed red for a second. The vampire made a fist and I swore he was going to take a swing at me, but Jezebel instantly appeared between us. She whispered in Sam's ear and he unclenched his hand. Without saying a word he walked away. Jezebel turned and stared hard at me for a second. She didn't say anything. I knew she wanted to kill me, but Katrina would have her head if she did. Jezebel followed after Sam while Selene and I continued for the exit.

Zack, Elizabeth, and Jean Luke were at a nearby table. Zack had a lady friend with him, but I couldn't tell if she was a vampire or not. When the vampire saw me walking by he gave me a big toothy grin and waved. I nodded to him as we pushed our way through the crowd. We finally made it to the exit and Tyrone was standing in his usual spot. The big vampire grinned and said, "Jacky boy. I heard you have an interesting night planned."

"I guess you could say that," I said as I opened the door. "Want to come and crash the party?"

"You know I would," Tyrone replied in a serious tone. "If Katrina didn't forbid it I would absolutely have your back."

"I know you would," I said with a laugh as we walked out into the night. "See ya Tyrone, at least I hope to."

Tyrone laughed loudly and I heard him say, "Happy hunting Jacky boy."

We got in my car and took off. We had fifteen minutes to get to Nathaniel's coven. It was going to be close. My house was on the way so I stopped off and ran inside. I grabbed my trench and shotgun, put a handful of shells in my pocket, grabbed the extra clip of bullets for the .380 and ran back to the car. I sped most of the way there, hoping there weren't any police lurking. I drove down Santa Fe until I came to Thirty Second Lane. I turned left onto a road lacking houses. On both sides of the road corn fields surrounded us. We drove for a mile until I saw a cast iron fence standing eight feet tall. The top of the fence was tipped and it looked razor sharp.

I followed the fence to a driveway. As soon as we stopped the gate opened automatically. We drove up the road until it ended in front of an enormous mansion. There were trees all around the mansion so it was completely concealed from Santa Fe. Unless you drove down Thirty Second Lane, there was no way of knowing it existed.

The estate was beautiful. It had three floors, with grand picture windows in the front. There were thick curtains on them so I couldn't see inside. The outside was white stucco and black trim. The grounds were gorgeously landscaped. All the ornate landscaping was full of luscious green grass and well maintained bushes which lined halfway down both sides of the outer wall. Flowers bloomed down the sides of the sidewalk that led up to the door. The mansion looked like a celebrity house that would be seen on TV or on the cover of a home magazine, not something belonging to a vampire.

As we pulled up, I glanced at my watch, we had a one minute left. Selene take her cell phone out of her pocket and put it in my glove compartment. I looked at her curiously and she said, "That's just in case I have to transform. I don't want to lose my phone when I rip out of my clothes."

It made sense to me. We got out of the car and walked up to the mansion. I knocked on the door and a few moments later it opened. I saw a man standing in front of us wearing a tuxedo. His black hair was balding and he had a snobbish air about him. His nose stuck up and he stared at me with black beady eyes. He was tall, at least six foot three inches and very skinny. He almost looked like a skeleton with skin.

"You must be Jack," the butler said haughtily. He looked at Selene. "I see you brought a guest."

"This is Selene," I said and the creepy butler fixed his beady black gaze on me again. "She is my dinner date."

"Please come in and sit any where you like," the butler said. "I'll let the master know you are here, but first you must relinquish your firearm."

"I don't think so," I said firmly. "There is no possible way I am gong anywhere without my gun."

"So be it," the butler said blankly. It was as if he could care less one way or the other. "I will let the master know of your decision to keep the firearm. Please wait here."

We watched the butler until he turned a corner and then I heard Selene say, "He was creepy."

We both laughed and then walked into a room that looked like a large sitting area. The walls were completely paneled. Nathaniel went with the darker wood instead of white paneling. There were several pieces of Victorian style furniture in this room. Against the wall as soon as we walked in there was a bench and on the opposite wall there was another. In the middle of the room were two love seats and four comfortable looking chairs surrounding a coffee table. On the table was a stack of magazines that made the room feel more like a doctor's waiting room rather than someone's home.

We sat on a loveseat and waited impatiently. I had a hard time sitting with the concealed shotgun fastened inside my trench coat, so I just let it hang open. Someone could possibly see the gun if they looked hard enough, but I thought just standing around might be even more conspicuous.

There were several paintings on the walls. A couple was of Nathaniel and a few more of other people I didn't know. One of the paintings had the vampire sitting on a white stallion in front of a mansion that looked a lot like this one. I found it amusing to see it was daytime in the picture and then I wondered if the painting was made before Nathaniel was turned into a vampire. The one painting that caught my interest was an ocean scene. In the foreground was an old ship, possibly a galleon. The ship looked to glide across the waves with the wind in its sails. In the background was either the setting or rising of the sun. The artist caught the vibrant colors of the sky and I found the painting utterly breathtaking.

I was so absorbed in the painting I didn't even notice the return of the butler until Selene jabbed me in the ribs with her elbow. I looked at her and she motioned towards the butler. He was standing at the edge of the room staring at me and when I looked at him he said, "Sorry to interrupt you sir, but my master is ready for you. He says you can keep the barbaric weapon, but if it is brandished your friend will die before the first bullet leaves the chamber."

We both stood up at the same time and followed the butler down a long hallway. There were two closed doors on the left side. I wondered what was behind the doors, but I didn't think Nathaniel would like me snooping through his home so I didn't open them.

At the end of the hall was a large room and I sensed supernatural from within. We were escorted into the room and saw it was a dining area. To our right there were four giant picture windows with the curtains wide open. They stood at least twelve feet tall and were four feet across. I was standing in the middle of the room and even from where I was I could see a lot of the grounds and all of the way out to the street. There was also a perfect view of the moon, even though the night sky was kind of cloudy.

There were a dozen wood tables in the room and each table seated four. The tables had white tablecloths on them and elegant designs were masterfully carved into woodwork. On the top of each table there was a candle, even though the crystal chandelier above us was large and bright enough to light up the whole room. To our left was a stage that rose a foot from the ground and up on a stage was a long twelve foot table that had the same elegant designs carved into it. The table had five chairs positioned behind it, each of them facing towards us. Three of the chairs were occupied and I recognized all of them. Sitting on the middle chair was Nathaniel and two chairs on his left was Kiki. The third occupant had my attention. He sat between the two vampires. It was Pascal. The elderly man looked down at me and in an astonished voice he asked, "What the heck are you doing here, Jack?"

"I invited him," Nathaniel said before I could reply. "But I don't remember inviting his guest."

"Selene's my date," I said and I felt the were-panther tense up when she looked at the vampire. "You didn't think I would come without my girlfriend."

"She's your girlfriend?" Pascal asked as he looked lustfully at Selene. "How the heck did you get her to fall for you?"

"Where's Danny?" I asked, ignoring Pascal. "You told me he was here, but all I see is Pascal."

"You were supposed to come alone Jack," Nathaniel said as he and Selene stared hatefully at each other. "No matter, I have a history with the were-panther that must be dealt with anyway."

"What?" Pascal said confounded. He looked back and forth between Nathaniel and Selene. "Were-panther, what the heck is that?"

"Bring him out," Nathaniel said as he ignored Pascal's question.

A hidden door opened behind the table. Out of it walked a vampire I didn't recognize. He was completely bald and he had piercing dark blue eyes. He wore a t-shirt and jeans, but the one thing that caught my attention was the tattoo he had on his forehead. It was a demonic looking smiley face.

The vampire dragged someone behind him. I couldn't tell it was Danny until the bloodsucker abruptly sat him on the chair next to Nathaniel. Danny looked around the room until his eyes stopped on me and then he asked, "What's going on here Jack? Who are these people?"

"Yeah," Pascal said looking at Danny. He was extremely naïve and dense. "What the heck is going on here? I was supposed to have dinner with Kiki and her father, but then Jack showed up and Danny gets dragged out of some kind of secret doorway."

"I grow tired of this old man's babbling," Nathaniel said as he looked at me. "Please Kiki, dispose of him so we can continue."

"Gladly," Kiki said giggling.

The vampire instantly rose from her chair and forcefully tilted Pascal's head to the side before the old man even knew she moved. Pascal had just enough time to cry out before Kiki sunk her fangs deeply into his neck. Her eyes glowed red as she stared at me. I didn't know if she expected me to try something or not. I wasn't here for Pascal. I tried to warn him earlier, but he was a foolish old man who wouldn't listen. My main concern was getting Danny, Selene and myself out of here alive.

Pascal's mouth was gaped in a silent scream and his eyes were beginning to dim as Kiki continued drinking. The process took less than a minute, but the look on his face implied it lasted an eternity. Once the vampire was done she released Pascal's head and he fell forward onto the table before tumbling to the floor. Kiki giggled again as she wiped the blood from her face with her fingers and then sucked them clean. She had a sadistic look on her blood splattered face as she stared at me and I found I couldn't meet her gaze.

"What's the matter, Jack?" Kiki asked laughing. "I like them well aged, but this one had a sour taste to him."

I didn't say anything to her. I just stared at Danny and saw he was looking directly at Kiki with a horrified expression. He had just been introduced to the supernatural world and I hoped he lived long enough to hate it as much as I did.

"Oh my God!" Danny yelled as he struggled to get up, but the vampire with the tattoo held him in his chair. "Oh my God! She killed Pascal! Jack, what's going on?!"

"Yes, Jack," Nathaniel said before I could reply. "Tell your friend what is happening. Tell him what kind of situation you got him into. Then I want you to tell him everything is going to be alright."

I didn't want to play Nathaniel's game. I just wanted to get us all out of here. I didn't know if Shaun was here or not. He said I wouldn't see him, but if I knew he had my back it would be a lot easier to play the tough guy. I delayed as long as I could, until Nathaniel lost his patience and screamed, "Tell him everything I said right now or I will rip out his throat and let my servants drink his blood!"

"Danny," I said and I had to swallow the lump in my throat before I continued. "I am sorry you got caught up in all of this. Vampires exist, and for the safety of my friends and family I have been forced to deal with them for the past several days. It wasn't a mountain lion that attacked me over a week ago, it was a vampire."

"If you dealt with them for my safety, then why am I here now?" Danny asked fearfully and I didn't know what to tell him. The deal I made with Katrina was supposed to keep everyone safe. I didn't expect a second master vampire to be part of the deal.

"Because my deal was with another vampire named Katrina," I replied and I couldn't look Danny in the eye. "Katrina conspired against Nathaniel and she forced me to join her side."

"You left out the part about killing two of my servants," Nathaniel said and I wanted to direly make him the third. "This is the real reason why Danny is here. You killed my servants so who better to fill that void than a friend of yours. A life for a life, Jack. Now, tell Danny its going to be alright."

I didn't want to say it. I knew what Nathaniel was planning. After I gave Danny a false hope of freedom Nathaniel was going to kill him. I looked at Selene and once again there was sorrow in her eyes. So much has happened to me and my friends over the past week and until all these vampires were out of my life it would never be the normal again.

Nathaniel stared at me and I saw he was losing his patience. I was about to tell Danny what the vampire wanted, but I saw a little red dot begin to move across Nathaniel's chest until it rested over his heart. I saw the same thing happen before on TV and recognized it as a targeting laser from a high powered sniper rifle. Shaun was in position and about to shoot Nathaniel. I acted like I didn't see anything, then heard the sound of breaking glass as the bullet rocketed towards its target. A microsecond before the wood bullet penetrated the vampire's chest, Sarah appeared behind Nathaniel and she spoke the word "Raield." The bullet slammed into an invisible barrier and shattered into several pieces.

Nathaniel snarled at me and with lightning speed he grabbed Danny by the throat and pulled him off his chair. The vampire sank his fangs into Danny's neck as more bullets hit the barrier. I pulled out my gun and started to shoot at Nathaniel as well, but with the same results. Nathaniel did something I'd never seen before. He bit his own wrist and placed it over Danny's mouth. I heard D-man begin to choke as the liquid ran down his throat.

Sarah pointed her finger in the direction the bullets were coming from and said "Ireall." A small ball of fire flew from her finger tip and out the broken window. A few moments later I heard a loud explosion behind me, coming from somewhere outside. I felt Selene tug on my arm after I took another shot at Nathaniel. I looked at her and she yelled, "Jack, we have to leave! Danny is dead! Let's get out of here while we still can!"

My body was numb as I started to run for the door. Katrina was right, but I fear Danny wasn't killed. Something far worse happened to him. He was drained to the point of death and then Nathaniel fed Danny his blood. In three days D-man will rise from his shallow grave as a vampire.

As we raced down the long hallway I pulled out my shotgun and then I heard Nathaniel yell from behind us, "Get them. Don't let them escape or I will extract punishment on you instead."

I ran as fast as I could with Selene by my side. For a moment I thought we might make it without a fight, but then I felt a breeze on the back of my neck and knew a vampire was right behind us. I felt a strong hand on my shoulder and then my momentum stopped as I was instantly slammed against the wall. My head hit hard and I saw stars. The room began to spin and my stomach started turning flips. Great, I had another concussion.

I heard Selene begin her transformation. I wanted to kill the bloodsucker, but the shotgun was pinned between me and the wall. I felt the vampire release me and I crumbled to the floor. I looked up in time to see Selene, in full panther form leap at the vampire with the smiley face tatoo. The were-panther latched onto the vampire with her front claws and began to bite at his throat as she raked with her back ones. I saw her try this stunt before on another vampire and the turnout was pretty much the same. The vampire did manage to unlatch Selene, but the damage was done. Blood gushed from its neck and it doubled over in pain as the vampire tried to hold it's organs in. I'm not sure if the wounds that Selene inflicted were fatal, but the vampire was definitely out of the fight.

Selene transformed into her half human form and then tried to help me to my feet. The room still spun a little, but at least the nauseous feeling was gone. If I did have a concussion it was only a slight one. Selene helped me down the hall and I found it very difficult to keep up. She was just about to pick me up when another vampire appeared at the sitting room doors.

The vampire hissed at us and I lifted my shotgun to shoot at the same time it charged us. I didn't waste precious time aiming, I just pointed in the direction I saw the vampire and pulled the trigger. Wood chips scattered in a wide arc in front of me and I heard the vampire scream. It staggered backwards with dozens of bleeding wounds. Pieces of wood were impaled throughout the vampire's body. Within a few moments the wounds began to smolder and then eventually smoke. The smell of burning flesh was nauseating and the vampire screamed again as it fell to its knees. The scream was mind piercing and my head already ached from being smashed against the wall. The vampire screamed a third time as parts of its body began to burst into flames. It reached forward, pleading for my help and I accommodated it with a bullet in its heart.

I leaned completely on Selene as she carried me the rest of the way down the hall into the sitting room. We stumbled to the door and flung it open. The evening air poured into the mansion as we ran out into the night.

My car was a mere ten steps away, but it seemed like an eternity before we reached it. Selene helped me into the passenger seat and ran around to the driver side. I fished the keys out of my pocket as Selene got in. She took the keys and quickly started the car and that was when I noticed she was completely naked. We didn't need to be driving through town without clothes, but we didn't have time to worry about that right now.

We sped down the road as several vampires stormed out after us. Selene had the gas peddle floored, but the Hyundai was only a four banger. I now wished I had bought the muscle car instead of the gas saver. The bloodsuckers kept up with us until we finally broke fifty miles per hour and then they trailed off. We turned back on Santa Fe and drove towards the city. We barely escaped with our lives, but I wasn't able to save Danny and quite possibly Shaun met his fate from the ball of fire as well.

I took off my shirt and handed it to Selene. I held the wheel as she slipped it on. It was long enough to look like a mini-dress so if anyone pulled up next to us they wouldn't think she was naked. It was late and very few people were on the road, but with my luck a cop would pull up next to us.

As we drove down the road my phone rang. I answered it without checking who was calling and smiled when I heard Shaun's voice on the other end say, "Why the heck didn't you tell me he had a spell caster?"

"I didn't think it mattered," I replied, happy to hear Shaun's voice. "I didn't know she could shoot balls of fire from her fingertips."

"They can do far worse than that," Shaun said and I heard the sound of a car starting up in the background. "I just barely got out of there in time. I saw that flaming ball coming towards me and I high tailed it. The hair on the back of my head got singed when that sucker exploded."

"Can she be beaten?" I asked since I didn't know anything about magic.

"Oh, we can beat her," Shaun replied, but he didn't sound very confident. "She's just going to be a wild one. We're going to have to take her by surprise and hope she doesn't know we're coming."

"Great," I said and then my cell phone beeped to let me know I had another call. "Hold on a second Shaun. I have another call."

I answered my phone and heard Detective Oswald's voice on the other end. She sounded very upset and frightened.

"Jack," Detective Oswald said as soon as I answered.

"What's up detective?" I asked and I wondered what had her freaked out.

"That kid from the Crimson Chateau is outside and he wants me to let him in," Detective Oswald said in a frantic voice. "I almost did. Oh God, I almost opened the door and let him in. I don't know what stopped me, but when I didn't invite him he started running around the house breaking windows."

"Stay away from the windows and if you see him don't look at him," I said as I tried to figure out a way to help the detective until we got there. "Don't listen to him either. If he can get you close enough to one of the windows all he has to do is pull you through."

I heard the detective scream and then a gun shot went off. I swore Joseph got her until I heard her voice say, "Please hurry Jack. I don't know how much longer I can keep him out of my head."

"What's you're address?" I asked and she told me. "We'll be right there."

"Hurry Jack," Detective Oswald said and then the line went dead.

I told Selene what the address was, then got back on the phone with Shaun. I told him what was going down and gave him the detective's address as well. We were about ten minutes from Detective Oswald's house and something told me Shaun was farther out than we were. Great, we escaped Nathaniel and now we have to face Joseph. An old phrase came to mind; Out of the frying pan and into the fire.

Chapter Thirteen

Ten minutes later we pulled up to Detective Oswald's house. My headache had subsided enough so I could think and function on my own. The detective had every light on, inside and out. The neighborhood she lived in looked peaceful. It was late so most neighbors were already sleeping, except for the ones that woke up from the commotion and gunshots. I was sure someone called the police by now, even though Detective Oswald one of them.

I loaded another shell in my shotgun. It still had two shots left, but you never know when you may need another shot with these crafty bloodsuckers. I also replaced the clip in my handgun. We got out of the car and Selene took off my shirt and tossed it to me. She began her transformation and I hoped no one was able to see her. Within a few seconds a panther stood in front of me.

As of right now Selene was the only supernatural I was sensing. We walked up to the house. Besides the windows being busted out, nothing seemed unusual. I looked at Selene and got her attention. I motioned for her to go around the house. I figured she knew what I meant when I saw her quietly walk off. I loved how silent she was in her panther form, then again Selene was very agile and quiet in any of her forms.

I watched Selene disappear around the corner of the house and then I walked up to the front door, shotgun in hand. I tried the knob but it was locked. The big picture window next to the front door was broken out so I stuck my head in and called out to the detective. I didn't get a response. The window was big enough to climb through, so I swung my leg over, while watching out for shards of broken glass, I maneuvered myself inside.

Once in I had a clear view of the front room. I looked around and saw a sectional facing the wall to my left. On the wall was a thirty two inch plasma TV. She had lots of pictures framing the television. As I walked around the sectional I saw a golf ball sized rock, lying on the floor. There was fresh blood on it and lying on the floor next to the rock was Detective Oswald. I knelt down and examined her neck for bite marks, but there wasn't any. At least she was still breathing, although she did have a really nasty lump on her head. Blood trickled down her face from the head wound and I figured the rock was the cause. I tried to wake the detective up, but she was out cold.

While kneeling over her body, I sensed supernatural coming from the window I entered through. I looked and saw Joseph staring at me. The vampire had a sadistic smile while showing off his fangs.

"Hi Jack," Joseph said while leaning through the window. "I see you escaped my father's clutches. Were you able to save your friends as well?"

"You piece of crap," I said seething. I jerked my head towards the detective. "What did you do to her?"

"She has a very strong will so she wasn't affected by my mind control," Joseph explained with an impressed look on his face. "Since I couldn't glamour her into letting me in, I decided to clip her with a rock. If she couldn't think straight it would weaken her defenses against me so I could break her will. How was I to know she would move directly into the rocks path as I threw it?"

"Why don't you come in so I can blow your freaking brains out?" I asked and I heard Joseph laugh.

"Sorry Jack, but this isn't your house and unless she wakes up and invites me in were at a stale mate," Joseph said and I was happy to know the rumor about vampires not being able to enter unless invited was true. "If you would like to come out here to me, then it would be a different story."

I stood up and looked at the smiling vampire. I wished Shaun was here as I started to walk towards the front door. I no sooner got half way there when I sensed a second supernatural presence. I opened the door in time to hear Selene growl as she crashed into Joseph. The were-panther began to claw at the vampire, ripping his flesh. I heard the bloodsucker hiss as they tumbled around the yard. I went outside and tried to sight in on the vampire, but he always managed to keep Selene in the line of fire.

Joseph was bleeding from several deep wounds, then I noticed Selene had a few of her own. A truck pull up across the street and Shaun got out. My attention was drawn back to the fight as I heard Joseph scream. Selene had bit deeply into the bloodsucker's shoulder. The vampire's eyes glowed red and it almost looked feral. I saw Joseph's fingernails extend into claws, then he repeatedly drove them deep into the panther's side. I heard Selene yowl from the pain and she released the vampire's shoulder. Selene struggled to break Joseph's grip, then she quit moving all together.

Blood was everywhere and I was sure most of it was Selene's. I was full of dread and feared for her life. I saw the were-panther return to her human form. I took aim at Joseph again and noticed Shaun did the same. Effortlessly the vampire threw Selene's body at me and even though I could have dodged it, I stood my ground and let my body absorb the impact.

Selene's body slammed into me and I heard her half cry half yowl from the pain. We fell to the ground. My body screamed in pain and I couldn't catch my breath, but Selene was still alive.

As I laid there catching my breath I heard a gunshot. I saw Shaun trying to get Joseph in his sights. I had very little problem following the vampire's movements, but I knew Shaun wasn't able to keep up. Joseph eluded every shot that came his way and when the opportunity was right Joseph went in for the kill.

After Shaun's last shot he had to reload. He fumbled for some shells in his pocket, then he quickly began to load the shotgun. Joseph saw this and dashed forward. I saw the attack coming, but wasn't able to maneuver with Selene laying on me. The most I was able to do was scream, "Look out Shaun!"

Anyone else would have hesitated or looked around for the apparent danger, but not Shaun. He skillfully dropped to the ground and avoided his throat being ripped out by Joseph's clawed hand.

I slowly moved out from beneath Selene and I heard her groan in pain as I did. I picked up my shotgun and looked around for the vampire. An instant later I felt supernatural behind me and I knew there was no way I was going to turn around in time. I braced for impact as I expected to see the vampire's hand erupt from my chest. Instead, I heard the loud booming sound of a gunshot, then a sharp pain in my arm as claws tore through leather and flesh.

Joseph's body crashed at my feet and I was confused from where the shot came from. I looked at Shaun but he was still on the ground as he attempted to reload his weapon. I saw movement out of the corner of my eye as Joseph's body began to turn to ash. I saw Detective Oswald standing in her doorway, smoking gun in her hand. She was staring at Joseph's body as it imploded into a little black marble.

Shaun got to his feet and walked over. He bent over and picked up the marble and then looked at the detective and said, "Nice shot."

Detective Oswald didn't respond, she put a hand to her head and staggered back a couple feet before she was able to regain her balance.

I knelt next to Selene and noticed she was still breathing, but lost a lot of blood. The detective noticed Selene was naked so she went inside and came back out with a blanket. I carefully covered her and then said, "She's lost a lot of blood. We need to get her to the hospital."

"There's nothing they can do for her there," Shaun said and I stared at him blankly. "She's a lycanthrope. Her blood type is totally different than anything the hospital would have. Her body would just reject it."

"There has to be some way to save her," I said and tears burned in my eyes.

"Unless you know another were-panther there is nothing we can do," Shaun said and the only person who came to mind was Xylon, but I didn't know how to contact him.

I put my lips close to Selene's ear and whispered, "Selene. Can you hear me?"

Her eyes flickered open for a second, then shut again. For that brief moment I noticed the beautiful green orbs I loved were starting to grow dim. I whispered again.

"Selene," I said, my voice cracking. "Just nod if you can hear me."

For a moment there was no movement, then I saw the slightest nod. For a moment I felt hope, then I asked her, "You lost a lot of blood. How do I contact Xylon?"

I saw her lips part for a moment, then in a voice even softer than a whisper I heard her reply, "Phone."

I remembered Selene put her cell phone in my glove compartment. I instantly jumped to my feet and ran to the car. I flung open the door and opened the glove compartment. I saw her phone lying under a street map. I picked it up and started scrolling through her contacts. I went through all of them and the last one was Xylon's. I pushed connect and the phone began to dial. A few rings later I heard Xylon's voice on the other side.

"Hi Selene, what's up?" Xylon asked and he sounded like he just woke up.

"Xylon, it's Jack," I said and my voice sounded urgent.

"What is it Jack?" Xylon asked and he didn't sound happy to hear my voice. "What are you doing with Selene's phone?"

"We had a run in with a vampire and Selene's badly hurt," I replied and I swore I heard Xylon growl. "She's lost a lot of blood."

"Can you get her to La Luna?" Xylon asked and his voice sounded stressed.

"Yes," I replied as I ran back to Selene. "We can be there in about ten minutes."

"I'll meet you there," Xylon said and then he hung up.

I stuffed Selene's phone in my pocket, looked at Shaun and said, "Help me put her in the back seat."

Shaun nodded and helped me pick her up. Once we had Selene in our arms Detective Oswald wrapped the blanket around her. We carried her carefully to my car and the detective opened the back door. I climbed through the door backwards as I held Selene's shoulders. Shaun laid her legs gently on the seat and then closed the door. I jumped into the driver's seat and felt in my pockets for the keys. They weren't there. I remembered Selene drove us here so I looked at the ignition and the keys were there. As I started the car I heard sirens in the distance. Detective Oswald must have seen the worried look on my face because she said, "Don't worry about the police. I'll take care of them."

I nodded, then made a u-turn in the street. I glimpsed Shaun get into his truck and follow me as I sped down the street. As I drove towards La Luna I hoped Detective Oswald was able to come up with a convincing story for her fellow police officers.

Minutes later I pulled up to La Luna and Shaun parked next to me. The door to the restaurant opened and Xylon walked out. His long black hair was uncombed and his eyes were bloodshot, but he looked very alert. As I got out of the car he was already opening the back door. I went around to the other side and opened that door. I carefully lifted Selene's legs as Xylon did the same to her upper body. I climbed through the car while holding her legs. Once I was out we carried her through the door Shaun was holding open.

Xylon led us through the dining area and through the kitchen door. It was dark so I trusted the were-panther to lead me through. We turned right and walked until we came to another door. Shaun moved ahead and opened it. As soon as the door was opened Xylon turned on the light.

We carried Selene down a flight of stairs to a makeshift operating room. Xylon led me to a bed and we gently laid Selene on it. The were-panther quickly went to work. The first thing he did was stop the bleeding. I assisted the best I could, but with no experience I was little more than useless. Shaun helped more than I did. I didn't know for sure, but I thought he may have been in the military at one time. He helped Xylon stitch the cuts, then dress some wounds.

Once they were finished I saw Xylon run to a refrigerator and grab a couple bags of plasma. Apparently he's done this before. I knew what was coming next and I couldn't watch. I turned my back and walked away. Shaun came over to me looking concerned. When I looked at him the world began to spin and I felt sick. My legs gave out and Shaun caught me. He helped me to a chair and I sat down.

"He's losing blood," Xylon said, as he finished hooking the I.V. up to Selene. "I can smell it from here."

Shaun helped me take off my coat and sure enough my arm was soaked with blood. Four deep claw marks in my right bicep bled freely. I knew I was hurt when Joseph's claws hit my arm, but I didn't know how badly. Shaun began to clean the wounds while Xylon filled a syringe with morphine. The were-panther walked over with the needle and my body tensed up. I guess he could sense my fear because Xylon just smiled at me and said, "Don't tell me you're afraid of needles?"

I was embarrassed by the remark, then I became angry. I looked up at the were-panther and said, "Just do it."

I turned my head as Xylon injected the painkiller into my arm. In my opinion it was the bravest thing I've ever done, well at least until he started to stitch me up. I felt like I was going to pass out, but I knew Xylon would enjoy it and I didn't want to give him the pleasure. I didn't feel any pain, but I gritted my teeth with every stitch. The tugging of the needle made me sick.

Once Xylon was finished Shaun helped me over to a gurney and I laid down. The morphine was making me drowsy and no matter how much I fought to stay awake it was a losing battle. I soon drifted off to sleep.

I dreamed of many disturbing things. I was walking through the same valley of white flowers I was in the dream from a few nights ago. The sun shone brightly upon me like before. On the other side of the valley I saw Selene waiting for me, but this time Danny was with her. I walked over to them and instead of Selene embracing me with a kiss; blood began to gush from her and Danny's eyes and mouths. I began to scream, then I heard laughing coming from all around. I recognized the laughter and knew it was Nathaniel cackle. I ran away, trying to escape the laughter, but no matter where I went it was all I kept hearing.

I woke gasping and covered in sweat. I saw I was still in the basement of La Luna. I looked over to where I last saw Selene and she was still there, but she no longer had the I.V. hooked up to her. Xylon walked in a few seconds later carrying a bucket and mop. He went to a floor sink and dumped the crimson liquid into the drain. Once Xylon was finished he noticed I was awake. He put the mop and bucket down, washed his hands and walked over to me.

"Have a good nap?" Xylon asked, checking the bandaging on my arm.

"I guess," I replied and I jumped when he hit a tender spot. "How long was I out?"

"A couple of hours," Xylon replied as he took off the bandages and assessed the stitches. "You're friend left after you passed out."

"How's Selene?" I asked, hopeful for good news.

"She's fine," Xylon said and I was relieved. "She came to about an hour ago and told me everything that happened. I can't believe you actually had the balls to go into Nathaniel's lair."

"Balls had nothing to do with it," I said, trying to ignore him messing with my arm. "I went in to save a friend. I am just sorry I wasn't successful."

"Looks like I misjudged you," Xylon said as he finished bandaging up my arm. "Now I know what Selene sees in you."

Xylon walked to the sink and washed his hands again as I got up from the bed and went over to Selene. The color returned to her face and most of her wounds were already healed. I guess the look of astonishment was very apparent on my face because after Xylon was finished drying his hands he said, "We heal at a much faster rate than humans. By noon all of Selene's injuries will be gone."

"Wow," I said, rubbing my bandaged arm. "That must be nice."

"The sun is coming up and I need some rest before I start work," Xylon said and I watched him grab some bedding out of a cabinet. "I'm going to crash on one of these beds until my shift starts. Feel free to do the same."

"Actually I'm dying for a shower," I said and I walked over and picked up my trench coat. "I'm going home and then I'll be back later."

I took Selene's cell phone out of my pocket and laid it on a stand next to her bed. I leaned over and gently kissed her on the forehead, then started towards the stairs. I made my way through the dark kitchen and through the dining area until I came to the front door. I got in my car and drove home. Once there I dragged myself up to the door. Since I knew vampires couldn't enter without permission I wasn't worried about one being inside. My supernatural sense would have gone off anyway..

I unlocked the door and went inside. I went straight to my bathroom and hopped in the shower. I tried not to get my bandages wet, but that was impossible.

Thirty minutes later I ran out of hot water so I got out and dried off. I put on my sweat pants I use as pajamas and staggered off to bed. No sooner than my head hit the pillow I passed out and remembered no more.

Chapter Fourteen

I didn't have any weird dreams, but I woke the next morning to someone knocking on my door. I sat up for a moment and waited for the groggy feeling to go away. The knock came again, but louder. I got out of bed and headed to the door. I wondered who it could be and my suspicions were leaning towards Detective Oswald. I dismissed the thought as I felt supernatural on the other side. It was daytime, which ruled out vampires, so I figured it had to be Selene. She must have healed faster than expected. I opened the door and was completely shocked and frightened by who I saw. Standing on my doorstep, smelling of dirt and blood was Danny.

His long black hair was a tangled rat's nest that was hanging loosely in his face. His Aces uniform was completely stained with dirt and dried blood. His skin was sallow and he resembled a zombie out of a horror movie. Which was what I thought seeing him on my doorstep looking completely ghoulish. Danny looked at me with his bloodshot eyes. He licked his chapped and cracked lips and then in a raspy voice he said, "Are you going to let me in or what?"

"Right now, I'm leaning towards, or what," I replied staring wide eyed at him. "It depends on if you are still alive or not."

"I'm still alive," Danny said. Then he coughed. When he did his body went into spasms and once the coughing fit was over there was blood on his lips.

"At least you think you are," I said watching Danny wipe the blood away with his hand. "You're not a vampire or you would have burned up from the sunlight. I'm thinking you're some kind of intelligent zombie or something."

"I'm not a zombie," Danny said sickly. "My heart is beating and I still need to breathe."

"I don't know D-man. I'm going to have to take your word on that," I said and then instantly with lightning speed, Danny had me by the neck with a vice-like grip. He lifted me off the ground and I couldn't breathe.

"I'm going to ask one more time Jack," Danny said wildly with desperation. "Can I come in?"

"I'll tell you what," I managed to squeak out and I wish I had my gun. "Put me down and let go of my neck."

Danny blinked his eyes, came back down to earth and realized what he was doing. He quickly put me down. I gasped for air and wished I had a dollar for every time someone grabbed my throat. I coughed a couple of times and noticed Danny looking down at his hands in amazement. I rubbed my throat and when I thought I was able I said, "Being able to do what you just did isn't entirely what a human can do. I'm not inviting you in Danny, but if you can enter without my permission, then by all means do so."

Danny looked at me, then walked past me and into the house. I knew from last night's experience, vampires couldn't enter a person's home without an invitation. One thing was for sure though, with the super speed and strength he acquired, Danny was definitely something other than human.

I shut the door and turned around. Danny was standing in the middle of my living room, staring at me. I thought he looked creepy out in the sun, but now in the dim light he looked totally nightmarish. Besides his hair being tangled and messy, he had dark rings around his eyes. Danny licked his lips and stared at me with his dark eyes and then asked, "What did you get me involved in Jack?"

I didn't know what to tell him. He now knows supernatural creatures exist, heck, he probably is one. As he stared at me I felt horrible for what happened to him. It was my fault, so I told Danny everything, from the first night I was attacked, through all the events leading up to last night. I told him the truth. When I was finished Danny sat down and stared down at his dirt stained hands. I sat across from D-man on my couch and watched him. I didn't know what else to say and he was at a loss of words as well. We sat in silence until Danny finally looked up at me and said, "I came here today to kill you because I thought you were to blame for this happening to me. Now that you told me the truth I see it wasn't your fault."

"I'm sorry Danny," I said with tremendous guilt. I couldn't bring myself to look at him anymore. "I did everything I could to not bring any of you guys into this. It seemed like the more I tried to keep everyone I knew safe, the more they got dragged in."

"You should have told all of us the truth in the first place," Danny said.

"You wouldn't have believed me," I said and he had no idea on how much I wanted to tell everyone.

"Probably not," Danny said with a glint of a smile. "At least when we'd visit you at the State Hospital you could have said you told us so."

I didn't know if I should laugh or not. It sounded like the old Danny making a joke. When I saw him smile I knew he was. I wished I could go back in time and in sick that day. If I had, what happened to me would have happened to someone else and since this ability I have is unique, they would have been traded to Boris and killed.

"I need to know something Danny," I said, with a curious tone in my voice. "I saw Nathaniel drain you, then make you drink his blood. Why aren't you a vampire?"

"I'm not sure," Danny replied thinking about last night. "I remember Nathaniel biting me and my life force beginning to drain away. I remember my heart beating so fast I thought it was going to explode. I concentrated on slowing my heart rate. With all my years of martial arts training I was able to slow it down, almost to nothing. I guess since my heart wasn't beating fast enough to pump blood through my veins, Nathaniel thought I was drained. I faintly remember his blood running down my throat, though I didn't know it was blood at the time. Next thing I remember was waking up in a shallow grave."

"That has to be the reason why," I said piecing everything together. "Since you were only half drained, you were only half transformed. Wait a minute! I read something about this on the internet. I think it was called a vampyre. You have the strength and speed of a vampire, but you can be out in the sunlight and you don't have the blood lust."

"I may be able to be out in the sun, but its uncomfortable," Danny said and I hoped there weren't any other drawbacks to his transformation. "I haven't craved blood. But since I haven't eaten for eighteen hours I could go for a bite."

I didn't think there was any pun intended, but you never know with Danny. I looked at the clock and saw it was almost noon. I wanted to get back to La Luna and find out how Selene was so I suggested lunch to Danny and with the ravenous look in his eyes he didn't decline the offer. We stopped off at his place so he could clean up and change. Forty five minutes later he looked human again. All the blood was washed away and the tangles were combed out of his long black hair. Danny slipped on some clean clothes and we were on our way. We pulled up to the restaurant just after three-o-clock and saw the lunch rush was still going strong.

We went inside and I noticed everyone was finely dressed. Men wore anything from a dress shirts and ties to full three piece suit. Women were wearing dresses or business suits. We were definitely under dressed in our blue jeans and t-shirts.

"After all the supernatural horrors you put me through," Danny said looking around the restaurant. "What type of nightmare did you bring me to?"

Once the hostess saw us she walked over and said, "I'm sorry gentlemen, but you need a dress shirt and tie to be seated."

She wasn't the same hostess from last time. She had dark brown hair and gorgeous blue eyes. She was heavy set, but it looked good on her. She wore a beautiful black cocktail dress and black heeled dress shoes. She topped off her outfit with an exquisite pearl necklace. By the looks of the pearls it was worth more than what she could afford on a hostess' salary. I figured it was a gift by an admirer. She wore a tag with Amber printed on it and personally I thought the name fitted her perfectly. There wasn't anything supernatural about her so she definitely wasn't a were-panther.

"We're here to see Selene," I said and she raised an eyebrow as she looked at us. "I'm her boyfriend Jack and this is Danny."

"Oh, so you're Jack," Amber said. Her face brightened as she smiled. "I heard a lot about you. I'll go get her. Would you like to have a seat and something to drink?"

"Were actually here to eat," I replied and I couldn't avoid all the displeased faces looking at us. "Though, I'm not sure we're dressed properly for fine dining."

"They can deal with it," Amber said airily as she led us to a table. "I'm sure they have enough money for all the therapy. Your waitress will be with you shortly. Nice meeting you Jack."

"Likewise," I said as Danny and I sat down.

I saw Amber walk over to a waitress and say a few words as she gestured in our direction. The other woman looked at us and they both giggled. I was starting to feel like a side show with everyone staring at me. A moment later Amber headed for the kitchen and the waitress walked over.

She was tall, almost a foot taller than Amber. She had black hair pulled back in a tail, dark brown eyes and dark skin, but not as dark as Tyrone. She wore a black cocktail dress that was similar to Amber's and black heels. Her face and body were pleasant to look at. When she came closer, I sensed supernatural from her. She smiled at us and said, "Hi, my name is Cleo and I'll be your waitress today."

"Hello Cleo," I said smiling up at the young woman. "I'm Jack and this is my friend Danny."

"I know," Cleo said, handing us menus. "Amber told me. I've heard a lot about you Jack."

"So I've been hearing," I said and I wondered what Selene has been saying about me.

"What can I get you two to drink?" Cleo asked and I couldn't help but notice her liveliness and sexual vibe.

"I'll have iced tea," I replied, which was what I usually ordered. I didn't care for soda very much and just plain water didn't have enough taste for me.

"I'll take whatever cola you have," Danny replied and I was happy to see his taste in drinks hadn't changed. Personally, I think it would have been embarrassing and extremely awkward if he asked for a glass of B positive.

"I'll be back in a minute with your drinks," Cleo said as she walked towards the kitchen.

"So you and Selene are actually a couple?" Danny asked, smiling as he looked through the menu. "I don't know what she sees in you. I'm sure it can't be for your looks or personality. You don't have any money, so what could it possibly be?"

"I don't know," I replied, deciding on the steak and shrimp combo. I always was a carnivore. I think any type of vegetable is for rabbits. "I guess she's into average looking guys with dull personalities and no money."

Cleo came back with our drinks and asked if we were ready to order. I ordered, then Danny asked for the ten ounce sirloin. There was nothing peculiar about that, but it caught me off guard when he asked for it rare. Last time Danny and I ate out, he wanted his hamburger well done. Personally, I like my steak medium rare to medium, but rare is a little to. bloody for me. It gives a new meaning to the saying, "If it's not mooing then I'm not chewing."

Once Cleo had our orders she returned to the kitchen. She was gone for a few minutes, then the door to the kitchen open again and Selene walked out. I was elated to see her walking instead of bleeding on a bed. I couldn't hide my excitement and I grinned at her as she approached. She was wearing a black skirt and white dress shirt with ruffles going down each side of the buttons. Her silky black hair was combed back. As soon as She reached our table she sat down next to me and kissed me gently on the lips.

I wanted to pull her close and return her kiss passionately, but I knew this was not the proper time or place.

I couldn't help myself. I was so happy to see Selene healed I couldn't take my eyes off of her. Selene on the other hand was staring at Danny and I knew why. We both saw Nathaniel start the vampire process, but yet here he is in broad daylight having lunch at La Luna.

Danny noticed Selene staring and she didn't have to ask, we both knew what was on her mind. D-man took a sip from his drink and said, "I know I should be dead, or undead, I guess"

Selene nodded. I was having a hard time accepting that Danny was alive; I could only imagine what she was thinking. Then again Selene was supernatural and has been in their world longer than I have, so I figured she may have ran into something like this before.

"Danny showed up on my doorstep this morning," I said after taking a drink. "He has extraordinary strength and speed, but he's not a vampire. He's no longer completely human either. I read something on the internet about vampyrs. Have you ever heard of such a thing? Could he be one?"

"Yes," Selene nodded. "Vampyrs are very rare and hated by vampires. They're what vampires want to be. A superhuman that can walk in the sunlight and don't have to survive off humans, although once in a while they do have the craving for rare meat."

The rare steak made sense now. I was wondering what Danny was feeling at the moment. Did he have more energy, feel more alive, or feel anything at all? I will have to remember to ask him another time.

Cleo brought out our meals and when Selene saw Danny's steak she smiled. He began to eat ravenously at first, but started chewing his food when he noticed people staring.

"Sorry," Danny said. "I haven't had anything to eat since yesterday afternoon."

"That's all right," Selene said as she snagged a shrimp off my plate. "After what you've been through I think you are entitled."

"So is Cleo a were-panther?" I asked as I watched Selene take a bite out of the shrimp.

Selene nodded, then after she swallowed she said, "She is one of our newer Pride members. She's been with us a little over a year now."

I started to cut my steak into bite sizes when Selene went in for another shrimp. I decided to let the steak wait, even though it was grilled perfectly. I began to eat the shrimp while I still had some. I took a bite out of one, it was totally mouth watering.

The three of us sat, talked, and ate. Selene was sure Nathaniel would cause problems tonight for either Katrina or myself, or quite possibly both of us. After the death of his son it was the least I was expecting. I hoped he kept it personal instead of going after family and friends. One thing was for sure, Katrina didn't know about the events that occurred last night and she wouldn't be expecting an attack by Nathaniel. She needed to know, so she could prepare for tonight, but until nightfall there wasn't any way to warn her. Personally, I didn't care. Let the bloodsuckers kill each other. The world would be a better place without them, but Selene was very concerned about the situation and insisted Katrina be warned.

After finishing our meal Cleo came with the bill, but before she was able to place it on the table Selene just waved her off.

"It's on the house," Selene said and Cleo began to turn and walk away.

"Wait a second Cleo," I said and the young were-panther turned and looked at me. "The least I can do is leave a tip since Selene is picking up the bill. What was the total, so I know how much to tip you?"

Cleo looked at Selene and she shrugged. The young were-panther showed me the bill and my face flushed. The total came up to almost eighty dollars. I looked at Selene and she just picked up my tea and took a sip. Even though she was trying to hide it I saw the slightest smile on her lips. Now I knew why people with suits and ties ate at La Luna. It wasn't called fine dining restaurant for nothing.

I pulled out fifteen dollars and handed the money to Cleo. She thanked me with a smile. I was used to eating fast food. Fifteen dollars was what I would have paid for two value meals, but here it was barely enough to cover the tip. I laughed and shook my head. Selene's profit margin must be incredible, yet nobody here complained about the prices. I now knew why we got nasty looks from the other patrons. Next time I dined here I was going to have to be dressed up. Yeah right, just as soon as I take out a loan to pay for dinner.

After Cleo left, Selene told me she needed to get back to work. Being the owner didn't mean she could slack off. I learned that from working with Tom all of those years. We stood and Selene kissed me again. This time there were fewer customers, so she did it a little more passionately. I longed for the day Nathaniel was no longer a factor in our relationship.

Danny and I headed to my car. I asked Danny where he wanted to go. He wanted to find his car, so I drove him back to the last delivery he remembered and there it was, still sitting where he parked it.

I figured I would let Danny take his car home while I took care of some personal matters, but he didn't want to be alone. Danny wouldn't tell me why, but I already knew. After what happened to him last night, he was scared to be alone right now. I didn't blame him. After I was attacked I felt the same way and right now I was Danny's link to the supernatural world. It's a lot to accept, if you can accept it at all.

Danny drove his car to his house and then got back in my car. I really didn't have a clue where to go so I started to drive back home until my phone rang. It was Shaun. I answered and heard him say, "Hey Jack, I just heard from my contact. Nathaniel is furious and he is coming after you tonight."

"I figured as much," I said and even though Detective Oswald killed Joseph, I was the one he was blaming.

"If we're going to be tangling with a master vampire and a spell caster, we better be well equipped," Shaun said and I couldn't argue with him on that.

I told Shaun about Danny and what Selene said about vampyrs. He was quiet for a few moments then said, "Bring him along. He's knee deep in this as much as we are and I'm sure Nathaniel will want to finish the job he started."

"Where should we meet you?" I asked and Shaun gave me his address, then hung up without a word.

I was getting used to that. He was a lot like Tom in that respect. He didn't like talking on the phone either.

I made a u-turn and headed to the West side. Shaun lived on the far West side across Pueblo Boulevard, near a sports bar. I don't visit bars very often so I couldn't remember the name of it, but I knew exactly where it was.

When we arrived I saw there were no other houses around Shaun's, just lots of trees. It was very secluded. His yard was nicely landscaped and the house looked immaculate. We got out and walked up to his porch. I didn't need to knock, Shaun was watching for us. He invited us in

Shaun led us into the kitchen. Besides the basic appliances and a microwave, the only other items in this room were a small table and two chairs. Behind the table was a door. I wouldn't have ever known it was there if Shaun didn't pull the table out of the way and push it. The door was hidden in plain sight.

"This is where I keep the good stuff," Shaun said before he starting down the stairs. "Come on down, but watch your head."

We followed Shaun to a big room. There were boxes lining the walls and a wide selection of firearms. I knew some had to be illegal, but with what we were going up against the extra firepower was appreciated.

There were other kinds of weapons as well. I saw a wooden sword, archery equipment, a crossbow and a quarterstaff which was sharp on both ends. Danny took the staff off the wall. He began to spin and twirl it around very skillfully. I recognized the technique as one he showed me before.

Shaun called me over and handed me a ring. The ring looked like it was made of silver and it had a large gem embedded into it. As I was examining it Shaun said, "It's a weapon against vampires."

I just looked at the ring and couldn't imagine how it could possibly be used as a weapon. I turned the ring over in my hand, then Shaun said, "Here, let me show you."

I handed the ring to Shaun and he popped the gem off. Under the gem was a needle. I stared at him with a very confused look on my face and then he said, "The ring is hollow. I put garlic essence inside and then it is injected into a vampire through the needle. It won't kill a vampire, but the bloodsucker will be subdued and seriously in pain. That's all the time you need to put a wood bullet in its heart. I don't know how it will work on a master. It may not have any effect at all. It's a one shot deal, so make sure it counts."

I took the ring from Shaun and slipped it on my finger. It was kind of bulky and awkward, but if it could save my life I was willing to put up with it.

I already had the two guns Shaun gave me so I didn't really need anymore. I wasn't worried about having more firepower, since at a distance I probably couldn't hit what I was aiming at anyway. So far everything I shot at was point blank. It's awfully hard to miss at that range.

Besides the staff Danny took a handgun. I saw him grab an ankle holster and strapped it on. I was tired of carrying the handgun in my pocket so I looked around for a holster as well. I couldn't find one that strapped to my ankle, but there was one that strapped to my shoulder. Unless I had a jacket, or something over the weapon, it would be hard to hide, but with my trench coat concealing the gun it would be a snap.

While I was looking at all the weapons I happen to notice a box on the ground which had some religious relics sticking out. I questioned Shaun about the religious items and he told me he used to adorn them before going up against vampires, but now since he knew they didn't work he just packed them away.

Once we had all the weapons we could conceal, Shaun took us back upstairs. When we were in his front room I happen to notice he was wearing some type of rosary. I kind of wondered why he wore it since all the other religious items were packed away in a box. I found it weird that the beads were black instead of white, but when I was able to get a closer look at the necklace I saw they weren't beads after all. They looked more like little black marbles. What Shaun was wearing wasn't a rosary at all, but what was left of all of the vampires he had killed.

"So how many bloodsuckers have you killed?" I asked as I gestured towards the necklace.

"With the one I got last night, I'm up to sixteen," Shaun replied as his hand unconsciously went to the necklace. "I'm hoping to reach twenty before the night is over."

"I appreciate your optimism," I said even though I wasn't as confident. "I would be happy to end this without bloodshed, but I guess that's not possible now."

"Especially since we killed Nathaniel's son," Shaun said and he smiled wryly.

I glanced outside while I was talking to Shaun and noticed it was starting to get dusk. In about thirty minutes the sun will be completely set and the bloodsuckers will be out on the prowl. I had a feeling Nathaniel was going to be after Selene as well so I wanted to make sure I was there to protect her. Yeah, right, I seriously doubt I would be challenge for anything she couldn't handle. The only thing I would be is extra canon fodder. Maybe if we were lucky, while the vampire was holding me up by my throat Selene would be able to take the bloodsucker out.

I called Selene and told her what Shaun explained to me about Nathaniel. She agreed that Katrina should be warned. I was a fairly long distance from the Crimson Chateau so Selene told me she would drive over and let Katrina know what happened last night and what could happen tonight.

I told Shaun I was heading to the Crimson Chateau so I could be with Selene if anything happened and he offered to tag along. I'm not sure how well that would turn out since Katrina wants Shaun dead. I was hoping everybody could remain neutral until this was over. Something told me there was no way it was going to be as simple as that.

I went outside to my car, followed by Danny. I saw Shaun get in his truck and begin to follow us. It was a good thirty minute drive to the Crimson Chateau, which should put us there just after sunset.

It was a little awkward driving the car with Danny's staff between us. My car wasn't very big and the staff had to have been six feet long. Good thing I didn't buy the stick shift.

When we were about a mile from the Crimson Chateau my phone rang. I was expecting either Selene or Katrina, but it was my mom. As soon as I answered I could tell something was wrong. She was extremely frantic, even more so than usual. It took me a moment to calm her down enough to understand what she was saying.

"Mom, what's wrong?" I asked as I tried to make out what she was saying. "Just slow down and tell me."

"A man came to my door," She replied and that was all I could get out of her at first.

"Did he try to hurt you?" I asked and I was starting to fear this man may have been one of Nathaniel's vampires.

"I saw him," she said and I knew since she was blind it wasn't possible. "He knocked on my door, when I answered he told me to let him in. I saw him in my head. His voice was in my head. I tried to block him out, but all I heard was his voice telling me to let him in."

To me it sounded like the vampire was trying to glamour my mom, but for some reason it didn't work on her. I figured it was because she was blind and wasn't able to see the bloodsucker's eyes.

"Is he still there?" I asked and I turned on the next street and headed towards her house.

"I don't know," She said in a little more calm and coherent voice. "When I didn't answer the door he screamed and then I heard something that sounded like wings flapping."

"Did you call Janet?" I asked and I wondered if vampires really turned into bats like they showed on TV.

"Not yet," she said and I really hoped Nathaniel wasn't going to send his goons after her as well. "I called you first because you live closer."

"Hold on mom," I said. "I'm going to give Janet a call real fast."

I borrowed Danny's cell phone and called my sister. The phone rang three times before she picked it up. As soon as she answered I asked, "Janet, are you at home?"

"Yeah," Janet said and I was relieved they were still ok. "We just got back from grocery shopping. What's wrong, you sound a little stressed?"

"Someone just tried to break into mom's house," I replied and I heard Janet gasp. "Don't ask me how or why, but I think they may try to break into yours next. Don't answer you're door if someone knocks on it tonight."

"What's going on Jack," Janet said and she sounded worried.

I was just about to tell her when I heard someone knocking in the background and Brian saying, "I'll get it."

"Don't let him open the door!" I screamed and I heard Janet tell Brian to wait.

For a moment there was silence and then I heard Janet's scream. A moment later a female's voice I didn't recognize came over the phone and said, "Is this Jack?"

"Who are you?" I asked even though I had a feeling I already knew.

"I think you already know the answer," the vampire said and a cold chill went down my spine. "Hurry Jack, before we become really hungry."

Nathaniel's servants were after my family and there was nothing I could do. I turned my car again, but this time in the direction of Janet's house. At that time I remembered I had my mom on the other phone. I picked it back up and said, "Mom, I need to call you back later. I'm sending someone over to your house to stay with you until I get there."

"What are you talking about?" She asked and she started to sound frantic again. "I thought you were coming here."

"I'm on my way to Janet's," I said and I knew she was going to ask me a lot of questions, but I didn't have time right now to answer them.

"Why are you going over there?" My mom asked and she was starting to work herself up into a frenzy. "Is there something wrong with Janet? Is she ok, Jack?"

"Mom, I don't have time to answer your questions right now," I replied and I was starting to be annoyed because I really needed to get off the phone. "I am sending a police officer over. Her name is Detective Oswald. She will stay with you until I can get there. Do you understand?"

"Why can't you come?" She asked and I heard her start to cry.

"Bye mom, I'll call you later," I said and hung up. I felt cold and heartless, but knew my sister needed me more.

I really didn't want to hang up on her like that, but she wouldn't have let me off the phone any other way. I called Detective Oswald right away and told her what was happening and asked if she could go over to my mom's until I could get there. She agreed, and then I thanked her and hung up.

Next I called Shaun, who was still behind me in his truck. As soon as he answered he said, "What the heck is going on Jack?"

"Nathaniel's servants are after my family," I replied and since my mind was in several places at once I ran a stop sign in the process. Luckily no one was coming from the other direction. "They just tried to get my mom and now they have my sister."

"It could be a trap Jack," Shaun said and the thought did run through my mind.

"I know," I said as I turned down the street which led to Janet's house. "I can't let them kill my sister so what choice do I have?"

"I've got your back," Shaun said and I was happy he and Danny were with me. "Just be careful."

I pulled up to Janet's house and got out. I saw Shaun get out of his truck and head around to the back. I knew the vampires heard us pull up so there wasn't any reason to sneak in. I pulled out my .380, then walked up to the front door and Danny followed behind with his gun in one hand and the staff in the other. There wasn't any sense knocking so we just went in.

As soon as we entered I saw signs of a struggle. The couch was turned over and a lamp lay shattered on the floor. To my right was a hall which went down to a bedroom and to my left was the kitchen. Another small hallway led from the kitchen to the laundry room. In this room was another door that led to the backyard.

Standing in the kitchen with tears running down her cheeks was Janet and Brian sat at the table next to her, but they were not alone. Standing behind my sister was the vampire with the demonic smiley face tattoo on his forehead. The vampire had a clawed hand on her neck and it looked at me with a sadistic smile. Brian had blood flowing from his head and the crimson liquid rolled freely down his cheek. Another vampire I haven't seen before was standing behind him. The bloodsucker was a female, probably the one on the phone. She had short spiky red hair and green eyes. She wore a t-shirt with the picture of a rock band on it and blue jeans with the knees ripped out. The vampire watched the blood roll down Brian's face, and then she leaned over and licked it off.

"Nice of you to show up Jack," the smiley faced vampire said. "I see you brought Danny with you. Nathaniel wanted him back so once we are finished here the master will be very pleased with us."

"I thought you were dead," I said as I looked at the vampire. "The last time I saw you you're guts were oozing out."

"We heal fast and even faster after we feed," the smiley face vampire said as he feigned going in for a bite on Janet's neck. "The worst off our wounds are the more we need to feed. Sadly the person I fed from didn't survive. As a matter of fact I think I still need a little more healing."

"Let my sister and Brian go, then I will make sure you're deaths are fast," I said and the vampires just laughed.

"You were no challenge for me last time Jack," the smiley faced vampire said. "And you're pet lycanthrope isn't here to save you this time."

I was just about to make another comment when I saw Shaun sneaking up behind the vampire with the spiky hair. He put the barrel of his shotgun to her head and as he cocked the hammer he said, "The kitty cat may not be here to save Jack, but I am."

Both vampires turned instantly to see Shaun. The female hissed as she stared down the shotgun barrel. Both vampires were surprised by Shaun's entrance and Danny didn't waist a moment of the opportunity. With the speed of a vampire Danny threw his sharpened staff at the smiley faced vampire. The bloodsucker must have sensed Danny's movement because it turned back toward us right in time for the staff to strike him in the forehead. The staff went straight through the smiley face and out the back of the bloodsucker's skull.

The vampire staggered back a few feet and screamed as it clutched the staff that was embedded in its skull. The vampire didn't know about Danny's increase in strength and speed so it was caught totally off guard. It would have been easy for the vampire to dodge out of the way if the staff had been thrown by a normal human, but Danny was anything other than normal anymore.

I saw the female vampire stare at her partner in horror as smoke began to rise from the puncture wound in its head. The bloodsucker screamed again as Danny walked over to it. Janet ran over to where I was and threw her arms around me. She was sobbing uncontrollably and I wasn't sure how I could console her. She just had her first glimpse into the supernatural world. I just hoped she was strong enough to deal with it.

I watched D-man grab the staff and pull it free from the vampire's head. The vampire screamed again for the last time as Danny thrust the staff into the bloodsucker's chest, penetrating its heart. The vampire fell to its knees as it turned to ash and then imploded into a little black marble.

"I love watching that happen," Shaun said and the female vampire just looked at him with dread in her eyes. "Jack, get your family out of here. I want to have a few words with this bloodsucker."

"Let's go Brian," I said and I watched as he tried to get up from the chair, only to crash back onto it.

"I can't get up," Brian said as he grimaced with pain. "She broke my leg."

Danny walked over to Brian and lifted him from the chair. I wasn't sure I was ever going to get used to what D-man has become, but one thing is for sure he didn't seem to mind the changes.

Danny helped Brian out to their car and I was right behind them with Janet. As soon as we got out to the car I looked at Janet and asked, "Are you fit to drive, because Brian needs to get to the hospital?"

"Yes," Janet replied and then we all looked up to the house as we heard the vampire scream in pain. "What are those things?"

"Vampires," I replied and I was sure Janet already knew the answer to her question. She just needed someone to confirm she wasn't going insane. "I'll tell you everything later."

Danny helped Brian into the car and I held the driver's door open for Janet as we heard the vampire scream again. I wondered what Shaun was doing to the bloodsucker and I was sure the same thought was going through everyone's mind as well.

I watched Janet and Brian drive off down the street and then I caught some movement out of the corner of my eye. I looked in that direction and saw Shaun coming out of the house. He held up a little black marble and with a smile he said, "Just three more to go."

"So what was all the screaming about?" I asked and I saw Shaun's smile become wider.

"I was trying to get some information from her," Shaun replied as he took a syringe out of his pocket and showed it to me. "I injected a little garlic essence into the vampire. Not enough to incapacitate them, but enough to make them wish they were."

"So what did you find out?" I asked and I didn't like what he told me.

"This was just a diversion to keep you busy," Shaun replied as he put the syringe away. "Nathaniel's going to attack the Crimson Chateau tonight and they wanted to make sure you weren't going to be there to help Katrina. Apparently with you as her human servant she is as powerful as Nathaniel, or maybe even more so."

"Great," I said as I pulled out my phone. "Selene is there. I better call and warn her."

I dialed Selene's cell number and I heard it ring three times before she answered. I heard her voice on the other end and she sounded stressed and a little out of breath.

"Jack, where are you?" Selene asked and I heard a lot of commotion in the background.

I was just about to respond when I heard a loud sound like something exploding. I pulled the phone away from my ear and for the next few moments all I heard was a ringing sound. Once the ringing stopped I put the phone back to my ear and there was nothing from the other end. I tried to call Selene again, but the phone just continued to ring until her voice mail answered.

"Sounds like the attack has begun and Selene's in danger," I said as I put the phone back in my pocket. "There was a loud explosion and the phone went dead."

"Let's go," Shaun said as he ran towards his truck.

I didn't need to be told twice. I ran to my car and opened the door. As soon as I got in I saw Danny was already sitting in the passenger seat. I was once again amazed on how fast he could move. I started the car and floored the gas pedal. Dirt and rock shot out from the back tires as we sped off towards the Crimson Chateau.

Chapter Fifteen

I drove as fast as I dared towards the Crimson Chateau. The only thing going through my mind was Selene's safety. I had to reach her before anything happened. I knew Selene's history with Nathaniel and she would attack on sight. She wanted revenge for the murder of her husband. I wanted to be by Selene's side to see it through so she could finally have peace. I've known her for only a short while, but I have grown to love her more than anything in the world.

I called Xylon and told him what was going down. He felt the same way I did. If it wasn't for Selene being involved we would let the vampires fight it out. Xylon said he'd meet me there. I was happy he decided to help. Seeing Selene in action was extremely impressive against vampires. I figured if Xylon was anything like her, he would be a great ally against Nathaniel.

Ten minutes later I pulled into the parking lot across from the Crimson Chateau and Shaun pulled up next to me. I saw the club long before we reached it. Flames stretched and smoked billowed into the sky. Xylon pulled up next to us in his car. It was a hot nineteen sixty nine Ford Mustang, one of my favorites. He had it painted cherry red and it was in pristine condition. Needless to say I was jealous.

Xylon got out and I noticed Cleo was with him. I was happy with that, two kitties were better than one. With Cleo, it was closer to a fair fight.

We stood across the street from the burning building where a small crowd began to form. We heard sirens in the distance and knew we didn't have much time before they arrived.

The front door to the club was missing and some windows were broken out. Flames leapt from the empty doorway and broken windows. Even from across the street, I could feel the heat from the inferno.

I knew when the police and firemen arrived they would restrict access to the Chateau. I also knew if we wanted to get inside we would have to find a way now. I crossed the street and everyone followed. Once across, the heat from the fire was unbearable. I was about to head to the alley and try the back entrance when I saw some movement to the side of the building. My hand went to my gun as I moved closer. If it was a vampire I wasn't too worried. I had a small army at my back.

I sensed supernatural as we got close to the area where I saw movement. Most likely it was a vampire, but I couldn't help hoping it was Selene. As we moved closer I stopped and everyone behind me followed suit.

"What is it Jack?" Shaun asked, staring into the same patch of shadows I was looking at.

"I sense supernatural there," I replied, pointing towards a shadowy corner.

Shaun pulled out his shotgun and we edged closer. Once we were closer I heard a recognizable voice from the darkness ask, "Is that you Jacky boy?"

It was Tyrone. The big vampire staggered from the shadows, holding his right arm. It was bent at an awkward angle. The bone was protruding through his skin and it was bleeding.

"What happened?" I asked and Tyrone's face went blank.

"I don't really know," Tyrone replied as he slowly shook his head. "I was standing in my regular spot, then there was an explosion and a fiery light. The next thing I remember was waking up here and seeing you."

"Apparently that magic using witch shot a ball of fire into the door," Shaun speculated, staring at the big vampire. "The blast blew the door off its hinges and shattered the windows. Apparently, you were caught in the blast and got propelled out here."

"Are we going to stake this vampire?" Danny asked, tightening his grip on the staff.

"No," I replied. I saw the big vampire stare at Danny. "Tyrone is my friend."

"That's something I never thought I would hear a human say," Tyrone said, turning his gaze towards me and smiling. "I knew there was some reason why I liked you Jacky boy."

I don't know why I spared Tyrone. Because he always treated me well, I guess. Even though he was a vampire, I wouldn't feel right allowing someone to hurt him. Also, the big guy might come in handy getting us into the Crimson Chateau without becoming charcoal.

"Is the back door open during business hours or lock?" I asked since we couldn't enter through the front.

"It only opens from the inside," Tyrone replied.

"Is there any other entrances?" I asked and the big vampire just grinned.

"Of course," Tyrone replied with a hearty laugh. "What type of vampire doesn't have an escape route?"

"Well, where is it?" I asked, impatiently. It was driving me nuts not knowing what was going on inside.

"Follow me," Tyrone replied. He started walking around the building to the back.

We followed Tyrone to the alley. By that time the sirens were getting very close. The big vampire stopped at a manhole cover and pointed towards it.

"Down there," Tyrone said and I grimaced. The big vampire chuckled when he saw my look of distaste. "What's the matter Jacky? Don't like roaming through the sewers?"

"Not really," I replied as I watched him cradling his mangled arm. "Are you going to be able to fight?"

"If someone helps me set the bone I can," Tyrone replied and I shrugged. I had no idea how to set bones.

"I'll set it," Xylon said as he walked over to Tyrone and looked at his arm. "Just try not to cry out."

The big vampire started to laugh, then stopped and grimaced in pain as Xylon grabbed Tyrone's arm. There was a loud popping sound as the were-panther pulled the bone back in place. Tyrone looked very pale and close to passing out. At first his arm hung loosely at his side, then it began to heal. Within a couple minutes Tyrone's arm completely healed and the big vampire stood there with a big goofy grin. He flexed it, then bent over and picked up the manhole cover.

"Let me go first," Tyrone said. "I'll see if I can find a dry spot for Jacky boy to stand in. "I don't think he wants to smell like someone's butt when he rescues his lady love."

I didn't find Tyrone's comment amusing, but apparently everyone else did since they were laughing. Tyrone lowered himself down into the sewer, then a moment later he called back up, "Come on down. It's mostly dry, just stay to the right."

One by one we lowered ourselves through the manhole. Once I was in I couldn't see anything. It was pitch dark, then I heard Tyrone's voice say, "Follow me."

"Follow you?" I sputtered. I can't even see you."

"My bad," Tyrone said with a chuckle. "I forget humans can't see in the dark."

"Hold on a second," Shaun said as I heard him shuffling around. "I have a flashlight."

A second later, I heard a clicking sound, then light filled the tunnel. Now that I was able to see I noticed we were in a metal pipe about four feet wide and seven feet high. There was a little stream of water flowing down the center of the tunnel and I don't know how we missed it when dropping in.

Tyrone led us down the tunnel. We walked about thirty feet until the big vampire stopped. He pushed on the wall and it moved inwards. We moved through the opening and Tyrone closed the door behind us.

With Shaun's flashlight I saw we were in another tunnel, but this one slanted down. Tyrone took the lead again and we followed. The tunnel continued onward at a slant until we came to a dead end. Tyrone pushed on the wall again and another door opened. We walked into a large room which was well lit by a few ceiling lights.

The room was carpeted with dark oak paneling covering the walls. The one thing that caught my attention were the coffins. As I looked around the room I counted twenty caskets. I figured this was where Katrina and her coven slept.

"So which one is yours?" I asked Tyrone, who was walking across the room to another door.

"Can't you tell?" Tyrone asked amused. I looked around, but I couldn't tell the differences between any of them, except for one. This coffin was polished pearl white and bigger than the others.

"Is it the big white one?" I asked, gesturing to it.

"No," Tyrone replied, unlocking the door with a key he pulled from his pocket. "That's Katrina's. Take a closer look."

When Tyrone mentioned Katrina's coffin I saw Shaun smile. I could surmise what devious plan was going through his head. I'm sure he was thrilled to know where Katrina's resting spot is and which coffin was her's, but I'm sure she's not stupid enough to leave the coffins where we know they are. If we survive this night I know Shaun would be back in the morning, hoping to do some staking.

I walked around the room looking at the coffins until I came to one with a big gold T on both sides. I shook my head when I saw it, then Tyrone said with a laugh, "It's all about style Jacky boy. Katrina may have the biggest one, but mine looks good and is stylish."

Tyrone opened the door, then we walked through to see we were in the big room with the black carpet. It was empty and I felt nothing supernatural..

Tyrone shut and locked the door behind us. A thin layer of smoke hung in the air. We made our way through the room to the door leading to the spiral staircase.

Tyrone opened the door. The smoke was thicker and breathing was a little harder. We made our way up the stairs until we came to the storage room. The smoke was acrid. I was forced to put my t-shirt over my nose and mouth to avoid choking. The door leading to the alley was shut and a couple black marbles were at the foot of the door. They must have been what was left of the chefs as they tried to escape.

As we walked to the kitchen the fire from the club was spreading inward. The smell of burning flesh was very apparent. Shaun pulled handkerchiefs out of his pocket and wet them down in the sink. He handed one to me and then wrapped the other around his nose and mouth. I took the wet handkerchief and tied it on. The water filtered out some of the smoke and I was able to breathe without coughing up a lung.

I looked at Danny, Xylon and Cleo saw they were affected by the smoke as well. Xylon picked up an apron and tore it into three pieces. He wet them down and handed a piece to Danny and Cleo.

When everyone was ready we started towards the double swinging doors. Before we got to them I felt supernatural from the other side. Over the roaring fire I heard a commotion coming from the club. My eyes were tearing as I saw Shaun walk ahead to the doors and peak out. It took him a moment to focus in the smoke, then he said, "There are several vampires in the room. I counted twenty with that spell caster of Nathaniel's. I don't know about the rest of you, but I say she is the most dangerous and should be taken out first."

"She's his human servant," I said agreeing with Shaun. "He is extremely powerful with her around. Were they touching?"

"No," Shaun replied shaking his head. "They're real close to each other though. Nathaniel's holding some vampire by the throat and Katrina is lying on the floor in front of him."

"Did you see Selene?" I asked because I was extremely worried.

"She is in her panther form standing between Nathaniel and Katrina," Shaun replied and I was relieved to know she was still alive. "She looked in bad shape though. I seriously doubt she has the strength to deal with Nathaniel."

I crept to the double doors and peeked out. The vampire Nathaniel had hoisted in the air was Sam. Katrina was half sitting as she supported herself on one arm. She looked like she was pleading with Nathaniel, but I couldn't hear what she was saying over the roaring fire.

Selene was crouched in front of Katrina, ready to pounce if Nathaniel attacked the vampire. I saw Zack laying on the floor a few feet from Katrina. A couple vampires were standing over him. Jean Luke and Elizabeth stood back to back away from the master vampires. They looked as if they were holding their own, but they were surrounded by six vampires. Jezebel stood off to the side with a wood stake protruding from her shoulder. She looked in agonizing pain as smoke smoldered from the wound. Standing close to her was Kiki. The vampire had a wicked look on her face and I knew she was waiting for the kill order from Nathaniel.

Other things caught my attention as well. There were several bodies lying on the floor. I figured they were customers of the Crimson Chateau who got caught in the vampire war. The bodies looked charred with some limbs missing. Like they were caught in a powerful explosion. I figured the fire and charred remains were Sarah's doing. I saw the ball of fire she cast at Shaun last night. The explosion from the spell could easily have done everything here.

I noticed the roof appeared to be weakening in certain areas. Even though the fire engulfed the room there was a circle around the vampires that was totally untouched by the flames. Apparently, one of Sarah's spells kept the fire out. It was the only part of the room that wasn't engulfed in flames and looked secure enough to stand on.

"It looks bleak at best out there," I said, feeling a sense of dread welling up inside of me. "It looks like Sarah cast a spell which is keeping the fire at bay. If we kill her the spell may dissipate and the whole room could burn up. Doesn't this place have sprinklers?"

"Now that you mention it, yeah it does," Tyrone replied sounding confused. "I don't know why they're not working."

"We need to do something soon," Xylon said stifling a cough. "Me and Cleo can't take much more of this smoke. Our lycanthrope senses are making it hard for us to breathe."

"Can vampires and lycanthropes survive in fire?" I asked as a plan began to form. "I didn't read anything about fire being used as a weapon."

"Everything is destroyed by fire in time," Tyrone replied, peeking into the club. "Since we heal quickly, we can survive longer than humans. If we can't escape we will burn to death as well. It's a very long and agonizing process."

"The fire is spreading rapidly into the kitchen, so we better do something fast," Shaun said, readjusting the handkerchief around his nose and mouth. "Not to mention the smoke is getting thicker."

"Xylon, was there anymore aprons back there?" I asked and the were-panther nodded. "Gather up as many as possible and soak them down."

Xylon took Cleo and Danny with him. A few minutes later the trio came back with several dripping aprons. I took one and wrapped myself in it. The apron was cold and it soaked my clothes on contact, but with the rising heat it actually felt good.

"We have to run through the flames to make it to the clearing," I explained. "Hopefully with the extra protection we won't get burned too bad."

"Xylon, Cleo and I should be ok," Tyrone said, watching me cover myself. "We're fast enough to get through the flames without getting burned too bad. Our regeneration will heal the burns in a matter of seconds."

"I may have vampire speed, but I don't know if I regenerate," Danny said, grabbing another apron. "I'm going to stick with Jack's plan."

"Somebody has to stay behind and snipe Sarah once we make it to the clearing," I said as water dripped down my face from the apron. "Hopefully whatever spell she is using to protect them isn't a force field or we could be trapped in the fire with no place to go. We also have to hope we don't get incinerated by the flames once Sarah is dead."

"I'll snipe her," Shaun volunteered as he began to install a sniper's scope on his rifle. "She's human, so I don't need to aim for her heart. A head shot will work just fine."

Shaun was the perfect person for the job. I was about to ask if everyone was ready when I heard cracking bones. I knew Xylon and Cleo were transforming. I watched Selene do it once and thought it was gross, so I decided not to watch them. Once they were finished I heard Danny say, "That was so cool."

"Everyone ready?" I asked. I looked down at the ring Shaun gave me and turned it so the needle was easily concealed by the palm of my hand. Everyone nodded including the panthers, which was weird for some reason. "Then let's do it."

I stormed out towards the clearing and was instantly bombarded by heat. It was like an oven in the kitchen, but out here in the flames it felt like I was being cremated.

I kept my head down and ran as fast as I could. I felt a couple gusts fly past me and knew it was Tyrone and Danny. I glanced up and saw Xylon and Cleo darting by, then leap over the flames I was about to run through.

The heat was almost unbearable. The apron I was wearing was drying extremely fast and parts were starting to catch fire. I heard the thundering sound of Shaun's rifle and knew he fired at the witch. I didn't dare look to see if my plan worked.

It was fifty feet from the kitchen to the clearing, but the heat from the fire made it feel like a mile. The unprotected parts of my body began to burn and blister, but I continued to run. I swore the floor was going to give out below me, but I kept my legs pumping until I finally burst through the flames. I immediately dropped to the floor and rolled around until the flames were out.

I was burnt in several places, but none of them were life threatening. I didn't notice before, but the fire sprinklers had gone off. I pulled the apron off my head, then I heard Katrina scream, "NOOO!"

I looked up in time to see Sam implode into a little black marble. I barely noticed Sarah's body lying in a puddle of her own blood before I was hoisted up by my throat.

Selene leaped towards Nathaniel as the vampire held me up. I watched helplessly as the bloodsucker backhanded her, sending the were-panther flying to the edge of the clearing.

With Sarah dead, the clearing was dissipating quickly and filling with smoke. As Nathaniel held me by the neck, my eyes began to water. Good thing I couldn't breathe at the moment or I would be choking on smoke.

I glanced around and saw Danny helping Zack, while Xylon and Cleo evened the odds for Jean Luke and Elizabeth. Jezebel was on her knees with one hand clenching the wooden stake protruding from her shoulder as Kiki walked behind her. She had her clawed hand on Jezebel's neck, waiting patiently for permission from her master to finish the job. Tyrone didn't join the fight. He was kneeling next to Katrina, helping his master back to her feet.

"You have interfered for the last time Jack," Nathaniel said, pulling me forward to rip out my throat. "You and Katrina will die and I will use your lycanthrope as my whore until I grow tired of her."

I didn't have time to go for my guns so I did the only thing I could. I jabbed Nathaniel in the back with the syringe from the ring. He stopped a centimeter away from ripping out my throat and looked at me. For a moment nothing happened, then the vampire's face contorted in pain. He dropped me and stumbled a few feet before falling to the floor.

I quickly jumped to my feet, pulling out my .380. I took aim at Nathaniel, but before I could pull the trigger a vampire slammed into me. The gun flew from my hand and was lost the inferno. The same would have happened to me, but before I flew out of the clearing Zack caught me. The impact took my breath away, but it was far better than burning alive. As the vampire set me back on the ground I heard him say, "Got you Jack."

"Thanks Zack," I said after I was able. "I owe you one."

"Just remember that the next time you feel like staking a vampire," Zack said with a laugh.

The vampire, who sent me flying, saw its plan was ruined by Zack so he charged me again. This time Zack stepped in and absorbed the impact. Nathaniel's bloodsucker was a head taller than Zack, but he held him to a stand still. The vampires struggled until I heard another thundering shot and Zack hollered in pain. Blood began to flow from a gunshot wound in his shoulder. For a moment, I figured Shaun missed his target until I the other vampire turned to ash and implode.

The gunshot wound to Zack's shoulder wasn't lethal, he'd recover from it by morning. The vampire stared at me in disbelief, then asked, "Who shot me?"

I knew it was Shaun, but shrugged. Shaun must have known the bullet would go through Zack's shoulder and penetrate the vampire's heart. Either that or he was just a really bad aim.

I looked around the and saw Nathaniel was still suffering the effects of the garlic essence, but looked like it was wearing off. I saw Selene struggling to get on her feet, so I ran to her. I got within a few feet of the panther I saw movement out of the corner of my eye. I got a glimpse of Nathaniel just as his hand slammed on my shoulder, his claws striking bone. The force drove me to my knees and I cried out in agony.

Selene looked at me and our eyes met. She had several spots on her body where the fur was singed away and the flesh had blistered. Blood was trickling from her nose where Nathaniel had hit her. Tears filled my eyes from pain and smoke. Selene also had tears in her eyes, but the expression on her cat face was of sorrow. Nathaniel was still too powerful for us to fight single handedly. I knew the only way we would be able to stop him is if the two of us made it to Katrina.

Nathaniel squeezed my shoulder and I heard something crack. I howled in pain again and heard the vampire laugh maniacally. Nathaniel began to lift me to my feet, then I heard him say, "Kill them all!"

Nathaniel bent my head with his free hand, exposing my throat. The vampire sank his fangs deeply into my neck and started to drain my life force.

Selene tried to get to her feet, but Nathaniel kicked her to the ground. Unless I did something fast the vampire was going to drain my life force and possibly force me to become one of his minions.

The ring was useless and my gun was lost. All I had left was the shotgun inside my trench coat. I saw Nathaniel's foot so I reached inside my trench until I felt the shotgun. I feigned a struggle to keep the vampire from expecting anything. Nathaniel tightened his grip on my shoulder and I heard more cracking sounds. I cried out as I lost all feeling in my shoulder and my left arm became useless.

I was quickly losing consciousness from the pain and blood loss. I got a firm grip on the shotgun with my right hand. I tilted it back so the barrel was over Nathaniel's foot, then pulled the trigger. There was a thundering bang and the vampire screamed as he let loose of my neck and shoulder. Nathaniel fell to the ground screaming, while looking at the bloody stump that used to be his foot and ankle.

I took this opportunity to reach Selene. The were-panther transformed back to her human form. I took off my trench coat to cover her naked body. I helped her up as I looked around the clearing to make sure no other vampires were about to attack us. Zack and Danny finished off the last vampire they were fighting. Jean Luke, Elizabeth, Xylon and Cleo were still very much out numbered and growing weary. Jezebel yanked the stake out of her shoulder and stabbed Kiki in the belly, but not without consequences. Kiki ripped out Jezebel's throat and she fell to the ground in a pool of her blood.

I saw Kiki pull the stake out of her belly and look around. She saw Nathaniel lying on the floor, bleeding profusely from his wound, then to me and Selene. Kiki knew if we reached Katrina it was all over. She applied pressure to her wound, then looked at me again. She smiled sweetly, then with incredible speed, sprinted out of the diminishing clearing into the fire.

I helped Selene towards Katrina. Nathaniel grabbed at my leg, but his wound made him so clumsy I was able to dodge his grasp. Tyrone saw us trying to reach Katrina so he carried her to where we were.

Nathaniel pulled himself across the floor, trying his best to stop us from making contact, but his efforts were in vain. Selene and Katrina grasped hands. I instantly felt their power. I let it build up inside me until my body could take no more. I didn't release it, instead I concentrated on every vampire's life force in the club until I distinguished Nathaniel's servants from Katrina's. I targeted only Nathaniel and his servants, then forced the power into Selene. I felt the power travel through the lycanthrope and into Katrina. I felt her try to contain it, but the power was mine to control.

The force of power burst from Katrina, engulfing the room. I saw Nathaniel and his servants writhe in agony. I felt the pain from the vampires reveled in it. One by one they dropped to the ground, their faces contorting. I searched around the Crimson Chateau for Kiki, but she was either dead or long gone. I looked at Tyrone and said in a voice that wasn't my own, "Kill them all except Nathaniel. He belongs to Selene."

Katrina's servants staked Nathaniel's minions, until all that remained was the master. I released Selene's hand and the power dissipated. Nathaniel looked from where he lay and laughed manically. Selene took off my coat, then began her transformation.

"You think this is over?" Nathaniel asked, watching Selene finish her transformation, then walk silently towards him. "I have told the council what you have done. I told them you murdered my son. They will hunt you down, Katrina, as well as your human servant and his lycanthrope whore."

Katrina neither spoke nor showed emotion. With those words Selene growled and clawed Nathaniel's face. The vampire put his arm up to deflect the blow, but at a cost. Nathaniel screamed as his arm was torn completely off at the elbow. Blood spurted from the bloody stump, his face contorted with agony. Selene stalked forward again for the killing blow and Nathaniel laughed insanely.

"Are you finally getting revenge for your mate?" Nathaniel asked, taunting the were-panther. "Then come and end my two thousand year reign of ---"

Before Nathaniel finished his sentence, Selene leapt at the vampire. Her powerful claws sliced, then connected with Nathaniel's throat. The master's eyes went wide. His mouth gaped open in a horrifying scream, no one could hear. The vampire's head toppled backwards and rolled onto the floor. Nathaniel's body turned to ash and imploded into a little black marble.

Selene walked over and transformed back to her human form. I handed my coat to her and she slipped it on. I looked around and saw everyone was on their feet, except Jezebel. The vampire lay on the ground in a puddle of blood. Her throat had been torn out and she was slowly bleeding to death. I walked over to the vampire and knelt down next to her. Jezebel's eyes flickered open and she tried to speak, but nothing came out.

"Jack," Zack said behind me. I looked back and he had a wood stake in his hand. "She's in agony. Do it."

I took the stake and looked at Jezebel. The vampire looked at the stake and I saw fear in her eyes. She then looked at me and a bloody tear rolled down her cheek. I saw a smile form on Jezebel's lips, then she nodded her head and closed her eyes. With a single powerful thrust I drove the stake deep into her chest, piercing her heart. Jezebel's mouth and eyes opened momentarily, then she looked at me and turned to ash. I stood as her body imploded into the little black marble that once was the supernatural energy which sustained her life force.

"Its over," Katrina said looking at me. "We need to get out of here. The firemen are trying to get in."

"It's not over yet," I said as I pulled out my shotgun and loaded another shell, awkwardly, with my good hand. I tried to point the gun at Katrina, but a shotgun was very hard to aim one handed. "There's still one bloodsucker I missed."

Katrina laughed, but I didn't see what she found so amusing. If she didn't think I was serious then she was very sadly mistaken. Once Katrina finished laughing she looked at me and said, "Are you going to kill us Jack?"

"Us," I replied, confused. "What do you mean us? I'm only going to kill you."

"Didn't anyone tell you? Once you become a master vampire's human servant you are bound to that master," Katrina said. She laughed again, seeing my confused expression. "If a human servant dies nothing happens, but if the master dies so does their servant. So, Jack, if you kill me you will die."

I looked at Selene and she shrugged. I was convinced Katrina would say anything to keep herself alive, but she sounded so assured. Knowing so little about vampires, I couldn't trust her. I was about to pull the trigger and call Katrina's bluff when Jean Luke said, "Wat she says is true, mon ami. I've seen it happen."

I looked at Katrina and she smirked. Her smile faded once I drove the butt of my shotgun into her face. In her weakened state, she couldn't dodge the blow and fell to the ground. Blood trickled from her nose, which she wiped away with the back of her hand.

"It's over Katrina," I said, towering over her. "After tonight I don't want to see you again, unless it's an emergency. The only reason why I'm not cutting you off completely is because Selene still has need of you."

Katrina looked furious, but in her weakened stage she knew even a mortal could defeat her. The vampire was humbled. She knew there was no way for her to win.

"So be it Jack," Katrina said as she got to her feet with Tyrone's assistance. "My power is weak from my looses, but since I am the only master in the city we should be sufficient. I will not call upon you unless it's an emergency."

I handed the shotgun to Selene, which she fastened inside my trench. I heard the firemen preparing to enter so they could fight the fire from the inside. The sprinklers had done a good job keeping back the flames, but they were not able to extinguish the inferno.

I didn't want to be on hand when the firemen burst through the doorway. I was tired of lying and didn't want to explain what happened here. There were no vampire bodies, but the club patrons were still here, badly charred and unrecognizable.

"Let's get out of here," I said, looking at Selene. "This is Katrina's mess. Let her explain it."

"I will give my report to your detective friend," Katrina said as she looked at me. "At least she knows what we are and maybe she can exaggerate a little on her report. We need to find another place to rest before sunrise. Luckily, I happen to know of a mansion that just became unoccupied. We will sleep there, then move our coffins tomorrow night."

Katrina took a step, but stumbled. Tyrone was there to catch her. The big vampire scooped the master in his arms and, in a blink of an eye, they were gone. I stared at the flames and knew there was no way I was going to make it without frying. A moment later I felt a hand on my shoulder, which belonged to Zack. With a big grin he looked at me and said, "This is going to be two you owe me, Jack. Unless you want to burn to death."

Before I could comment the vampire scooped me up and sprinted through the flames. Wind flew around me and everything was a blur. Within a few seconds we were in the storage room. I followed Zack down the winding stairs and into the big room. We waited for everyone else at the door to the sleeping chamber. Once everyone was present, Zack unlocked it and we went in.

Jean Luke opened the secret passage while Zack locked the door. We didn't have Shaun or his flash light so Danny and I could see. Selene took my hand and Cleo grabbed Danny. They led us through the darkness until we came to the manhole cover. Jean Luke opened it and we crawled out into the night.

There were firemen near the back entrance of the Crimson Chateau. They were trying to break down the door with little success. They didn't see us climb out of the sewer. We left the alley, blending in with the crowd that had gathered to watch the fire. Zack, Jean Luke and Elizabeth disappeared into the night, probably to meet up with Katrina. We tried to make it to our cars, but the parking lot was crowded. We decided to pick them up in the morning and walked the few blocks to La Luna where Cleo had her car parked. She parked it there when she caught a ride with Xylon. Otherwise, we would have to take a cab.

Blood oozed down my arm from my shoulder wound. The gash was deep, but at least blood wasn't gushing out. I was going to need stitches again, which meant more needles. Great, I detested shots. I wished my healing factor was as fast as Selene's. During the fight she was hurt badly. By the time we reached La Luna she was almost fully healed.

Selene took me to the basement where all the medical supplies were. Xylon checked my shoulder and said, "It's dislocated. I'll set it and bandage you up, but you're going to be in a lot of pain for a while."

I never knew what pain was until Xylon set my shoulder. I screamed and nearly passed out. Xylon gave me some pain medicine and stitched up my arm. Once he was done he put it in a sling and advised me not to use it.

When I was patched up and ready to go, Cleo offered to give everyone a ride home. It was almost sunrise so Xylon declined the offer and decided to sleep here until his shift. I admired the stamina of lycanthropes. If I was expected to work after a night like this, I would either end up being a zombie all day or crash my car into a tree.

Our first stop was Danny's. He thanked Cleo for the ride and then started up the walk. I got out of the car and followed him. Once we got to the door Danny turned, looked at me and said, "I take it things will never be the same again."

"They haven't been for me," I said, realizing those weren't the words Danny was hoping for.

"What am I going to tell my girlfriend?" Danny asked with doubt in his eyes.

"The truth," I replied. It may not be the best thing for him to do, but in a good relationship honesty was all there was.

"See ya at work?" Danny asked and I didn't know what to tell him. I doubted Tom wanted me back.

"I don't know," I replied. "It depends if Tom will let me have my job back."

"Laters Daaaack," Danny said.

"See ya D-man," I said as I walked back towards the car.

Getting into the car, Selene looked at me and smiled. As soon as I shut the door Cleo asked, "Where to?"

"Would you mind if we make an unexpected stop?" Selene asked and Cleo shook her head. "Could you please take me to Hillview Cemetery?"

I knew why she wanted to go to the cemetery. Nathaniel was dead and the time had come for her to end a chapter in her life. She avenged her husband and could find closure.

Selene was quiet and I knew she had a lot on her mind. I didn't push the matter. When we arrived Selene gave Cleo directions and when we stopped she said, "Wait for me here, I will just be a moment."

I watched Selene from the car as she stopped at Dante's grave. I knew she was saying her goodbyes before she started her life over. I don't know what she was planning to do, but I planned on being a big part of it.

While waiting for Selene I called Detective Oswald. I told her everything and that it was safe for her and my mom. I let my mom know I would call her in the morning and the man who tried to break in was apprehended.

Ten minutes later Selene walked back to the car and got in. Cleo looked back at us and asked, "Where to now guys?"

I looked into Selene's big green eyes and could tell she had been crying. She smiled at me and said, "Take us to Jack's."

I gave Cleo directions and wondered if I was healthy enough for what Selene had on her mind. One thing's for sure, I was aiming to please.

Once we pulled up, I thanked Cleo for the ride and got out. I met Selene and as we walked towards the house I heard Cleo say, "Hey Selene, try not to hurt Jack too much. Not unless he's into that."

I don't know who blushed harder, Selene or me. We ignored the young were-panther and went inside.

My body suffered several more injuries, but after seeing the wild look in Selene's eyes, I had a feeling the real pain was about to begin. However, if all pain was like what I was about to experience I would become a masochist.

Chapter Sixteen

The next morning I was awoken by my phone ringing. I sat up in bed and felt Selene stirring next to me. I took a moment to indulge in her beauty, but the phone continued to ring. I got up and quickly slipped on some pants. I made my way to the front room, stubbing my toe on the couch in the process. I answered and heard Shaun's voice on the other end.

"Jack," Shaun said jovially. "What happened last night?"

"You were there," I yawned. "You probably saw more than I did."

"I only saw up to when you blew off Nathaniel's foot," Shaun said. "The vampire girl with pig tails ran past me, and when she did she knocked the air out of my lungs by slamming me into the wall. Once I was able to breathe I went after her, but the bloodsucker was long gone."

"Nathaniel and his minions are dead," I said and I heard Shaun hoot for joy.

"What about Katrina?" Shaun asked sounding excited. "Did you get her too?"

"I was about to, but she had an ace up her sleeve," I replied. There was stunned silence from Shaun.

"What do you mean?" Shaun asked.

"It turns out when she dies, I die. Being her human servant and all," I explained and once again there was silence from the other end.

"That sucks," Shaun finally said. "What are you going to do about her?"

"Nothing," I said yawning again. "We have an agreement. I won't kill us if she leaves me alone. The only way she is allowed to contact me is if she has no other choice."

"Do you actually think she'll keep her word?" Shaun asked. Neither of us trusted Katrina. I had no choice but to let her live.

"Not really, but maybe it'll keep her away long enough for me to straighten out my life," I replied and my cell phone began to ring. "Hey, my cell is ringing so I need to let you go."

"I hope you know what you're doing," Shaun said and like usual I really didn't. "See ya Jack."

I hung up and made it half way to my bedroom before the phone stopped ringing. I entered the room and saw Selene had answered it. As soon as she saw me, she said, "Hold on a second he's right here."

Selene handed me the phone. I looked at the number on the screen and saw it was Tom. I was totally surprised to hear from him, but something told me it wasn't work related.

"What's up Tom?" I asked. It didn't feel right to use his nickname.

"Alan's dead," Tom said and I could hear the sorrow in his voice. "The doctor said he died sometime last night."

For a few moments I couldn't speak. I liked Alan and he would be sorrowfully missed. I felt bad for Steve too. I could only imagine what he was going through.

"When's the funeral?" I asked.

"In a few days," Tom replied, choking back tears. "The funeral announcement should be in tomorrow's paper."

"Danny's alive," I said, hoping to lighten some of the sorrow Tom was feeling.

"I know," Tom said and I was kind of amazed on how fast he heard. "Danny called me this morning and told me everything that happened the past couple nights."

"Then you know it's over," I said, wishing I felt as convinced as I sounded.

"Is it really, Jack?" Tom asked and he didn't sound convinced at all. "Katrina still lives and apparently you are permanently tied to her. I'm afraid until the bonds you share with the supernatural are severed it will never be over. I need to go Jack. See ya."

Tom hung up before I was able to say anything else. I sat on my bed and couldn't help but feel responsible for everything. All I was trying to do was protect everyone I cared for. Instead all I managed to do was get Alan killed and lose my job.

Selene sensed the strong emotions I was feeling, because she put her arms around me and snuggled her head into my neck. I returned her embrace, then I lost my composure. Tears rolled down my cheeks and for a while we sat in sorrowful silence. I don't know how long we sat there and I didn't care. I had Selene in my arms and that was all that mattered.

The emotions we were feeling were abruptly brought to an end when someone knocked on the front door. I softly kissed Selene on the lips and got up. The knock came again as I opened the door. Standing on my doorstep was Detective Oswald. I smiled and said, "Good morning Detective. How are you doing today?"

"I'm fine Jack," Detective Oswald replied and her voice sounded a little stressed. "Can I talk to you for a moment?"

"Sure," I replied, stepping aside and let her by. "What's up?"

"We've been through a lot over the past few days," Detective Oswald said as I shut the door. "I wanted to wait until it was over before I did what I came here to do. First of all, I want you to know I appreciated everything you have done for me and to let you know what happens next is not personal. It pains me to say this Jack and I'm sorry for doing it, but you're under arrest for the murder of Sebastian Saint Clair."

I definitely wasn't expecting this. My jaw dropped and I broke into a cold sweat. I was sure I had a very funny expression on my face.

The End???